UNVEILING BEULAH

DANA WAYNE

Book Liftoff
1209 South Main Street
PMB 126
Lindale, Texas 75771

Book design by Champagne Book Design
Cover design by Just Write.Creations

Library of Congress Control Number Data
Wayne, Dana
Unveiling Beulah / Dana Wayne.
1. American—Historical—Romance—Fiction.
2. General—Historical—Romance—Fiction.
3. General—Romance—Fiction.

BISAC:
FIC 027360 FICTION / Romance / Historical / American.
FIC 027050 FICTION / Romance / Historical / General.
FIC 027000 FICTION / Romance / General.

2021902363

ISBN: 978-1-947946-69-9 (Amazon/Kindle Direct)
ISBN: 978-1-947946-70-5 (Ingram Spark)

www.danawayne.com
www.bookliftoff.com

BOOKS BY
DANA WAYNE

Secrets Of The Heart

Mail Order Groom

Whispers On The Wind

Chasing Hope

Coming in 2021

The Detail

PRAISE FOR DANA WAYNE BOOKS

"Dana Wayne's characters don't live on the printed page. They live in your heart for a long time." Caleb Pirtle, III award-winning author

Chasing Hope
"A feel-good romance at its finest!"—KayBees Bookshelf

"My kind of romance!"—Readers Favorite

"A truly special book that deserves a place of honor on your bookshelf."—InD'tale Magazine

"Strong characters, a sweet romance, and a hopeful examination of real-world issues."—BookLife Prize

"…(can) draw out a plot that is predictable in all the right places yet still offers twists that surprise, delight and keep the story moving."—Ruthie Jones Reviews

Whispers on The Wind
"Excellent mix for chilling read!"—InD'tale Magazine

"Truly a joy to read!"—Readers Favorite

"…both sizzles and gives you chills."—Book Chick Blog

"If you love romantic suspense, you are in for a treat!"—Nicole Laverdue Reviews

Mail Order Groom

"…brings the characters to life in a way that has you leaning against the fence post watching it all unfold. Five Stars!"—Coffee in The Morning Blog

"…well written, romantic and suspenseful!"—Books and Benches Magazine

"A gripping story that cannot be ignored for a second!"—Readers Favorite

"Intricately crafted story with many curves along the trail that the reader never anticipates!"—InD'tale Magazine

"…exceptional piece of literature from a well-accomplished writer who is now one of my favorite writers of all time!" Redheaded Book Blog

Secrets of the Heart

"…a good romance, storyline with substance, and very interesting well-developed characters." Linda Thompson, The Author Show

"…stands out for originality…characters are strong and the work well-written." Kevin Cooper

"…she blends heartbreak and despair with love and hope." Coffee In The Morning Blog

"…a romantic winner that touches all the emotions and touches them with love and compassion."—The Book Editor

"For all lovers of romance, get this book!"—Amazon Reader

"One of the few books in my life I can't wait to read again!"—Amazon Reader

To my wonderful mother, Mickie Barnett, who made me believe
I could do anything. I love you, and I miss you every day.

CHAPTER ONE

East Texas, Late February 1879

A RAIN-SLEET MIXTURE PELTED THE GRIME-COATED window of the train car, leaving a trail of muddy streaks puddled at the bottom. Beulah Mae Lockhart considered this less-than-auspicious welcome to Texas a good omen. Start bad end well was her philosophy. At least, she tried to make it so.

She pulled the oft folded piece of paper from her handbag and smoothed it over her lap. A newly awakened sense of strength bolstered her spirits, and her body vibrated with new life as she reread it. *I, Frank Barker, owner of Bakersville General Store, Bakersville, Texas, do hereby sell said business, building, and all contents to B.M. Lockhart of New York City. Sale includes the inventory listed below, the house located behind the store, and any items left behind.*

Bea scanned the list already committed to memory, which was nothing like the items stocked by her father's upscale mercantile in New York. Basic frontier supplies: farm tools, flour, sugar, lard, seed. No silk or satin. No crystal or silver service. Nothing extravagant. Nothing special.

But it was hers. And one day, it would be special.

She returned the treasured document to her bag and shivered as frigid air seeped around the edge of the window. The heavy wool coat was no match for the deep chill ingrained into the wooden floor that leached into her feet despite her leather boots and thick stockings. *Only another hour or so. I can stand it that long.*

A woman seated across the aisle ducked her head when Bea caught her staring at the jagged scar on her right cheek. Bea didn't bother to adjust the hat's veil to cover it. She refused to hide anymore. People would accept her as is, disfigurement and all, or they could go to, well, they could go away and leave her be.

Bea sat up straighter and addressed the woman. "Are you from Bakersville?"

Startled, the woman flinched and looked at the scar again rather than meeting Bea's gaze. "Um, yes. We live in town." She shifted in the seat, eyes finally making contact. "I've not seen you around before."

"I recently purchased some property there."

The woman's eyes lit up. "I'm Eunice Martin. My Jeb runs the post office and telegraph. The only thing I know for sale around here is the mercantile, but I heard someone named B.M. Lockhart from New York bought it. Is that your husband?"

Bea countered the question with one of her own. "How long have you lived there?"

The look of disappointment on her companion's face was so acute, Bea almost felt sorry for her.

"About six years." The woman cocked her head to one side. "You're not from around here, are you?"

"New York."

Mrs. Martin's eyes lingered over the scar, and Bea struggled to stifle the angry retort hovering on the tip of her tongue. She refused to explain it to anyone, especially someone so noticeably rude. "I understand there is a rather nice hotel in town."

"There is." She blustered and sat up straighter, gloved hands clasped over an expansive waistline. One bushy brow arched upward. "If you don't mind associating with…well, her kind."

Bea's protective instinct kicked in with a vengeance. A victim of unwarranted bias because of the scar, she had no tolerance for discrimination or prejudice. "And just what kind is that, Mrs. Martin?" She made no effort to temper the iciness in her voice.

Seemingly unaware of Bea's disapproval, the woman's face became infused with what appeared to be misguided happiness.

"She's not married." She leaned forward, and her voice dropped though no other passengers were close enough to hear. "And has a child." She straightened and sucked in a self-righteous breath. "And you know what that means."

It took Bea a moment to regain her composure. "No, I don't know." Before the nasty woman could say more, she cut her off. "And neither do you."

Mrs. Martin sputtered and sat back in the seat, blinking rapidly. "I'm merely trying to help."

"Are you now? By implying the owner of the hotel is somehow unworthy of my patronage simply because she has a child?"

"She doesn't have a husband," snapped Mrs. Martin, "and no one knows why."

"Meaning *you* don't know, and for that reason alone, you supposed the worst-case scenario." Bea sat up straighter. "I do not listen to gossip and prefer to evaluate people based on how they treat me. And others." With that stiff reprimand, she turned and looked out the window, effectively ending the conversation.

Unfairly shunned by her family and society as well, Bea quickly related to the unknown woman's plight. Ever since the accident when Bea was thirteen, she stoically endured her mother's declaration that the scar somehow made her unworthy of love or even affection. Tutors and other household staff tried to fill the emotional void caused by her parents' coldness.

But, thanks to her grandmother's steadfast love and support, Bea managed to grow up relatively well-adjusted but painfully shy. Her sudden death eight years ago left Bea inconsolable for weeks.

Until that surprise visit from Granny's lawyer. The sizeable and unexpected inheritance provided a much-needed boost of self-confidence and initiated a series of long-overdue changes. The first one being her refusal to relinquish control of the money to her father, who believed women in general, were ill-suited for such things.

Thanks to the guidance and support of her late grandmother's lawyer and banker, Bea discovered she possessed a shrewd head for business. Using her beloved grandmother as inspiration, Bea began to consider a future away from New York and her parents.

Still, after years of being told she was somehow defective, it took time to gain the confidence to not only venture outside the home but convince her father to teach her how to run his fashionable mercantile, albeit from the back rooms. The only reason he relented was her mother's declaration that since Bea was completely unmarriageable, "She may as well make herself useful." Under Bea's leadership, Lockhart's quickly became *the* place for the social elite to purchase whatever the most current rage happened to be.

Until disaster struck in the form of one Edmund Wilshire Abernathy III. Surprised and flattered by the handsome aristocrat's attention, Bea fell hard and fast. Three months later, they became engaged.

Even now, her face burned with shame as she recalled the debacle. *One would think a woman thirty years of age would be smart enough to see past the smooth-talking Englishman to the scoundrel lurking beneath the surface.*

Thankfully, Bea ignored her mother's insistence she grant Edmond control of her finances before they married. Otherwise, he would have likely squandered it all on his worthless schemes before his real character became known. Some of her parents' friends and her father were not so lucky.

Image was everything to her parents, and the subsequent scandal rocked their world. They placed full blame on Bea for the debacle, despite the fact it was her father who brought Edmond into their home and encouraged their relationship and subsequent engagement.

That disastrous event set her feet on the path she now trod.

She wasn't surprised when her parents' first concern upon hearing of her plan to leave was if she intended to replace the money Edmond swindled from them.

She suffered no qualms in refusing their request.

The screech of the train's whistle interrupted her musings. She stiffened her back and inhaled. *The past is gone. My future starts today.*

The steam engine's dirty window and swirling smoke obscured her view as the train rolled to a stop.

She allowed herself only a moment's hesitation before rising to meet her future.

"Can I help you, Miss?"

Bea turned to the gruff voice behind the counter to her right.

An older gentleman, reed thin and slightly stooped, squinted at her with faded blue eyes. A thick wool overcoat hung on his wiry frame, and a scraggly beard covered a weathered face.

"I'm looking for the station manager or someone who can assist me."

"Well, depending on what you need, I reckon that'd be me."

She took a step toward him and deliberately let the veil slip to show the scar.

His gaze never wavered.

"Name's Silas Upton, ma'am. How can I help you?"

She stepped closer and turned her head to inspect the small space. "Mr. Upton, I wonder if I might temporarily store my things here. Or is there someplace else I should take them?"

"How much stuff you talking about?"

"A couple of large trunks and some boxes."

"How long is temporary?" His toothy grin was charming.

She returned the smile. "Just until I get set up in town. Shouldn't be more than a couple of days."

His finger made a raspy sound as it raked against his bearded cheek. "I reckon that'd be all right."

"Perhaps you could see that the smaller trunk is taken to the hotel." She paused, and one gloved finger tapped her chin. "Or maybe I should check to see if they have a room first."

"Miss Lizzie will have room. Ain't nothing going on this time of year. I'll get it sent over for you. What name do I give her?"

"Bea Lockhart, please. And thank you for your assistance, Mr. Upton." She turned for the door and stopped. "Oh, can you direct me to the general store, please?"

"Turn right and go down past Doc Morton's office. The store will be on the other side of the road across from The Hanging Tree."

"The Hanging Tree?"

He nodded. "The big oak in the middle of the road. Used to be for hangin's, but we ain't had one of them in years."

It took a moment to mask her surprise before Bea thanked him again and stepped out on the rough plank walkway. The rain and sleet were gone, but an icy wind remained. Though cold, it was nothing like winter in New York, and the heavy wool traveling coat protected against the chill. However, she doubted her feet would ever be warm again.

She straightened her shoulders and looked around. The train station marked the southern edge of town. Across the street stood an empty wood-frame building, its weathered exterior badly in need of repair. Next to it was a wooden barbershop and bathhouse, its faded sign boasting a hot bath and shave for twenty-five cents. A narrow alley separated that establishment from the two-story Broken Spur Saloon that covered the block. An outside staircase led upstairs, and a simple balcony wrapped around the three sides visible from her vantage point. Movement from an open door drew her eye, and she watched as a cowboy exited one of the rooms, a scantily clad young woman hanging on his arm.

Face flaming, Bea jerked her gaze away and continued to survey her new home.

Further down, she saw the oak Mr. Upton mentioned. Squarely in the middle of the muddy boulevard, it towered at least fifty feet in the air. Gnarled, massive branches, barren of leaves, stretched over the road on either side. Easily three feet in diameter, the trunk was surrounded by twisted roots and patchy dead grass.

One could easily imagine it providing shade during the hot summer months for buildings in its shadow, one of which was the general store. *Mother would have a heart attack if I told her shade came from The Hanging Tree.* Thoughts of her mother dampened Bea's rising euphoria. She would no doubt have little good to say about any of it.

Shaking off the encroaching melancholy, Bea looked around. Worlds apart from New York, Bakersville sported an eclectic mix of structures. A brick-and-mortar bank sat next to a wooden apothecary. The hotel boasted a white stone façade and a large oak door, its glass heavily etched with an intricate design she could not determine at this distance and accented by dark blue trim. Another building was connected to the hotel, its bright yellow exterior shining in the drab, grey morning. Horses waited at scattered hitching posts, and an assortment of the town's inhabitants hurried about their business, no doubt anxious to get out of the weather.

On this side of the street, the telegraph office sat next to the station. A small alley on either side separated the blacksmith shop and livery stable from other buildings in the block. A sign hanging from the roof indicated the jail was up ahead, though she could see no further details from this angle.

She took a breath and headed in the direction of her new venture. At the end of the boardwalk, she stifled a groan. There was no walkway again until she got past the blacksmith shop.

She sighed and debated options. *Walking through the muck in the alley will ruin my shoes and my skirt.* She looked around, expecting to see a coach for hire. She sighed deeply and reminded herself she was no longer in the big city where carriages were the norm.

"Something wrong, ma'am?"

The deep voice came from a bear of a man standing in front of the smithy.

By his attire, a long leather apron and gloves, she assumed he was the proprietor and quickly pasted on a polite smile. "I don't suppose there is a carriage or something I could rent to get me to the general store?"

When he didn't reply right away, she wondered if he heard her question.

His slow, patronizing smile said he did. "No point in hitching up a carriage just to go there."

His voice, low-pitched and clear, held the faintest accent. French maybe? And more than a hint of disdain.

Miffed, Bea fixed him with her coldest glare. "I see. Well, thank you anyway." She bunched up her skirts and prepared to step into the muck.

"Hold up." He tossed his gloves onto a shelf behind him and walked toward her.

When he stopped at the foot of the single step, she found herself transfixed by sky-blue eyes framed by long, sooty lashes. The shadow of a beard on sun-bronzed skin added a rakish aura. Ebony hair was secured at the nape by a strip of leather while one wayward curl fell casually across his forehead, and masculine wisps coiled against the open V of his homespun shirt. Despite the cold air, perspiration hovered above full, sensual lips. She was acutely conscious of a broad, muscular chest and shoulders that appeared a yard wide. A quick inhale brought heady traces of sweat, leather, manure, and something she couldn't identify. It was rude to stare, but she couldn't help it.

He was the most handsome man she had ever seen in her life.

"*Je vous donne une semaine, jolie dame.*"

Thanks to a determined nanny, Bea spoke fluent French and taught herself German as well. His French was smooth, refined, and totally out of place with his surroundings, so it took a moment for her surprised brain to translate the slight. Spine rigid, she looked down at him. "You give me a week for what, sir?"

Eyes wide, his head tilted back. "You speak French." The terse statement carried no hint of apology.

"*Oui Monsieur. Couramment.*"

The sexy smile appeared slowly, and she sucked in a breath only to have it lodge in her throat when he scooped her up in his arms as though she weighed nothing and started across the street.

"What are you doing? Put me down this instant!" Even as she protested, she grabbed his apron for balance with one hand while the other remained pinned against a rock-solid chest.

He didn't stop. "You really want to walk in this muck?"

She jerked her head around, saw they were in the middle of the road, and bit her lip. "No. I don't."

They reached the other side in silence, and he set her feet on the boardwalk past the saloon. Face burning, she forced herself to meet his gaze. "Thank you."

He tipped his head slightly, murmured, "*Mon plaisir, Madame,*" and turned back to his shop.

Heart racing, she watched until he picked up his gloves and disappeared into the smithy.

Just then, Bea noticed Mrs. Martin gaping at her from the doorway of the telegraph office. The firm set of her mouth said the smithy was someone else of whom she disapproved.

CHAPTER TWO

Lucian caught the glare of Little Mole as he crossed the muddy street back to his shop. He smiled inwardly at the secret name he gave Mrs. Martin some time ago. She talked without thinking and made no apologies when the gossip she spread at will turned out to be false, nor did she cease her constant meddling. He shook his head, unable to understand a behavior he'd witnessed most of his life.

He entered the livery and picked up the gloves he'd tossed aside when the woman appeared. His first thought was Bakersville was no place for her. Mature, but not so much so, she carried herself with all the grace and elegance of any European aristocrat. The wintry wind whipped color into pale cheeks, and there was both delicacy and strength in her face. Dark hair glistening like polished mahogany peeked under the stylish bonnet, and rich, hazel eyes gleamed with purpose. He found himself intrigued at first glance. When she responded to his comment in French without the slightest hint of insult, his interest grew.

He didn't notice the scar at first. Though visible, it didn't detract from her beauty. Some people wore their marks on the outside. Others carried them deep in their core.

Despite his determination not to think about it, his mind drifted to the crumpled letter resting atop his dresser. It arrived two weeks ago and sat on the table another week before he opened it. He had no idea his grandfather even knew where he was. Not that Luc tried to hide his trek to Texas. He simply thought the old man had written him off for good this time.

Apparently not. He would arrive mid-March and expected Luc to return to New York with him and assume control of the vast shipping empire that was the Moreau legacy. He even hinted that his broken engagement should proceed as planned.

"Not bloody likely," he murmured as his trip down memory lane continued.

Luc's father was a trapper, taking to the trade during an expedition to buy furs. During his second winter running traps, he met and fell in love with a Choctaw woman, and they eventually married. Luc remembered his father as a happy, smiling man who adored his wife and son. They did everything together. His father taught him to hunt, trap, fish, and his mother instilled in him the belief that family was everything.

While his grandfather never entirely accepted Luc's mother, he was civil when they visited him in New York. On such a visit when Luc was twelve, an outbreak of cholera robbed him of both parents and forced him into his grandfather's care.

A stern, taciturn man, Henry Moreau had no time for a grieving child and immediately sent him to a boarding school, followed by college and trips abroad.

Visits with his mother's people faded to a cherished memory as Luc traveled the world and rubbed elbows with nobles and the social elite.

It wasn't until his near engagement to Annabelle Blankenship two years ago that he finally realized something was missing from his life. And it wasn't marriage to a spoiled socialite.

Things came to a head at his grandfather's seventy-fifth

birthday party, where the older Moreau planned to announce Luc's betrothal to Annabelle, a marriage arranged and agreed to by both families.

Luc didn't love her, wasn't sure he ever would, but she was beautiful and sophisticated, and they got on well enough. Plus, she came from a wealthy family with connections, a necessity in the world he traveled.

And he was thirty-three years old. He wanted to settle down with a wife and family of his own. He wasn't particularly interested in the shipping business but felt obligated to his grandfather. Reluctantly, he resigned himself to a life in which he had little voice in planning.

Until he overheard a conversation between Annabelle and her best friend, Charlotte Ambrose, which revealed her true character and told him exactly how big a mistake he was about to make.

Even now, her cruel words sent anger coursing through his veins.

"You know his mother was a red savage," said Charlotte. "How can you bear to, you know, bed him."

Annabelle's laugh was cold and callous. "Darling, I'd bed the devil himself to get my hands on the Moreau fortune."

"What if you get with child?"

"Trust me," she murmured, "there will be no child in this marriage."

Luc barely heard their sharp gasps as he walked toward them from the shadows where he'd caught the conversation. "It is fortunate I found this out now." He couldn't keep the anger from his voice. Just this morning, she pledged to give him a child as soon as possible. But it was all a lie.

"Lucian, darling," she stammered, momentarily abashed,

one gloved hand reaching for his arm. "I did not mean that the way it sounded."

He pushed her hand away. "And what way did you mean it, Belle?" He deliberately used the nickname she hated. "What else can one infer from it?" He took a step toward her, his steady voice filled with cold contempt. "You want my money. I've always known that. But you would deny me a child in return?"

"I-I, no, of course not." Face flaming, she glanced at Charlotte. "I merely meant I might not be able to conceive. My mother had great difficulty, you know, and I might as well."

Tension coiled around them like a snake, its bands growing tighter by the second as startled hurt turned to white-hot anger. "You are quite the liar, Belle."

He left her standing there, a protest dying on trembling lips.

Luc found his grandfather, told him the engagement was off, and walked out, leaving him to explain things to her family.

Their conversation the next day quickly escalated into a shouting match. His grandfather didn't care about what Annabelle said. He wanted the power that merging his empire with the Blankenship's lessor one would bring.

Luc's happiness meant nothing. And that hurt most of all.

When his grandfather calmly suggested Luc get a mistress, he walked out and never looked back.

Now, for whatever reason, he'd tracked him down and expected things to pick up where they left off.

Luc snapped tongs around a horseshoe and plunged it into the hot coals, working the bellows with his other hand. "Like bloody hell."

"You get that shoe any hotter you gonna ruin it."

The comment from Amos Bigelow, his friend and previous

owner of the smithy, brought Luc up with a start. "I didn't hear you walk in."

"Some injun you are." He spit brown liquid toward a bucket in the corner. It hit the top and rolled down the side. "Thought you could hear a pin drop." Amos shuffled into the livery and lowered himself onto his favorite perch—an upturned barrel and sighed. "What's her name?"

Luc tapped the edge of the horseshoe with his hammer. "Who?"

"Don't play dumb with me, boy," he snipped. "The woman I seen you totin' across the road."

"No idea."

"What?"

He stuck the shoe back in the coals. "She came in on the train, needed to get to the other side. Couldn't let her walk through the mud."

"And you didn't ask her name? What's wrong with you?"

He ignored the dig.

Amos sighed. "I bet she smelled real good."

Like roses and honeysuckle.

"Well, did she?"

Amos's croaky voice drew him out of his reflections. "Did she what?"

"Hell, boy, ain't you listenin'? Did she smell good?"

He pulled the shoe out and pounded the edges again. "Fine."

"Fine? That's all I get? Fine?"

Luc stopped and looked at his friend. "Yes." He threw the shoe in a bucket of water beside him. "That's all you get."

Amos smacked his lips. "I seen her go into the general store. Mable said some man from New York bought it. Wonder if she's his wife?" He leaned over to look out the door. "Did you see him?"

It never occurred to Luc she might be married since she appeared to travel alone. Now, he found the thought rather disheartening. "Only folks who got off were her and Mrs. Martin."

"Hmm."

"Hey, Frenchy," came a gravelly voice from the doorway. "Can you do me a favor?"

He turned toward the voice. "Sure, Silas. What do you need?"

"That lady who came in on the train today, Miss Lockhart, needs a trunk taken to the hotel. It's a mite heavy for me. Would you mind taking it over?"

"No problem. She need it right away?"

"Well, now, she didn't say. She was headed to the general store. That's all I know."

"Give me an hour or so. I have to finish two shoes, then feed the stock."

"Thanks, Frenchy."

"If you find out she needs it sooner, let me know."

"I will. I sent that Martin boy over to tell Miss Lizzie she was gonna need a room, so she'll be expecting the trunk."

Luc watched him shuffle off, wondering not for the first time, why the gusty wind didn't topple him end over end.

"He's got rocks in his pockets."

Amos's comment drew Luc's gaze.

"To keep him from blowing away." Amos slapped his knee and cackled, the sound bordering on a hen's cluck.

"You're a fine one to talk, Old Man," teased Luc.

The cackle ceased abruptly. "She's a fine lookin' woman, though, ain't she?"

A grunt sufficed for a reply. This wasn't a conversation he wanted to get into at the moment.

"I watched her walk up the street, struttin' like a queen." He smacked his lips again. "Think I'll mosey over to the store and see what she smells like." He grimaced as he pushed himself up from the barrel. "These old bones are just gonna stop working one day."

He hobbled out, and Luc swallowed past the lump in his throat. Despite all his bluster and sass, Amos was the salt of the earth and the closest thing to family he had now.

Except for a grandfather who expected him to return to a place he hated and marry a woman he could never love. Or trust.

CHAPTER THREE

THE HEAVY CLANG OF A COWBELL OVER THE DOOR caused Bea to look up in surprise as she entered the general store. A variety of rich aromas inundated her with each breath. Leather, tobacco, oil, and others she did not recognize. Yet.

She scanned the room, mentally making a list of things to change. The big windows on either side of the door overlooking the boardwalk would be first. An enticing display to lure people in was a necessity. Right now, an assortment of tools and crates crowded the small space in no discernable order. That would never do. Neat and tidy was a must in her book.

A large pot-belly stove in the middle of the room provided blessed heat, and she moved toward it as she examined the rest of the room. An open door on the right led to an alcove she would explore later. A large counter ran the back length of the rear wall and contained shelves filled with an assortment of items. Overall, the layout was acceptable, with a diverse mixture of items available for purchase, most of which were functional and sturdy and a far cry from what she was accustomed to.

"I'll be right out," came a loud voice from the back.

Once the heat dissolved some of the chill from her bones, Bea inspected the fabric table nearby and fingered a bolt of drab blue cotton. Her first thought was to add some silk, or perhaps satin. Quick on the heels of that came the reproach, *You're not in New York, Bea, you're in Texas. Adjust your ideas accordingly.* She looked around the selections and knew she needed to add color if nothing else, to the choices. *A woman can be practical in a lemon yellow dress just as well as a drab blue one.*

She thought of the various supplies waiting in the trunks at the station and smiled. The bright yellow cotton would come out first.

"Sorry to keep you waiting," said the woman exiting the back. "We're still trying to get packed up." She stopped and eyed Bea up and down. "Mrs. Lockhart?"

Bea nodded and took a step forward. "Mrs. Barker?"

"Mable Barker." She wiped her hands on the apron around her waist and extended her right one, looking past Bea to the door. "Is your husband with you, Mrs. Lockhart?"

Bea took a breath. "I'm not married, Mrs. Barker. My solicitor and your cousin, Mr. James, arranged this purchase for me. I'm B.M. Lockhart. Beulah Mae Lockhart."

The woman gaped a moment, then clapped her hands and smiled. "Don't that beat all? I hope you know what you're getting into, honey. Bakersville ain't nothing like New York."

More at ease, Bea returned the smile. "I can assure you, Mrs. Barker, I'm well aware of the differences."

She eyed Bea's stylish traveling attire. "People around here are plain, simple folks, Miss Lockhart. We don't have fancy hotels or operas and such as that."

"Please, call me Bea." Her fingers tightened around the reticule she clutched. "Do you have a concern about selling to a woman?"

"Heck, no." Mable's hands rested on ample hips. "From what I understand, you grew up in a store and know what you're getting into."

Thank you, Mr. James.

"My only concern is if you really want to take over a business in the middle of Nowhere, Texas with only cowboys, farmers, and ranchers for customers." She shook her head and eyed Bea's fashionable clothes again. "The women aren't exactly the kind you see in New York."

Bea thought of Mrs. Martin's crass comments and immediately took exception. "I can assure you, madame, anyone who walks into my store will be welcomed, regardless of who they are or what they wish to purchase."

Taken aback, Mrs. Barker stammered. "Now, don't go getting all riled up, Miss Lockhart. I only meant that, with a few exceptions, most of the womenfolk around here are wives of small ranchers and farmers who don't have a lot of money to spend."

Chagrined, Bea took a breath. "I beg your pardon. I spoke with Mrs. Martin on the train, and…"

"She's a busybody. Don't believe anything that comes out of her mouth." Her hostess turned and headed toward a counter on the left. "Come on. I'll show you the books I've kept, so you know what's what." She took a breath and continued. "Most folks depend on selling crops or beef in the spring for their money, so we sell a lot on credit. I also allow folks to barter."

"What is that?"

Mable frowned, then gave a light laugh. "I guess you don't get much call for that in New York. Barter means someone can bring something in to trade for whatever they need. Eggs, butter, whatever. I have a price sheet here that says what I allow for each item, but you can do it any way you like."

Bea nodded. "I like that idea."

"Good cause a lot of folks depend on that. Now, I collected what I could off the book before we settled on a price." She pulled a well-worn ledger from under the counter. "It's up to you to collect the rest."

By the time an hour had passed, Bea's head swam with facts, figures, and names. *I'll never remember all this.*

"I know I give you a lot of stuff in a short amount of time," said Mable, "but we plan to be on the train Sunday, so we only got a few days."

"Oh," said Bea, "I wasn't aware you were leaving so soon after my arrival."

"Well, we were going to stay till you got situated, but my Frank's consumption is worse now, and we need to get to Santa Fe as soon as possible."

"Of course. I'm so sorry your husband is not well."

"Mr. James said you know all about running a store, so I don't think you'll have any trouble. And we gave him a list of where we get our supplies. You got any questions about who some of these folks are, just ask Lizzie Myers at the hotel." She paused for a deep breath. "The house out back is part of the deal. We left most of the furniture since we will be living with my sister once we get to Santa Fe. There's a bed, a stove, table and chairs, and some odds and ends." Her smile was genuine and heartfelt. "God sent you to us, Miss Lockhart. The money we got for this place will be more than enough to take care of things once we get there. Thank you."

"I'm the thankful one, Mrs. Barker. You have no idea what having a place of my own means to me."

"I know you must be tired from the trip and all, but if you're agreeable, we can keep going." She paused for a breath. "Today is Thursday, so we only got three days to get you started."

"Of course." Bea smothered the rising panic. Three days! "Mr. Upton is having my things sent to the hotel, so we can work as long as you care to."

Over the next three hours, a few customers came and went. While her reception was somewhat cool, no one blatantly shunned her, and a couple even smiled in welcome. Happily exhausted, Bea gathered her things in preparation for the short walk to the hotel.

"Oh, and if you need anything fixed, just call on Luc down at the blacksmith shop. He's handy as a pocket on a shirt. Don't know what we'd have done without him when Frank took sick."

"The blacksmith?"

She smiled. "His name is Lucian, but most folks call him Luc or Frenchy." She paused a moment and continued. "His Pa was a Frenchman. His Ma was Indian."

The look she gave Bea said she expected her to have an issue with all or part of that statement. Undaunted, Bea pulled on her gloves. "I guess that explains why he spoke to me in French." At her companion's confused look, Bea added, "I met him briefly when I arrived."

Mable chuckled. "Yeah, he does that sometimes. He may be cussing your sorry bones to the devil, but it sure sounds pretty."

Bea smiled. "I had a French nanny when I was young who insisted I learn the language. He was surprised when I understood him."

That comment produced a husky laugh. "I bet it did. He's a little gruff at times, but don't let that bother you. He might look like a bear, but he's really a lamb."

All she could manage was a quick nod. Somehow, picturing Luc as a lamb produced a wolf in sheep's clothing. She'd never met anyone who affected her the way he did. After the fiasco with Edmund, Bea didn't trust her female instincts anymore.

If she ever had any to trust in the first place.

CHAPTER FOUR

B EA STOOD OUTSIDE THE GENERAL STORE AND buttoned her coat against the frosty air. Dusk crept in while she and Mable finished for the day and shrouded the town in shadows. Lanterns glowed in a few of the windows up and down the main street, but few people were outside. Lively piano music drifted from the tavern down the block, along with boisterous voices. Her face burned as she recalled the young cowboy seen earlier above the saloon. *Oh, for heaven's sake, Bea,* she chided herself, *you're not a child, and this is not New York.*

She stiffened her spine and turned toward the hotel, her mind digesting the afternoon with Mable, and mentally added to her checklist of things to be done. A stiff wind blustered through the darkened alley between the mercantile and the next building, bringing with it a myriad of smells she preferred not to analyze. But at least this side of the street had a boardwalk connecting the buildings, and she picked up the pace.

The bright yellow structure adjacent to the hotel appeared to be a restaurant that hosted a sparse supper crowd. Aroma's drifting outside reminded her she'd eaten little the last two days. She stopped and debated whether to go to the hotel and freshen up or dine while the restaurant wasn't so busy. The need to be clean won the battle, and she walked to the hotel.

She reached for the ornate brass handle, and the door swung

open. Luc's muscular frame suddenly filled the entryway. Startled, she uttered a soft squeal, one hand pressed against her rapidly beating heart. "Oh my, you startled me."

"My apologies, *Mademoiselle.*" He took a step back for her to enter, then closed the door. "Or is it *Madame?*"

Bea sucked in a quick breath before she could speak. The soft glow of the lobby lanterns softened the rough edges around his face and made him even more attractive. She blinked twice and recovered her balance. "*Mademoiselle.* Though I prefer Miss Lockhart."

He bowed at the waist. "As you wish, Miss Lockhart." He straightened and nodded toward the stairs. "Silas asked me to deliver your trunk. It is in the room assigned to you."

Perhaps it was the accent that made his low baritone voice so pleasant, for she found herself hanging on every word. "Thank you, um, Mr., um, Mr. Lucian. Once again, I am in your debt."

His lips parted in a dazzling smile revealing straight, white teeth, and butterflies took flight in her stomach.

"No mister. Just Luc or Lucian. And the pleasure was mine."

Before she could reply, he spun around and was gone.

She stared at the closed door for several heartbeats, his smiling face still visible in her mind's eye. She blinked and turned around to inspect the spacious lobby. The furnishings were a diverse mixture of elegant Victorian chairs and settees seamlessly blended with sturdy and functional wood and leather chairs. Small tables, strategically placed, allowed groups to sit together and converse. Intricately woven rugs covered the polished wooden floor and added a high degree of color to the room. Utilitarian stairs covered in a deep, burgundy-colored carpet were to the right of the clerk's counter. An ornate grandfather clock rested beside a mahogany library table at the bottom of the stairs.

Nothing at all like the hotels in New York, it was, nonetheless, an inviting space.

Bea walked toward the woman behind the counter and smiled.

"Good evening, Miss Lockhart," said the woman. "I'm Lizzie Myers. Welcome to Bakersville."

Bea stared at the woman a moment. Curls like polished copper framed a perfectly oval face, and her smooth skin glowed with golden undertones. Emerald green eyes sparkled with fire and life, and her smile of welcome was genuine.

Instantly aware of her own disfigurement, dismay washed over Bea, and she forced herself to smile. "I'm amazed at how many people know who I am when I just arrived today."

"We are a small town, Miss Lockhart, and this time of year have very few visitors. And nothing sparks conversation like a new arrival in town." She pulled a key from the wall behind her and spun the ledger for Bea to sign in. "I have you in Room Eight. It's larger and has a separate bathing area. Top of the stairs, last door on the right." She paused a moment, crossed and uncrossed her arms. "We don't get many ladies here. Mostly cattle buyers and drovers, so our accommodations are rather plain."

"I'm sure it will be fine, Miss Myers. And I'll only be here until after the Barkers leave town."

"Please call me Lizzie. If there is anything you need, just let me know."

Bea signed the register and took the key. "I will. Thank you, Lizzie. And please, call me Bea."

"I took the liberty of scheduling a bath for you since you went directly from the train to the store, but it's going to be about an hour before they will have it ready."

"Oh." Bea gnawed her lower lip. "Then perhaps I'll go next door and eat."

"If you would rather, I can have something sent up to your room."

After a moment's consideration, Bea declined. No more hiding from the world. "Thank you, but I think I'll walk over there."

"You can enter through that door across from the stairs and not have to walk back outside," said Lizzie. "The Yellow Rose is attached to the hotel."

"Thank you. I'll go upstairs and freshen up first."

Twenty minutes later, she entered the restaurant minus the coat and bonnet she left upstairs, opting for a woolen shawl and nothing to hide the scar.

"Have a seat wherever you like," said a matronly woman serving a table on the right. "I'll be right with you."

Bea chose a table in the corner and sat down.

"You must be Miss Lockhart."

Bea looked up to the woman who stood beside her chair. Dressed in a faded blue cotton blouse and darker skirt, a white apron around her ample waist, she was full-bosomed and curvy. A wreath of salt and pepper curls circled a round face, anchored by sparkling blue eyes and a genial smile. "Welcome to Bakersville. I'm Viola Davis." She made a swipe across the table with a cloth pulled from inside her apron. "But folks 'round here call me Miss Vi or just plain Vi. What can I get for you?"

"I don't know what you're cooking back there, but it smells divine."

"Tonight's special is beef stew with cornbread and apple pie for dessert. Or steak with potatoes and beans." She took in Bea's slender frame. "I can whip up something lighter if you'd prefer."

"The stew is fine. And coffee, please."

"I'll have that out right away." Miss Vi spun around and headed through a door at the back.

Bea glanced around and recognized a couple, the Walkers, with their young son, who were in the store earlier today. She remembered them because the mother struggled to keep her son corralled while she shopped. He wanted to touch everything. Bea finally gave him a licorice stick and talked to him while his mother completed her purchases. While the child eyed her scar with curiosity, he said nothing.

The woman smiled a greeting as her son fidgeted as though he sat on hot coals.

The man spoke to someone at the table beside him while the boy continued to wiggle. A stern look from his father and the child instantly stilled, hands folded in his lap, but he looked at Bea again and grinned, one small hand lifted in a slight wave.

A draft of cold air announced a new customer, and Bea looked toward the newcomer.

Luc stepped inside and closed the door. He started for a nearby table but turned and headed toward Bea.

Her heart gave an unfamiliar flip, and her breath hitched when he stopped beside her table.

"Silas said you still had things at the station. Let me know when you need them brought to the hotel."

"Thank you, Mr. Lucian, but –"

"No mister, remember? Just Luc."

She opened her mouth to speak, but the young boy managed to escape his mother's watchful eye and now stood beside her table.

"What happened to your face?"

Unprepared for the question, Bea gasped.

"Joshua!" His embarrassed mother pulled him backward.

Undeterred, he pulled his hand free and stood beside Bea. "Does it hurt?"

Spine rigid, Bea kept a smile in place. "No, it doesn't."

"What happened?"

"Joshua!"

The boy's father joined the circus at her table, drawing the attention of the other patrons.

"Apologize. Now." The man turned to Bea, his face beet red. His mouth moved, but nothing came out.

"I'm sorry, ma'am," said Joshua softly.

Aware the time would come sooner or later, Bea leaned forward. Now was as good a time as any. "Many years ago, I was in an accident." She refused to look at Luc or Joshua's parents. "This was the result. Perhaps I should have covered it up because it's well, not very pretty to look at."

"I think you're really pretty, ma'am," said Joshua earnestly. "I just wondered how you got it."

Bea sat back. "You think I'm pretty?"

"Well, sure. You smile a lot, and your eyes sparkle."

It took Bea two breaths to speak. "Thank you, Joshua. That's a lovely thing to say."

"People only call me Joshua when I'm in trouble," he said. "Rest of the time, I'm just Josh."

For the first time in way too many years, Bea's smile came from the heart. "Thank you, Josh."

The man snapped his hat on his head and nodded at Bea. "Miss Lockhart." He turned to Luc. "Evenin', Luc. Thanks for fixing those shoes so fast today."

"No problem, Bob."

Bob grabbed his son by the hand and pulled him toward the door, his wife following behind.

"The boy's right," said Luc.

Luc spoke before he thought and gave himself a mental kick. *I shouldn't have said that. Too late now.*

Lips pursed, her head tipped to the side, as she met his steady gaze.

He searched for words. "Your eyes do sparkle."

About then, Miss Vi returned, and with a flourish, placed the savory stew in front of Bea, followed by a plate with cornbread, a dish of fresh butter, and a cup of steaming coffee. She turned to Luc. "Evening, Luc. Glad to see you joining our new neighbor so she doesn't have to eat alone. Sit down. I'll bring your dinner." She whirled and headed back to the kitchen.

A long moment passed before Bea spoke up. "Please. Sit down."

Luc didn't think the offer sounded all that sincere, but he sat anyway.

"Thank you for taking my things to the hotel."

"No problem. Glad to help." He didn't mention she'd thanked him at the hotel.

Her eyes darted around the room, not settling on any one thing. "I can't get over how friendly everyone is here."

Her voice took on a faint hint of melancholy, and Luc wondered why. "Well, we try to make folks feel welcome."

This time, her eyes met his, and she smiled. "And I appreciate that. To be honest, I wasn't sure what to expect."

"Why is that?"

She shrugged. "My father is convinced this is a waste of time and money. He insists a woman alone cannot operate a business even though I ran his for the last five years."

"What business was that?"

She paused while Miss Vi placed Luc's steak in front of him. When he cut into it with relish and took a bite, her gaze fixed on his mouth as he chewed.

She skimmed her lower lip with her tongue, and a flood of heat settled below his belt. Shocked by his immediate reaction, he forced himself to look away.

"My father owns a large mercantile in New York." She took a bite of her stew, then dotted her mouth with a napkin. "Oh my, this is very good. Perfect for a day like today." She spooned another bite and continued. "Lockhart's is one of the largest in the city."

He downed his half-chewed steak and washed it down with coffee. *It can't be the same Lockhart's.* The one Annabelle dragged him to time and again. The imposing structure covered two floors and boasted a wide assortment of finery that even the picky Annabelle appreciated.

"What made you decide to buy a store here?" He sawed off another bite of meat. "We're a long way from New York."

"Precisely." The moment she spoke, her face turned a deep scarlet, and she ducked her head.

So, she wanted to be away from New York? I wonder why? "I spoke to Mable earlier. She mentioned you might need help getting your things into the house."

She hesitated, then nodded. "Yes. I will." She placed the spoon beside her bowl. "They plan to be on the train Sunday morning. It will take me a couple of days to get things in order, but I'd like to get moved in as soon as possible."

"The train leaves around eleven. I'll see that the items left at the station are delivered to the house by, say, two o'clock?"

"Thank you. I appreciate that."

There was a slight tremble to her hands when she picked up the spoon.

"That stew is better hot," he said, "Best eat before it gets cold."

The remainder of the meal passed in stilted conversation as she deflected questions about her family with observations about the town and hopes for the store.

She's Jeremiah Lockhart's daughter. The Lockharts moved within his grandfather's social circle, and they'd met a few times, but he found them pompous, self-centered, and generally unlikeable. Luc traveled a lot, so thankfully was spared much interaction with them. Nothing was ever said about a daughter until he overheard Belle and friends talking about her one evening.

He couldn't believe this was the same woman they spoke of so callously. They delighted in regaling everyone with stories of the hideously disfigured daughter and heir to the vast Lockhart fortune. According to Belle, the family was so embarrassed by her appearance, she rarely attended balls or parties and spent her days locked in her room. He'd heard from others that she attended a few functions but always alone. She never stayed long and always wore a veil that covered the scarred side of her face.

It was difficult to reconcile Belle's account with the woman in front of him. While the scar was noticeable, it certainly wasn't as Belle described and in no way detracted from the beauty of the woman behind it.

Without question, she was a lady. But she was also strong, self-confident, educated, and refined. He watched in fascination as her expression changed from subdued to excited as she spoke of her plans for the store, and he wondered how on earth that vivacious spirit survived in isolation.

Is that why you ran here? Or perhaps there is something or someone else from whom you ran?

CHAPTER FIVE

Bea bid the Barkers farewell at the station and headed for the store bright and early Sunday morning.

Her store.

She couldn't wait to begin the changes she envisioned. The inside was chilly, but after seeing the small amount of wood at the back, she decided to forego a fire in the big pot-bellied stove, reasoning she would keep warm by activity.

After less than an hour of trying to work with her hair pinned up and, in a dress, she stopped and rummaged through the men's clothing section and selected jeans and a plaid flannel shirt. She kept her modified soft corset and added a pair of long johns under the jeans, which fit a bit snug in the hips but allowed for effortless movement. A length of rope served as a belt. The shirt hugged her full bosom, but since no one would be around to notice, she wasn't concerned about propriety. Next, she added a pair of lightweight work boots, then removed the pins from her hair, and tied it at her nape with a piece of string. Satisfied with her attire, she went to work.

First up, the junk in front of the windows. After moving everything out of the way, she washed the inside of the windows and began her displays.

A small table and chair replaced the clutter on the right. A piece of the drab blue cotton, an assortment of sewing notions and ribbons, and a bonnet sat atop the table along with the latest copy of the Montgomery Ward catalog she brought with her. A search for a teapot proved fruitless, so she settled for a cup and saucer.

She placed assorted tools, a rack of seeds, and another table with coffee, tobacco, a hat, and gloves on the left side.

Inspired, she grabbed a broom and swept away the dust and grime. It took several trips out back to the well, but the floors and counters were soon dust-free and relatively clean.

Next came the arduous task of cleaning and rearranging the shelves. The pants made climbing the ladder to reach the top shelves easier to accomplish. She finished the last one behind the counter and stopped to take a breath before descending the ladder.

"Sure looks different in here."

Startled by Luc's voice, she jumped and lost her footing. Strong hands grabbed her waist and set her feet on the floor.

"My apologies, Miss Lockhart," said Luc, the hint of a smile on his face. "I did not mean to surprise you. I thought you heard me enter."

Flustered by the weight of his hands on her waist, she stood mute and stared.

"Mademoiselle? Are you all right?"

It took a moment to gather her wits, and she stepped back. "Yes. Yes, of course. I didn't hear you enter."

One heavy brow arched up as he took in her appearance. "I have never seen a woman in jeans before."

Heat rushed to her face, but she held her ground—no more hiding. "I needed something more practical for work. I did not expect anyone to see me."

"I have your things from the station. Where would you like me to put them?"

She placed the rag in her hand on the counter. "Oh, dear. I completely forgot."

"You have made good use of your time," he said as he looked around the store. "Don't recall ever seeing it this neat and organized." He nodded toward the big pot-bellied stove in the center. "Why didn't you light a fire to warm the place while you worked?"

"There was only a little wood out back, so I thought I should save it for tomorrow." A stray tendril of hair tickled her cheek, and she pushed it behind her ear. "Perhaps you can direct me to someone who can fill the wood box."

He nodded. "I usually bring the wood for Mable when she needs it. I'll take care of that later."

"I couldn't ask you to do that," she hastened. "I have imposed on you too much already."

He started for the back door. "It's no imposition. I did it for Mable. I'll do it for you." He stopped when she didn't follow. "Where would you like your things?"

She grabbed her shawl from the counter where she tossed it earlier and wrapped it around her shoulders. "There are two trunks marked for the store. The rest goes to the house. This way."

Jeremiah Lockhart's daughter. He shook his head as he watched the gentle sway of her hips when she walked away, confident she had no idea how seductive he found her choice of clothing.

Buttons on the red plaid shirt strained to hold in a full bosom, and the shirttail knotted at the waist emphasized its smallness and the generous curve of her hips. Luc's fingers itched to touch the thick, mahogany-colored curls that trailed midway down her back.

He snapped his mind away from curls and jean-clad legs and focused on the task at hand. The small, white frame house was a big box, twenty feet by twenty feet. Both the front and back had deep porches that ran its length, and a picket fence outlined the yard. As they approached the front steps, he pointed to the bushes gracing the edge of the porch. "Those are gardenias. Mable sent off for them a couple of years ago."

A smile lit up her face. "I love gardenias. My grandmother's gardener grew them in the greenhouse. The fragrance in the summer was quite intoxicating."

She stepped onto the porch and opened the front door. "Mable left the place pretty clean, so I don't have to do that." She stood in the middle of the living room and pulled the thin shawl tight around her shoulders. "I guess just put everything in here until I have time to unpack."

"I saw one of the crates marked *fragile,* and I'm guessing that's dishes?"

Her smile grew pensive, and she hugged herself tighter. "My grandmother's china."

"I'll put it on the table in the kitchen."

"Thank you again…Luc. For everything."

He nodded. "It won't take long to unload the wagon." He looked around the cozy room where he'd spent many an evening with the Barkers. The wood box beside the fireplace was empty, and he made a mental note to fill it before he left. The home was well built, and a fire in the fireplace usually provided sufficient warmth in the winter.

"I guess I'll get back to work, then." She headed for the door, and he followed. When she stopped and turned suddenly, he ran into her, throwing her off balance.

Instinctively, he grabbed for her waist and pulled her to him.

Her body melded seamlessly against him, her head touching his chin. Wide, hazel eyes stared up at him. She drew in a slow breath and turned her scarred cheek away from view.

A jumble of emotions raced through him. Gone was the happy, self-confident woman he admired. In her place stood the ostracized woman Belle ridiculed. An outcast himself for most of his life, he could guess what she endured and refused to let her think he found her wanting in any way. He placed his finger under her chin and turned her face toward him.

She resisted, but he waited.

Slowly, she turned and faced him again.

He hesitated, then his index finger traced the path of puckered flesh that extended from above her right ear, over the cheekbone, to the bottom of her chin.

Jaw clamped tight, she flinched but did not pull away.

"There are many kinds of beauty, *mon chère,* and yours outshines any scar."

Her chest rose and fell on several ragged breaths. Tears crowded the corner of her eyes but did not fall. Instead, she graced him with a timid smile and stiffened her spine. "*Merci, mon ami.*"

He released her, and she stepped back. Pulling the shawl tighter, she left him to his work.

CHAPTER SIX

Luc's words played through Bea's mind as she finished her tasks at the store. *There are many kinds of beauty, and yours outshines any scar.* Try as she might, she could not envision herself as pretty, much less beautiful. But his words nonetheless bolstered her flagging spirit.

She gathered up her discarded clothing, opting to stay in her jeans, and locked up. The day remained overcast and cold, so she was thrilled to see the wood box by the back door almost full and a smaller one with kindling resting beside it. She smiled and crossed to her soon-to-be home. The fireplace in the living room had wood ready for a fire. She debated burning it tonight, then opted to wait. She did not plan to be here long. Instead, she lit the lantern on the mantle and looked around. Items from the station sat in one corner, and the crate with her grandmother's china rested on the kitchen table.

A light floral-patterned paper on the living room walls was a nice surprise. The fireplace needed a rug in front to add a touch of color to the dark hardwood floor. A lone rocker sat off to the side.

The bedroom sat across from the living room and boasted wood walls painted a pale blue. A beautiful walnut bed rested between the front windows. The squared headboard and footboard each contained three panels with an intricate, carved floral design. On the opposite wall sat a matching dresser with a beveled mirror and a small armoire. The down-filled mattress was another pleasant surprise, and Bea easily pictured the room with curtains, a colorful spread, and pictures on the walls. Rustic and smaller than her room at Lockhart Manor, she loved it already.

Driven by a sudden need to put her mark on the place, she pushed the trunk with bedding and some personal items into the bedroom. Thirty minutes later, the bed freshly made and covered with the spread brought from New York, she looked around. Going back to the trunk, she pulled a carefully packed box from the middle and unwrapped it. The contents brought a tightness to her throat. A gift from her grandmother on her sixteenth birthday, the beautifully etched silver dresser set contained a brush, comb, mirror, and perfume bottle. She dug out two doilies she embroidered years ago and smoothed them on the dresser, then carefully placed the cherished items on top.

Next, she tucked the clothing away in the armoire and rechecked the trunk, pulling out the quilt Grandmother made for her. Cut from items she wore as a child; its brightly colored shapes held many treasured memories. A beautifully embroidered *B* on a red silk background, surrounded by flowers painstakingly stitched by her grandmother, filled the center. Throat tight, she ran tired fingers over the image. "Thank you, Granny," she whispered. "Thank you for loving me for who I am." She draped the beloved coverlet over the foot of the bed and walked to the kitchen.

A round oak table, small and free of design, sat in the center, surrounded by three matching straight-backed chairs. A cookstove, complete with upper warming oven, sat against one wall, and a freestanding wooden counter with a dry sink filled the back wall. Bea eyed the crate on the table and longed to pull out the contents but needed a hammer to open it—another thing to add to the to-do list.

A smaller room off the kitchen served as a pantry of sorts and contained a copper bathing tub surrounded by an overhead line suspended from the ceiling, probably used to shield the bather. A quick look out the back showed a deep porch ran the length of the house. A shelf attached to the wall near the door held a metal pan and hooks above it, no doubt intended for towels. A cistern sat on the east side of the porch, and on the west sat two simple wooden rockers with fading white paint.

She wondered how her mother would react to her new abode and frowned. It was doubtful she would ever see it and would undoubtedly disapprove.

She bolted the door and made another slow pass through the house. "It's mine, Grandmother. Thanks to you." She blew out the lantern and stepped onto the front porch.

A woman stood in the path to the gate. As Bea got closer, she recognized her as the one she'd seen with the cowboy above the saloon. She was young, maybe nineteen or so. Bea kept her expression neutral. "Good evening."

"Excuse the intrusion, ma'am," she said quickly, "but I seen the light on inside."

Bea hugged her clothes tighter, unsure of the woman's purpose. "What can I do for you, Miss…?"

"Reynolds. Daisy Reynolds." She ducked her head, then stood up straight and met Bea's gaze. "I work at the saloon." She paused as though waiting for a reaction.

Bea showed none. "And?"

A puzzled expression clouded Daisy's face, but she took a breath and continued. "I don't have much choice in what I do, Miss Lockhart." She nodded back toward the saloon. "But I ain't always gonna do it." She paused, the deep tint on her cheeks visible even in the failing light. "When Pa died, it was just me, Ma, and my little brother to work the farm. I tried to work it alone." She swallowed hard. "Ma's sickly and can't do much. And Levi, well, he's only ten, so we sold it and moved to town. There ain't much work here for women."

That simple statement explained a lot. Petite, with golden blond hair and blue eyes too old for her years, Bea immediately felt sorry for the girl's plight. What should be the best days of her young life were stolen away by circumstances. Who was Bea to condemn the choices one made to survive? "What can I do for you, Miss Reynolds?"

Daisy's eyes widened, and she pulled in a quick breath. "I like to sew." She looked down at her flashy green dress. "I make dresses like this for the other girls and me. Mrs. Barker ordered material when I got the money. Sometimes, she'd buy something I made and put it in the store." She hastened to add, "But we didn't tell anyone I made it 'cause most of the women wouldn't buy it if they knew."

Bea couldn't see much in the growing darkness, but the basic design was impressive, so she quickly decided on a plan. "A good seamstress is difficult to find. As it happens, I require a couple of dresses, something a little more casual than what I brought with me." She didn't bother to mention the rest of her belongings would arrive soon.

"I can do that," Daisy said quickly. "I'm really good, Miss Lockhart. I know I shouldn't brag, but I love to sew. If you show me a picture of what you want, I can make it."

"Drop by the store when you get a chance, and we'll discuss the particulars."

Daisy ducked her head again, then looked at Bea, and

managed a sad smile. "Thank you, Miss Lockhart. Don't worry; I won't come when anyone is there."

Bea knew first-hand what it was like to suffer unwarranted rejection, and her protective instincts roared to life. "You are welcome in my store anytime, Daisy," she said firmly, "whether anyone else is there or not."

Daisy nodded and walked away.

Heart heavy, Bea watched her leave. *She's just a child. I have to do something. One way or another, Daisy needs to leave that life behind.*

A gust of cold air sent her scurrying for the warmth of the hotel. Inside, she nodded to Lizzy, who stood behind the counter. "Good Evening, Lizzy."

Her new friend smiled. "Pants are a good look for you, Bea."

Lizzy's son, Michael, or Mikey for short, peeked over the counter. "Wow, Miss Bea. I never seen a woman wear pants before." A curious child of eight with curly red hair and hazel eyes, he was rarely without a smile. He came around the corner and inspected her attire.

"Wow. A woman in pants," he repeated, awestruck.

Bea chuckled despite another bout of embarrassment. "Well, now you have."

"I'll have your bath sent up right away," said Lizzy.

"Thank you." She smiled and walked up the stairs. The joy of having a friend, a real friend, put some pep in her step.

"Oh, and I left a box in your room with some stuff you might be able to use in the house." Her cheeks turned red, and she looked down, then back to Bea. "If you don't mind, I mean. It's nothing fancy. You don't have to take them if you don't need them."

"I appreciate your thoughtfulness, Lizzy, and I'm sure I will be able to use whatever it is. Thank you."

"I helped, too," said Mikey with a grin.

She touched his nose with her finger. "Well, thank you very much, Mikey."

An hour later, clean and wearing the clothing tossed aside earlier, Bea brushed her hair and wound it in a bun at her nape before walking to The Yellow Rose.

"Evening, Miss Lockhart," said Vi warmly, "just sit wherever you like. I'll bring you some coffee."

Bea chose the same table she shared with Luc and looked around. Silas Upton sat near the door. Eunice Martin and her husband occupied a table in the center. An older gentleman she didn't know shuffled over to Silas's table and sat down. Three other tabletops contained lone cowboys who nodded or smiled a greeting when their eyes met.

Miss Vi placed her coffee on the table. "I saw you working at the store earlier today."

She nodded. "A little cleaning and some reorganizing."

"I'll be over in the morning to pick up a few things."

Bea smiled. "I don't suppose there is any more of that wonderful beef stew, is there?"

"Yes, ma'am. I'll bring it right out."

One of the cowboys rose and walked by her table just as Miss Vi delivered her dinner. He tipped his hat and grinned. "Evening, ma'am."

Surprised, she returned the smile. "Good evening."

He paused as though about to say something else, then nodded and headed for the door. He opened it, then stepped aside as Daisy and another woman entered.

Mrs. Martin's face clouded with self-righteous indignation.

Unable to stop herself, Bea spoke when they walked by. "Good evening, Daisy. It's nice to see you again."

Startled, the young girl glanced at the Martin woman, then back to Bea. "Evening, Miss Lockhart."

A loud harrumph came from Eunice, and Daisy's face turned scarlet.

Bea teetered on the edge of making a scene. There was no call to be so rude to the child. "Enjoy your dinner, Daisy."

"Thank you, ma'am."

Bea ignored Mrs. Martin's glare and focused on the food in front of her.

The savory stew's first taste brought back memories of sitting in her grandmother's kitchen while the family matriarch and her namesake worked side-by-side with Cook to prepare their meals. Though wealthy in her own right, Beatrice Mae Lockhart was a kind and straightforward soul who never met a stranger. A widow for many years, she possessed an endless capacity for love and compassion, always helped those in need, usually anonymously, and instilled that kindness toward others in her only grandchild. Visits to her New Jersey home were the highlight of Bea's life, especially after the accident.

Bea never understood why her mother cared more about what her social group thought than how the injury affected her only child. Granny made an otherwise sad and lonely life bearable. Everything she valued, everything that mattered, came from her. She alone took the time to feed her inquisitive mind and shower her with the unconditional love and support withheld by her parents. With the clarity of adulthood, Bea decided they were simply incapable of thinking of anyone but themselves.

The sharp jingle of the bell above the door pulled Bea back from the painful memories that threatened to crush the joy of being on her own at last.

She heard Mrs. Martin mumble something about "eating with decent folks" as she stomped out the door.

Daisy and her friend kept their heads down and ate.

Granny's sage advice rippled through her head: *You can't save the world, Bea, but you can always make your corner of it a nicer place to be.*

And so I shall, Granny. So I shall.

CHAPTER SEVEN

ONDAY MORNING DAWNED COLD AND DREARY, BUT that didn't dampen Bea's excitement as she opened the store. A pot of coffee warmed on the side of the pot-bellied stove. A couple of chairs sat on either side.

Thanks to her talks with Mable, Bea didn't anticipate a rush of customers. But winter was winding down, and it wouldn't be long until spring rounds ups and planting season started. Things would pick up then.

She spent most of the morning gathering items she'd transfer to the house later and stacked them by the back door.

Vi Davis dropped in and placed an order, advising someone would pick it up later. Silas Upton came in for tobacco and saw the coffee pot. "How much for a cup?"

"Help yourself. Everyone needs a good cup of coffee in this weather." She pulled a tin cup from the shelf. "Use this today if you like. Or you can bring your own tomorrow. The coffee will always be on."

He looked at the cup like it was a snake. "No charge?"

"It's not a big deal. I drink coffee all day, and I'm happy to share."

Several townspeople drifted through by mid-afternoon, mainly to check out the changes, though a few bought things. Bea made it a point to tell everyone she would happily order anything they might need if they just let her know. That prompted a couple of special orders, which bolstered her spirits even more.

After lunch, several old codgers gathered around the stove, cups in hand, led by Silas Upton and another man he introduced as Amos Bigelow, the gentleman she saw him with at The Yellow Rose.

More than one offered to assist in gathering up goods or moving things around, and for the first time since her grandmother died, Bea felt accepted. Normal.

Home.

Late in the afternoon, Daisy came to the back door. Bea sketched a picture of the dress she wanted, and Daisy left with notions and a bolt of light green cotton with tiny yellow flowers she pulled from the supplies she brought along.

Satisfied with her first official day, Bea gathered up the empty cups used by Silas and his friends. They would be washed and set out for tomorrow. The bell over the front door clanged, and she looked up.

Luc's muscular frame filled the doorway. She ignored her heart's little stutter-step and the resulting heat that warmed her from the inside out. "Good evening, Luc." She placed the cup she held on the counter and walked toward him.

"Evening, ma'am." He tilted his head toward the stove. "I heard about the new gathering place."

"It would not be so inviting if you had not filled the wood box. Thank you." She was unable to keep the smile from her face or her voice. She stood in front of him, crossed and uncrossed her arms. "It's been a wonderful first day."

"I'm happy for you, *Chère*." He shoved his hands in his pants pockets. "I wanted to let you know there is plenty of wood at the house, and I added more to the box for tomorrow. I'll check it often, so don't worry about it."

"I'm very grateful. Please, just let me know what I owe for your trouble."

"Like your coffee, it is something one does for neighbors without a charge."

She started to protest, then nodded. "Thank you." After a moment, she asked, "I do need another favor if you don't mind. Well, two, actually."

"Of course. What can I do?"

"I'd like something I can put near the stove to hold the cups. Maybe a wooden rod of some kind with pegs so the cups can hang on it. I thought about a table, but that would take up too much room, and suspending it from the ceiling isn't an option."

"Give me a couple of days. I'm sure I can come up with something suitable."

They discussed the size and placement, then Luc asked. "You said two favors. What is the other?"

"I'm sorry. I know I am imposing on your hospitality, but do you have time to take some things to the house for me while I lock up?"

"But of course. Where are they?"

She showed him where the items were stacked and went about closing up the store. Before she walked out, she stood behind the counter and smiled. *I'm thirty years old and finally have a life of my own.*

A few minutes later, she stepped up on the porch as Luc exited the house.

"I made a small fire in the fireplace. I assumed you might want to put some of your things away."

"I do, so thank you again."

He stepped off the porch.

"I…um…I plan to try and move in this weekend." Bea hesitated, unsure how to proceed.

"Would you like some help?"

"Maybe. Probably. Um…I thought…I might." Flustered, she closed her eyes and tried again. "I will be at the restaurant around eight tonight. I would not object to company."

His intense gaze shifted from her eyes to her lips, and a slow, seductive smile tugged up the corners of his mouth. "I never turn down an opportunity to dine with a beautiful woman." He bowed at the waist and turned toward the gate. Two steps later, he stopped and looked back, his face unreadable. "That was a good thing you did for Daisy."

Luc waited five minutes before he entered The Yellow Rose after Bea and spotted her right away. Four long strides took him to the table they shared before. She looked up at his approach, cheeks a lovely shade of pink.

Back stiff, she kept her hands in her lap. "Please," she said, her voice a bit shaky, "Sit down."

She shifted in her seat and cleared her throat, eyes darting all around the restaurant. Finally, her gaze connected with his, and one hand fingered the napkin in front of her. The color on her cheeks deepened, and she looked away.

Some women can fake that kind of coyness, but he knew she did not. "You look lovely this evening, *mon ami*," he said softly.

Her fingers pulled on the napkin. "Thank you…Luc."

Miss Vi arrived with two cups of coffee. "Saw y'all come in and knew you'd want this." Hands resting on her hips, she looked between them. "You folks wanna order now or chat first?"

"Thank you." He looked at Bea. "I think we would like to drink our coffee first if you don't mind."

"I'll check back in a bit. We got venison steak with potatoes and green beans tonight."

Bea picked up her cup, cradling it between trembling hands. "Thank you for the fire in the fireplace. It made working at home more comfortable."

"Glad I could help. I noticed you got some work done already."

The evening passed in pleasant conversation. Stiff at first, Bea eventually relaxed enough that her smiles reached those alluring eyes. She talked freely about her day, surprised and honored when several townspeople brought gifts and things for the house.

"I now have a couch and a chair for the living room," she said happily, "and a small table to sit beside the bed. I still have things coming from New York, but I don't have to wait to move in. And Lizzy gave me the most beautiful curtains for my bedroom."

At the mention of her bedroom, an immediate flush stained her cheeks, and her gaze drifted downward.

Does your mind see what mine does, Chère?

She regained her composure and continued discussing plans for the house.

Her contagious enthusiasm elicited a smile in return even as he wondered about it. He knew the family was wealthy and lived in a stately mansion. Why would this place make her happy?

Belle told him that once Bea enjoyed a sizeable inheritance. So, why was she so willing to live in a small frame house with hand-me-down furniture?

"I still can't believe how nice everyone is," she said, shaking her head in wonder. "I mean, to just bring me things for the house."

She sat back in her chair. Voice lowered, one hand fingered the gold locket around her neck, and awe transformed her face. "I don't know why they did it. I know they're not big or expensive things, Luc, but they mean the world to me."

She looked at him with honest, open eyes, and something turned over inside. Never had he expected to find such a jewel in this place.

"Why would they do that?" she asked, her soft voice filled with surprise. "For a stranger?"

He thought it odd someone of her upbringing would find such examples of kindness unusual. "We are a small town, *Chère*. And you are now a part of it. We look out for each other and help where we can."

The glow of her smile warmed him from across the table.

Vi walked by, and they ordered supper. The remainder of the meal passed in casual conversation, neither getting off into personal topics.

Dessert was warm apple pie, and they ate with relish.

"I can cook," said Bea as she forked up the last bite, "but I don't think I'll ever be able to make a pie this good." She dabbed the edges of her mouth with a napkin then took another drink of coffee.

The action drew his gaze to plump, strawberry-colored lips, still moist from her drink. He quickly masked the unexpected groan that bubbled in his throat with a cough. *She has no idea how beautiful she is.* "So, when do you plan on moving in?"

"Saturday. If I work a little each night this week, I'll have all my things put away, get the pantry stocked from the store, and be ready to move. I could probably go before then, but if I wait until Saturday, I can sleep in on Sunday."

The small talk continued until they were the only two people seated in the dining room.

He couldn't remember the last time he'd enjoyed the company of a woman so much. She was unpretentious, open, and honest, with a keen sense of humor, and didn't mind laughing at herself.

When she barely covered a second yawn, he knew the evening must end. He pushed his cup aside. "You have had a busy day, Miss Lockhart, and I have selfishly kept you too long."

"Bea," she said hurriedly, "my friends call me Bea."

It pleased him she would allow this degree of familiarity, and he smiled in response. "Bea…I have enjoyed our evening immensely. And I hope to have the pleasure of your company again. Soon."

The blush returned to her cheeks. "I'd like that, too."

He stood and held her chair as she joined him. The subtle fragrance of roses touched his nose as they walked toward the hotel. At the foot of the stairs, she turned and graced him with a smile.

"I seem to be saying this a lot today, but thank you, Luc, for… this evening. For everything."

He allowed his gaze to drift from her eyes to her lips. "It is nothing, *Chère.*"

A quick intake of breath said she noticed his bold move. But she did not object.

"Maybe to you. But to me, well, it made today special."

He doubted she realized how sensual her quivering voice sounded. When he looked up to find her staring at his mouth, a sudden flash of desire swept through him. And with it came a powerful urge to see if her lips tasted like apple pie or coffee.

Before he could act on the impulse, the front door opened, and two cowboys swaggered in.

Luc took a step back. "I am glad the day turned out well for you." He bowed at the waist. "*Bonne nuit, Bea. Rêves agréables.*"

He hoped her sweet dreams included him. He had no doubt his would include her.

CHAPTER EIGHT

IT TOOK BEA HALF THE NIGHT TO GET OVER THE disappointment of Luc not kissing her on Monday. The unmasked look of desire she caught in his eyes surprised and thrilled her at the same time and left her wanting more. The moment did not present itself again, and the week passed in a blur of activity.

Customers came and went, and the stove became a regular gathering place for townspeople, young and old. The pole Luc made to hold the cups gained a new one every day.

Fatigue and lousy weather cost her two nights working on the house. However, she was determined to move in tonight and finish things tomorrow.

Luc promised to have the house warm for her, and she smiled at his thoughtfulness. While she secretly enjoyed comments from customers who quickly assumed them to be a couple, she wondered how he felt about it. Still, he did join her most nights at The Rose for dinner, which pleased her and helped fuel the gossip mill.

He always arrived after her, and neither made any pretense of it being accidental. The wished-for-kiss from Monday stayed at the forefront of her mind. More than once, she hoped the moment would present itself again, but to no avail, which made her wonder if perhaps she imagined it or maybe she should encourage him in some way, though she lacked the nerve to try.

While her mother discouraged Bea's attendance at parties, particularly at home, her grandmother always ensured she had the opportunity to socialize at every visit to her New Jersey home. Shy and self-conscious at these events, Bea's skill at flirting was woefully inadequate. What little she did know came from hiding in the shadows during the few parties she attended and marveled at how some women used their beauty as a tool.

Like Annabelle Blankenship.

A year younger than Bea, she and Annabelle were friends at one time. Beautiful, sophisticated, and pampered, when Belle simpered and smiled, men groveled at her feet, seemingly unaware of her lack of sincerity.

But Bea knew first-hand that inside the golden-haired beauty with sky blue eyes and a stunning smile lay a mean and spiteful person who took great delight in demeaning others.

Six months after the accident that changed Bea's life forever, Annabelle slipped into Bea's room. She made no effort to hide her shock at seeing the jagged scar which had not yet healed. The resulting scene had the entire household staff in a wild-eyed panic.

Later, Bea discovered Belle spread all manner of lies and exaggerations among their mutual friends. She called the scar hideous and vowed she now understood why her parents kept her hidden away. Bea seldom attended social events, so her contact with Belle was infrequent over the ensuing years. But, thanks to household staff, she kept up with her and others in their circle of past friends.

Rumor had it that Annabelle became engaged a couple of years ago. Bea remembered feeling sorry for the man and hoped he came to his senses in time. Perhaps he did because the marriage never took place.

She shook her head to dispel the painful memories threatening to cast a cloud over her big day. *Tonight, I sleep in my new home.*

A cold rain began Saturday morning, and by late afternoon, Bea decided to close early. She placed a note on the door advising anyone who needed something to come to the house. Lizzy, Miss Vi, and a lady she didn't know came in just before she locked the door.

"We're here to help you get settled," said Miss Vi. She indicated the other lady with them. "This is Mavis Morton. Doc's wife." She pointed to the basket Mavis held. "And that's fresh bread and a cake."

Caught off-guard, Bea stared. "I don't know what to say except thank you. But, well, there isn't much left to move except my things at the hotel."

"I hope you don't mind," said Lizzy, "I had Luc take your things to the house earlier since I knew you wanted to stay there tonight."

"And supper's all ready for you and Luc, so you won't have to cook when you get home," said Vi.

Home.

Bea's throat constricted. She had a home now and friends. "I decided to close early, so I guess there isn't anything to do but go home."

A few minutes later, they entered the brightly lit house.

Bea stopped inside the door and gasped.

The house was full of people.

A colorful rug lay in front of a blazing fire. The couch, a new chair, and the rocker were positioned to enjoy the warmth. A beautiful landscape painting hung over the mantle. Curtains covered the windows, and two small tables with glowing lamps sat on each end of the couch.

In the kitchen, a lace cloth covered the table set for two with her grandmother's china, and pleasant aromas drifted from containers resting on the stove.

"Welcome home!" the gathering shouted in unison.

She turned to the ladies behind her, unable to stop the flow of happy tears. "Thank you," she sniffed, then turning to the people inside, she repeated, "Thank you. Thank you all so much."

A sea of excited voices quickly overwhelmed her as they reported on their efforts to *spruce up the place* as a surprise. Each room held a unique contribution from someone in the group. The curtains in the living room came from Mavis Morton, and Lizzy added the painting. The banker's wife donated the tablecloth and Silas the rocker. No one seemed to know who gave the small settee in the bedroom, and the sconces on the walls came from a lawyer in town.

There were so many canned foods, decorative items, and such, she soon lost track of her benefactors and settled for a heartfelt "thank you" to everyone present. The group milled around munching cookies and drinking coffee supplied by someone, though Bea couldn't remember who.

At length, she got an opportunity to speak to the crowd. "I can't thank you all enough for this evening. You have no idea how much your thoughtfulness means to me."

"Now, missy," groused Amos, "If you're gonna go gettin' all mushy and sentimental, I'm goin' home."

Everyone laughed, and Vi spoke up. "Okay, folks, time to let Miss Bea and Luc enjoy their supper and some peace and quiet."

Luc stood at the back of the crowd, and Bea refused to look his way, afraid her reddened face would intensify and give away her thoughts.

The people filed out one-by-one, offering congratulations and well wishes. She couldn't be happier.

Lizzy was last out the door. "I'm so glad you decided to make Bakersville your home. I can't tell you how much I appreciate your friendship." Looking back at Luc, she continued. "Thanks for helping us set this up."

Luc observed from the open doorway between the kitchen and living room. Bea fascinated him. The joy on her face and the delight in her voice transformed her completely. If he thought her beautiful before, tonight she was stunning.

There wasn't a person in the room untouched by her sincerity or the magic of her smile.

That smile. Those lips. He found his gaze drawn to them again and again, trying to suppress the desire to taste them.

After Lizzy left, Bea shut the door, then leaned against it as her gaze traveled over the living room. She walked to the mantle and touched an oddly shaped vase of some kind with embellished flowers painted on it. He thought it gaudy. The look on her face said it was priceless.

She sighed and walked to him. "I understand I have you to thank for this evening."

He shrugged. "Actually, it was Lizzy's idea. I just help spread the word."

He didn't miss the tremble in her hands as she clasped them demurely in front of her. "It seems I am indebted to you again." Her chest rose and fell on one long, measured breath. "Thank you, Lucian."

His heart skipped a beat when she met his steady gaze. "It is not your thanks I want, *Chère*," he said hoarsely and took a step toward her.

Her eyes widened slightly, and her nostrils flared. "Then what?"

He took another step, giving her time to retreat. She didn't.

He was close enough to note the green flecks in her eyes and to smell the lingering scent of tobacco and oil from the store.

"This," he said hoarsely and, cupping her face in his hands, leaned down. He intended the kiss to be gentle, persuasive, meant to entice her to want more. That plan disintegrated the moment the soft fullness of her lips touched his.

He crushed his mouth against hers, firm and searching, unable to get close enough, to taste deep enough.

She gripped the front of his shirt and moaned deep in her throat. A shudder shook her body.

Suddenly, the part of his brain still functioning recognized she did not return the kiss as much as she endured it. He pulled back and rested his forehead against hers, breath coming in jerky gasps. "I am so sorry, *Chère*. I did not mean to be rough."

She sucked in a breath, still gripping his shirt. "I'm sorry…I'm not very good at—at kissing."

"The only fault here is mine." He pulled back a little more, hands still cupping her face. "The thought of kissing you has driven me to distraction for days."

"It has?"

He nodded. "The kiss in my mind was to be gentle, but…" he expelled a deep breath. "One taste was more than I could handle. Forgive me. Please."

Blinking rapidly, she unclenched his shirt and smoothed out the wrinkles. "Perhaps," she said softly, "We could try the kiss in your mind next time."

Despite the tension coiled inside him, he smiled and lowered his head and traced the outline of her lips with his tongue. "You ate the oatmeal cookies tonight."

She trembled, and her hands grabbed his shirt again. "Do you like oatmeal?"

"I do now."

He touched her lips lightly, caressing more than kissing, and his hands slid down her shoulders to her hips and pulled her close.

Her arms slid around his waist. Tentative at first, she soon gave herself freely to the hunger of his kiss.

The sweet tenderness of her acceptance nearly undid him, and he deepened the kiss, his tongue exploring the recesses of her mouth while his hands kept her hips firmly against him. Lost in the sensation, he didn't want to stop.

How long they stayed that way, he could not guess, but when it ended, their heavy breathing was the only sound in the room.

BEA'S MIND SWAM THROUGH A SEA OF TANGLED EMOTIONS. Nothing she'd ever experienced equaled the last few minutes in Luc's arms. The roughness of his first kiss surprised and disappointed her. But this, ah, this more than made up for it.

When he pulled back and folded her in his arms, she sighed in contentment and rested her head on his chest. The rapid thump of his heart against her ear echoed her own erratic pulse. *Who knew a kiss could be so potent?*

She thought briefly of Edmond. Where his lips were chaste and cold, Luc's ran white-hot and full of passion, and she idly wondered if that same fire occurred in the bedroom. Shocked at her thoughts, she buried her nose in his chest. He smelled like leather and wood and something she could not define.

A light chuckle resonated in his chest. "That was more what I had in my mind, *Chère*."

"Me, too." She squeezed her eyes shut. *I didn't mean to say that out loud.*

He leaned back, and she reluctantly met his steady gaze.

"So, you thought of kissing me, too, eh?" The smile in his eyes held a sensual flame.

She hesitated. To agree would be improper; to disagree, a lie. The twinkle in his eye spurred her on. "The thought crossed my mind."

His smile widened in approval. Then his stomach growled loud enough to be heard. "I think maybe we should eat before I pass out from hunger." He took her hand in his and led the way to the kitchen.

Bea took the lid off the pot on the stove. "Mmmm…I love this stew." A check of the warming oven revealed cornbread and apple pie. "My favorites," sighed Bea.

Within minutes, they were seated at the table, enjoying the tasty meal.

"I truly enjoy her cooking, but I'm looking forward to preparing meals in my own kitchen," said Bea, between bites.

"You cook?"

The expression on his face said the comment surprised him. "Of course. My grandmother taught me."

The beginnings of a smile curled up the corners of his mouth. "Perhaps I can sample your efforts some time."

Keenly aware of his scrutiny, she cursed the heat rising from her neck. "After all you've done for me since I arrived, the least I can do is cook you a meal."

"I shall look forward to it."

A secretive smile softened his lips, and Bea's heart skipped again. He was so handsome it took her breath away. Immediately, troubling questions arose. *Is he like Edmund? Will he use his looks to take advantage? Is he handsome on the outside but ugly on the inside?*

Unhappy with the direction of her thoughts, she sat up straighter and changed the subject. "I still can't believe everyone took the time to come by this evening and bring gifts. I'm afraid I lost track of who brought what. And no one seemed to know where the settee in the bedroom came from."

Luc stopped eating and placed his spoon inside the bowl. A tight frown replaced his smile.

"Luc? What's wrong?"

"I was asked to bring it here."

"By whom?"

He hesitated. "Daisy." He pushed his bowl aside and folded his hands on the table. "She wanted to do something to repay the kindness you extended." Expression unreadable, he continued. "It came from her room above the saloon."

Bea's mind raced with questions and assumptions. *Did Luc visit her there?* He was a man, and men did such things, but, in her mind, Daisy was a child.

"She didn't want you to know where it came from for fear of rejection." His gaze did not waver. "Daisy is a child forced into a woman's role who has received little kindness from most in town." He paused. "You and Lizzy are about the only women who speak to her."

Before Bea could form a reply, he spoke again. "And no, I do not visit her there."

Face flaming, she wanted to deny the thought crossed her mind, but Bea hated deception. Gaze lowered in shame, she took a breath and looked up. "You look out for her." She inhaled deeply. "I'm sorry for my thoughts, Lucian. Please tell Daisy I am very grateful for her gift."

He nodded, pulled the bowl back in front of him, and scooped up a spoonful of stew. "I like my name on your lips."

She blinked, then smiled. "I'm glad…Lucian."

When the meal was over, he insisted on helping put the kitchen to rights. Afterward, he added wood to the fireplace, and they sat side-by-side on the couch, his arm draped over the back behind her, long legs stretched out in front.

"I would very much like to know more about you, *Chère*," said Luc at last.

She lifted one shoulder, let it drop, very conscious of his nearness. "Not much to tell. I grew up in New York. Spent a lot of time with my grandmother in Newark—that's in New Jersey—until she died eight years ago."

"You were close?"

Fond memories washed over her, and she leaned back, the warmth of his arm reaching her neck. "Yes, we were. Especially after the accident." Thoughts of her parents' initial reaction, especially her mother, still made her heart ache. "It was difficult for my mother to deal with, so Granny took care of me for several months." She resisted the urge to nestle against his side, the lure of his heat more inviting than was probably wise. "Afterwards, I spent as much time there as I could." *Because my parents and their friends treated me like a leper.*

"And you never married?"

She flinched. "I was engaged once. Until I discovered his only interest was my money." She angled her head to look up at him. "What about you?"

He stared straight ahead, his beautifully expressive eyes cold and intense. "It would seem we have a similar past."

She understood his discomfort. Her breakup with Edmund happened months ago, yet the anger and hurt at being so gullible remained an open sore. "I'm sorry. I did not mean to cause you pain."

He shook his head. "The only pain is knowing I was a fool, *Chère.*"

She sighed. "Something else we have in common." She paused. "He was a new associate of my father's and stayed with us occasionally. One night I thought everyone had gone to bed, so I went to the library for a book, and he found me there. Said he'd been hoping to meet me. He didn't look away when—anyway, I was surprised at his interest." Even now, the shame at being so fooled by Edmund's attention retained the power to render her speechless. It didn't help that her mother insisted she should be grateful someone came along who would have her despite her disfigurement.

Luc slid his arm off the back of the couch and around her shoulder to pull her close.

"I should have seen through such an obvious pretense," she said, her gentle voice filled with self-reproach.

His fingers caressed her upper arm. "The heart can be blind, *Chère*." He paused. "It is his loss."

She remained silent a moment. "You know what I find strange now?"

"What?"

"I've been here for two weeks." She stopped and gathered her thoughts. "Very few people even appear to notice my scar, but back home, everyone did." *And always made me feel defective and ugly.*

"It is because they see the beauty inside you, *Chère*," he said softly. "They see your heart."

She swallowed hard as a tear found its way down her cheek. No one but Granny ever made her feel special. Even Edmond, who professed undying devotion "despite your scar," never called her pretty, let alone beautiful. Luc, who barely knew her, told her that several times in their short acquaintance.

Voice choked with emotion, she murmured, "Thank you, Lucian."

He tipped her chin up and lowered his head. "No sadness tonight, *Chère*," he whispered.

She held her breath and waited. The touch of his lips sent the pit of her stomach into a wild swirl, and she gave herself freely to the sensation.

Her only kiss before now came from Edmund. The cold and chaste brush of his lips did not compare. This—this was heaven, and she savored every moment.

He shifted on the couch, pulling her to him, chest-to-chest, while his lips worked their magic. His tongue teased her mouth open, then thrust inside.

Shock gave way to pleasure as dormant nerve endings stirred and sprang to life.

Flooded with unfamiliar yet thrilling sensations, she moaned softly and clutched his shirt, returning the kiss with reckless abandon.

He growled low in his throat and moved his mouth over hers, turning her insides to mush.

All too soon, he pulled back, his ragged breath and racing heart a match for her own. He sighed deeply and tucked her against his side.

She rested her head on his shoulder and waited for balance to return.

Despair vanished, and a new sense of life and strength emerged. *My place is here. With him.*

For the first time in her life, she knew what it was like to be desired by a man, to *feel* desire for him in return. The doubts she suffered earlier disappeared. Lucian was not Edmund. He had no hidden agenda. He cared for *her.*

Regardless of what may happen tomorrow, tonight, she was at peace and happy with her life.

CHAPTER TEN

BEA STOOD AT THE BACK DOOR AND SCANNED THE woods behind the house. Saturday's dreary weather gave way to sunny skies and slightly warmer temperatures on Sunday. She caught sight of the firewood by the back door and thought of Luc, who insisted on leaving via the back last night. His departure followed a lengthy goodbye kiss that, even in memory, sent shock waves through her body. Delicious, forbidden dreams made sleep all but impossible.

The desire he ignited was a new sensation and something she longed to explore. "He is the most handsome, kindest, and sincere man I have ever known," she whispered to the wind. "But I trusted my heart once, and look what happened. I don't know what to do."

She enjoyed his companionship, his laughter, even the silence. She told him more about herself in their short acquaintance than she ever told anyone, even Edmund. While he hadn't yet opened up about his past, she didn't think he hid secrets. Still, he intrigued her. He made her feel good about herself and happy to be in his company.

Always honest with herself, she recognized the longing in her soul and knew such an attraction could prove dangerous. The feelings he stirred to life clouded her judgment. Her upbringing said resist, but her body craved more. What if she gave in to temptation? Was she prepared for the consequences? What if he used her and left? A *fallen woman* label would ruin her only chance at independence.

But a life alone would destroy her soul.

She stood a moment longer, then closed the door and went back to the kitchen where hot biscuits waited along with freshly cooked bacon and gravy. She had more than enough to last for several meals, unless, of course, Luc dropped by. Just the thought was enough to send a ripple of excitement through her body.

She reached for eggs from the basket on the counter but stopped at the soft knock on the back door.

Luc.

Her pulse skittered, and she made herself take a slow, deep breath before answering the door, surprised to find Daisy on the other side.

The young girl held a bundle against her chest, her eyes darting around. "I'm sorry to come in the daytime, Miss Lockhart, but I wanted to see if you had time to try on the dress to see if I need to make any adjustments."

Bea took the bundle from her outstretched hands. "Thank you, Daisy. Please. Come in."

She took a step back, her face scarlet. "Oh, no, miss. Someone might see me."

Bea's heart ached for the young girl's plight. "Please, Daisy. Come inside."

Head bowed, Daisy walked in, and Bea shut the door.

"I'm glad you stopped by so I can thank you for the settee. It's perfect for getting dressed in the mornings."

The young woman's eyes clouded with unshed tears. "Oh, miss, it was—I didn't ..."

Bea stepped forward and placed a hand on Daisy's arm.

"The only thing that matters to me is that it was something you wanted me to have."

A heartbreaking sob escaped as Daisy stood there.

Bea didn't think about it. She put the package on the table and pulled the girl into her arms. Daisy's distraught cries increased in volume, and she hugged her tighter.

When at last the tears subsided, Daisy took a step back, her eyes red and swollen. "I'm so sorry, Miss Lockhart. I didn't mean to do that."

Bea pulled a handkerchief from her pocket and passed it to the girl. "We all need a good cry now and then, Daisy. There is no shame in that." Bea noted the dark circles under her eyes and the gauntness in her cheeks. *She's lost weight. And she isn't getting enough rest. I hope it's not because she was busy making my dress instead of taking care of herself.*

She saw Daisy's eyes widen slightly at the food on the stove.

"I was just about to have breakfast. Please, sit. Would you like coffee? I'm afraid that's all I have at the moment. Someone is bringing me fresh milk later today."

Daisy glanced at the food then to the door. "I really shouldn't stay."

She eased Daisy into a chair. "As you can readily see, I have made way more than one person can eat." She picked the dress up from the table and took it to the bedroom. "I'll try it on after we eat."

She returned and placed the coffee on the table along with plates and forks, then went back to the eggs.

Daisy sipped her coffee. "I really shouldn't stay long, ma'am. Ma's expecting me." Her voice dropped lower, and she ducked her head. "I don't...I don't work on Sundays, so I help her do things around the house, and she's gonna help me finish your dress."

"She's lucky to have you to help her," said Bea as she cracked eggs into a skillet.

Daisy said nothing more as Bea finished putting food on the table.

A soft grumble from Daisy's stomach as she looked at the bounty put a knot in Bea's throat.

"Thank you, ma'am. I ain't had biscuits and gravy in some time." Her hands shook as she picked up a biscuit and carefully added butter. "Ma cooks some when she can, but…"

The knot in Bea's throat grew. "Well, I hope they're edible. It's been a while."

Daisy focused her attention on the food. She ate slowly as though savoring each bite. When half the eggs and bacon were gone, she sat back. "Um, I think I'm full. It was near as good as what Ma used to cook."

"Why, thank you, Daisy. That is high praise indeed."

The girl shifted in her chair, and her eyes looked everywhere but at Bea. "Uh, um, since I'm full, I wondered if might take this to Levi. My little brother." She finally made eye contact. "If you don't mind, I mean."

By now, the knot in her throat nearly choked off her breath. "Of course, I don't. In fact, why don't you take what's left to your family." She gave a little laugh. "Obviously, I don't know how to cook for one person, and it will likely go to waste."

The look on the girl's face clearly said she was torn between accepting Bea's offer or being insulted by it.

Before Bea could think of a way to soften the blow to her dignity, Daisy sat up straighter, her voice barely above a whisper, as though she spoke to herself. "Sometimes you gotta put pride aside and do what must be done." She inhaled deeply. "Ma and Levi will be grateful for the food."

Bea nodded. "Finish your breakfast, child, while I try on the dress."

"Watch out for the pins."

Once in her bedroom, she shut the door and leaned against it, willing the tears away. *Just how destitute is her family?*

Once she regained her composure, she quickly donned the outfit, being careful of the pins, and went back to the kitchen. Daisy sat facing the back door, her plate empty. She jumped up and came around the table. "Oh, ma'am, this color is so pretty on you."

"You did a wonderful job, Daisy. And I like that you made the bottom and top separate." She lifted the sides of the skirt. "And it's not too full. Just like I wanted."

Daisy circled her, checking the ivory lace that edged the square collar, the bell sleeves' length, and the hooks down the front. "I have more lace for the sleeves, and I want to add buttons on the front for looks." She knelt on the floor, marked the hem with a pin, and then stood and checked the skirt's fit. "I need to take this in a bit more." Her smile was radiant. "You have such a tiny waist."

After a few more adjustments, she stepped back. "I added some pockets to the skirt. I know that's not normal, but with you working and all, I thought you might need them."

Bea found them and stuck her hands inside. "I love it! Thank you so much."

Red-faced, Daisy smiled. "You're welcome. I'm glad you like it."

"You said your mother helped you. Is that where you learned to sew?"

She nodded. "Before Pa died and she took sick, Ma used to sew for folks, and she taught me. Now, she helps me sew when she's up to it."

"May I ask what ails her?"

"Doc doesn't really know." She paused. "I think she just misses Pa too much." She ducked her head. "I reckon me working at the saloon don't help none, neither. If it wasn't for Levi, I think she would have joined Pa by now."

Bea didn't know how to respond to her comment. "Help yourself to more coffee or whatever while I change."

A few minutes later, she found Daisy back at the table, a cup of coffee in her hands.

Bea placed the folded outfit on the table and handed Daisy some money. "It is customary in New York to pay half the cost for a dress at this point with the balance being due when it's delivered." A little white lie to save what remained of the girl's pride.

Daisy looked at the money, and her eyes grew wide. "Miss, this is too much."

Bea turned around and began gathering the food. "It is less than what I would have paid my seamstress in New York because I furnished the material."

"Really?"

Bea nodded. "I told you. A good seamstress is difficult to find. And since I cannot sew a stitch, I'm happy to find someone who can." She pointed to the bathing room across the hall. "There is a small basket over in the corner. Would you get it, please? We'll use it for the food."

In no time, the basket was full of leftovers along with some items Bea slipped in when Daisy wasn't looking. She covered it all with the dress and handed it to the girl.

"I don't know how to thank you, Miss Lockhart."

"My friends call me Bea. And you owe me no thanks. You're doing me a favor by taking this."

Daisy's expression said she knew otherwise, but she didn't argue. "Thank you just the same." She hugged the basket to her and turned for the back door.

"Wait."

"Yes, ma'am?"

"My friends are always welcome in my home or my store."

"...Thank you, miss."

"And Daisy?"

"Ma'am?"

"I hope you will let me know if there is ever anything I can do to help you or your family."

She looked down at the basket and smiled. "You already did."

CHAPTER ELEVEN

ONDAY DAWNED SUNNY AND MILD, AND MORE
people came into the store. The laughter and
conversation reinforced her connection to the town
and its people. Each new contact solidified her feeling of belonging.

Despite the constant activity, Luc was never far from her
mind. She couldn't deny the spark of excitement that came when a
whiff of leather or wood smoke reignited the memory of their first
kiss. Like a breathless girl of eighteen, he brought undeveloped
senses to life and filled her with such yearning, clear thought fled.
It was apparent they shared an intense physical awareness of each
other, but what did that mean? What could come of it?

I can't let my emotions govern my actions again.

"Bea? Is something wrong?"

Lizzy's soft question jerked her back to reality. "What? No,
just thinking."

Lizzy's smile said she knew what occupied her mind, but
thankfully, she did not voice it. "I said, that was a good thing you
did for Daisy yesterday." Lizzy stood in front of the counter and
passed Bea a list of items she wanted.

"It was nothing," said Bea, glancing at the list.

"To you, maybe, not to her."

"I can't help but feel sorry for her. I wish there were more I
could do to help."

"I know. I'm the same way."

Bea pointed to the small list of items. "Do you want to wait for these or pick them up later?"

"I'll wait. I have someone minding the hotel, and I needed some fresh air."

"Daisy really is an excellent seamstress," said Bea as she pulled items from a shelf and placed them in a basket.

Lizzy nodded. "Mavis Morton told me her mother used to sew for extra money, but after her husband died, and she got sick, that stopped."

The beginning of an idea formed, and Bea pursed her lips in thought, glad the store was empty at the moment.

"I can see the wheels turning, Bea," said Lizzy with a smile. "What's up?"

Bea put the basket on the counter and tallied up the items. "Daisy told me she sometimes made things that Mrs. Barker sold in the store."

She nodded. "I bought a couple of them."

"I can continue to do that."

Lizzy's face clouded with concern. "Thanks to the likes of Eunice Martin, if people know she made it, they may be reluctant to buy."

"What if they didn't know? What if I kept her name out of it? Or maybe I could say her mother—what's her name, by the way?"

"Della. Della Reynolds."

The clang of the bell over the door stopped any reply as Mrs. Martin walked in. When she spotted Lizzy, she stopped. "I'll come back another time."

"There's no need for that, Mrs. Martin." Lizzy picked up her basket and walked toward her. "I was just leaving."

Eunice side-stepped too fast and stumbled against the mug stand, rattling the contents.

Lizzy grabbed her elbow to keep her upright.

The snippy woman stared at the hand on her arm.

"Don't worry, Mrs. Martin," said Lizzy with a smile. "I'm not poisonous."

The busybody huffed and jerked her arm free.

"You're welcome, by the way," said Lizzy and walked out.

Bea watched the exchange and forced her face into a neutral expression. Never in her life had she met someone so totally unlikeable as Eunice Martin. "What can I do for you today, Mrs. Martin?"

She slapped a piece of paper on the counter as the cowbell above the door announced another customer.

Amos Bigelow shuffled in and grabbed a cup from the stand next to the stove. "Morning, Miss Lockhart, Missus Martin."

"Good morning, Amos," said Bea. "Thank you again for the beautiful rug. It's perfect in front of the fireplace."

Amos nodded and filled his cup. "Glad to get shed of it," he grumbled.

Bea didn't miss the flush on his cheek or the tiny smile that edged up one corner of his mouth before he turned and sat in one of the chairs by the stove.

Bea scanned the list Eunice placed on the counter. "I'll have these items ready shortly. Do you wish to wait, or will someone pick them up later?"

"Mable always delivered my orders," came the righteous reply.

"Well, I can do that as well, but it will be after I close."

"I need it this afternoon. I'm baking for the church social this weekend."

Bea took a deep breath. "I will see what I can do."

Mrs. Martin's glare turned frosty. "If you want to stay in business in this town, Miss Lockhart, you need to be mindful of who you allow in your store."

That was the last straw. Bea summoned every ounce of control she possessed and looked at the snobbish woman. "Perhaps you are right, Mrs. Martin."

Nose in the air, back straight, she glared at Bea. "Of course, I am."

"However, as a businesswoman, I cannot afford to restrict who comes into my store. So, perhaps you may want to send someone in with your list next time. That way, you won't be subjected to those you deem unworthy." Bea kept her voice cordial, a forced smile in place.

The woman scowled at her. "I'll expect my order delivered by this afternoon." She sucked in air and turned to leave.

"Good riddance," barked Amos. "Now I can enjoy my coffee in peace."

"Wretched old man," she snapped and stomped out the door.

Bea suffered a tiny bit of regret. It was not in her nature to be unkind to anyone, but that woman pushed too far. "I'm probably going to regret that," she mumbled.

"Don't worry 'bout her, Miss Lockhart," said Amos. "She's so spiteful, even the devil don't like her."

The damage was done either way. "I better get her order together."

"I'll watch the place for you if you want to deliver it so she don't get all grumpy again."

"Thanks, Amos. I appreciate that."

The rest of the day passed in a flurry of activity, leaving

Bea little time to worry about Eunice Martin or to dwell on her growing feelings for Luc. Unchartered territory, she couldn't decide on an appropriate path. Her heart told her one thing, her mind another.

Focus on work, Beulah Mae, focus on work. The rest will take care of itself in time.

She had just locked the front when Daisy and her brother Levi came to the back.

"I finished your dress, Miss Lockhart," said Daisy. "I hope you like it."

Bea unfolded the garment and smiled. "I love it. Your work is excellent."

Daisy released a deep breath. "Thank you, ma'am."

Bea reached for the cash box to pay her.

"Um, ma'am, if you don't mind, instead of paying me, could I maybe trade for some stuff?"

Remembering what Mable said about bartering, Bea quickly agreed. "Of course. What would you like?"

Bea wasn't surprised when Daisy's items were kitchen staples.

"I think that's all for now," said Daisy.

"Based on what I owe you," said Bea, "there is still money remaining." Bea saw Levi eyeing the assorted candy on the counter. "Maybe some candy for Levi or perhaps some coffee or tea?"

Levi's eyes widened and quickly shuttered. "I don't need any candy, Daisy."

"Yes," she said firmly. "You do." She looked at Bea. "Please add some licorice and peppermint sticks. And if there's enough left, some coffee for Ma."

Bea filled a basket with their order and added the coffee

and some canned peaches. "I'm glad you stopped by. I wanted to talk to you about making some things for the store."

"Like what?"

"I've ordered some new material in brighter colors for spring." She pushed the wrapped packages toward Daisy. "I wondered if you and your mother could make a couple of simple dresses that I might put out to sell. Something a young farmer's wife would be able to wear for maybe church or socials. I'll furnish the material and pay you to make them."

Daisy's smile faded almost as fast as it started. "But no one will buy them if…"

"You let me worry about that." Bea saw the indecision on her face. "Why don't you discuss it with your mother and let me know. There's this one bolt of green silk I would love to see made into a nice evening dress. I have a pattern for it, too."

"Okay. I'll let you know." She turned to Levi, who held candy in each hand. "Come on. We have to hurry. I need to get to work."

Head bowed, he mumbled. "I wish you didn't have to work there."

Daisy closed her eyes and inhaled. "I know, Levi, but I do."

He looked up, and Bea's heart broke at the pain in his eyes.

"If I was older, I could work, and you wouldn't have to do that."

"One day, things will be different. I promise. But, right now, it has to be."

He nodded and followed her out the back door.

Luc approached Bea's door with a little trepidation and a lot of anticipation. He hadn't seen her since Saturday. Yet, the memory of their kiss still caused his breath to quicken and his heart rate to jump. His fingers tingled with the need to touch her face, the silkiness of her hair, her lips. He drew in a deep breath, blew it out slowly, then did it again before knocking.

The door opened, and there she stood, face flushed, eyes bright and excited, a tentative smile tipping up the corners of her mouth.

"Hi," she said softly, then stepped to the side. "Please come in."

She closed the door behind him. "Let me take your coat."

She placed it on a hook by the door, and the thought crossed his mind that it looked at home there.

"Supper's ready."

A few minutes later, they sat at the table, plates full of roast pork, potatoes, and beans.

"You are an accomplished cook, *Chère*," he said between bites. "This is delicious."

The color on her cheeks deepened, and she smiled. "Thank you, Lucian."

Small talk filled the time as they ate. He enjoyed watching her animated face when she talked about the different people who came into the store or the open amusement when she related the lively conversations between Silas and Amos. She was incredibly proud of the sign he installed for her today: *Lockhart's General Store*.

But it was her voice that mesmerized him. Sophisticated, yet intoxicatingly soft and mellow, it soothed and calmed like a bubbling brook. Troubles vanished, and life suddenly became new and exciting once more, and he found himself wishing for things that could never be. She was too good for the likes of him.

Wasn't she?

The meal over and dishes done, they once again sat

side-by-side on the couch. The warming glow of the fireplace cast her face in muted shadows. The intimate silence lasted for several minutes.

"We were coming back from dinner in town," Bea said softly, "my thirteenth birthday."

He knew without being told the story she was about to relate. When she paused, he draped an arm around her shoulders.

"There was a storm. Old Grover, the carriage driver, didn't see the tree across the road until it was too late. One minute we were racing to get home before the storm worsened. The next, we rolled down an embankment. The horses…" She took a breath. "Then, just blackness."

He pulled her closer, and she rested her head on his shoulder.

"I was unconscious for three days." She picked at some lint on her skirt. "The doctor did the best he could, but the cut was deep, and some skin was too far gone to save."

"That must have been very painful for you."

She lifted one shoulder, let it drop. "It was. But I think what hurt more was my parents' reaction." She drew in a shaky breath. "I still don't understand it."

He caressed her upper arm with his fingers. "Discovering people are human can be a disappointment."

She remained silent for so long he wondered if he'd said the wrong thing.

"What about your parents?" Bea asked at last, "Where are they?"

"My mother was part Choctaw, my father a French fur trapper. He was injured by a bear, and my grandfather brought him to their village. My mother helped nurse him back to health, and they fell in love." He couldn't keep the smile from his voice as he recalled his father's tale of meeting his mother and falling in love with the beautiful maiden. Their courtship lasted two winters because her parents didn't look kindly on a white man marrying their only daughter. "It took some convincing to get her parents to allow them to marry." He took a breath. "Cholera took them both when I was twelve."

"I'm so sorry, Lucian."

"No need, *Chère*. My parents had a good life. We had a good life." He stopped, unsure how much more to tell at this point. Chances were good that she knew his grandfather and thus would know of his worth. He had to know she cared about him and not the money. He settled for a partial truth. "I was left in the care of my grandfather on my father's side and rarely saw my mother's people again."

"How awful that must have been for you."

"As we all do, *Chère*, I adapted. Now, no more sad talk. Tell me more about Daisy and the dressmaking business idea."

Her expression brightened, and she turned to face him. "Well, I wanted to—"

A soft knock on the door stopped her.

"Who on earth would be coming by at this hour," mused Bea.

When she opened the door, a battered and bruised Daisy collapsed in front of her.

CHAPTER TWELVE

"How is she, Doc?"

Luc stared at the young girl asleep in Bea's bed, her delicate complexion marred by varying shades of black and purple bruises. Anger and vengeance fired his blood.

Someone would pay.

"Nothing appears broken, a couple of bruised ribs," said Doc sadly, "took several blows to the head and face. She won't be able to see out of her right eye until the swelling goes down, probably several days." He closed his bag. "I gave her some laudanum. She should sleep till morning."

"What can I do for her?" Bea sat on the edge of the bed, holding Daisy's hand.

"Just keep her comfortable," said Doc. "She's gonna feel every one of those blows tomorrow." He placed a brown bottle on the table beside the bed. "She's small, so start with six drops of this in some water for pain. No more than ten at a time." He took another long look at her and shook his head. "Damn shame. I'll check on her tomorrow."

Luc walked him out, and they stood on the porch in silence as another man strode up the path.

"Evening, Luc. Doc," said Sheriff Jeff Dawson. "How is she?"

Doc repeated what he told Luc.

"I talked to some folks at the saloon, but no one actually saw what happened," said Dawson. "Last seen talking to this new guy from the Circle B. One of the girls told me no one liked him because he tended to get rough."

"What's his name?" snapped Luc.

Voice firm, Dawson locked eyes with Luc. "This is my job, son, and I'll take care of it."

A former Texas Ranger, Dawson's looks fooled many an unsuspecting lawbreaker. Tall and slender with snow-white hair, he was tough as boot leather and meant what he said. So did Luc. "Good." *Cause I will if you don't* was the unspoken end to that sentence.

Doc walked back toward town, and Luc stared at Dawson. "Dammit, Jeff, he could have killed her. She ain't big as nothing. And she's a kid."

Jeff took off his hat and ran long fingers through his hair. "I know. I feel sorry for her, but she made a choice."

Luc's anger rose a notch. "She didn't have a choice, and you damn well know it."

"I'll find who did this, Luc. And the law will punish him." He put his hat back on his head. "Not you."

"Then you better find him first."

Neither spoke for several heartbeats, then Dawson nodded. "I'll be by tomorrow to talk with her."

Luc turned and stalked back to the bedroom.

Bea stood at the foot of the bed, silent tears rolling down her cheeks.

He walked over and placed an arm around her waist, pulling her against him. "She's going to be all right, *Chère*," he said softly.

She sniffed, then looked at him. "She can't go back there, Lucian. I won't let her go back there."

The next week passed in an exhausted blur for Bea. Lizzy, Vi, and Mavis Morton helped when they could, but most of the burden for Daisy's care rested on Bea, who split her time between caring for Daisy and the store. Amos or Silas always appeared when she needed to leave, and she was grateful for their help. A couple of the women in town asked about Daisy or brought food, but did not offer to sit with her, not that Bea expected them to since doing so would bring on Eunice's wrath. Something they all wished to avoid.

Levi was so worried about his sister he couldn't go to school, so Bea put him to work around the store and let him sit with Daisy afterward. He was overjoyed when she insisted on paying him to sweep the store and boardwalk each day.

By the time Bea got home Friday evening, Daisy had managed to cook a light supper on her own and was anxious to be back with her mother.

"I can't keep taking advantage of your hospitality, ma'am," she said. "You been real good to take care of me, ma'am, but I should go home now."

Before Bea could argue, Daisy continued. "Sheriff Dawson arrested the man that beat me up, but I don't see anything happening to him, and I gotta work."

Indignant, Bea snapped, "What do you mean nothing will happen to him? He assaulted you."

Daisy's smile held more sadness than joy. "In the eyes of most folks, ma'am, I'm a whore and got what I deserved. Folks ain't likely to find him guilty of anything."

Bea wanted to argue but remembered Lucian said basically the same thing yesterday and held her tongue.

But that didn't make it right.

"Are you sure you're ready to go home?"

"Yes, ma'am. I can't work looking like this, but I can help Ma out around the house, maybe do a couple of those dresses you wanted." She cast a quick look at Bea as she made that last statement. "That is if you still want me to."

"Of course I do. And I want you to give serious thought to my offer to sew for me at the store." She took another bite of her soup. "In fact…" Her mind raced with possibilities. Lockhart's wasn't the only department store in New York, and she had contacts with several. "I might be able to get some items into a store in New York."

Daisy jerked her head up, and her mouth dropped open. "You can't be serious?"

"Of course I am. You're an excellent seamstress." She sat up straighter as a new idea formed. "I know just the thing to start with."

Luc's mood on Monday was touchy at best. His mind was preoccupied with two different women; he couldn't stay focused on the metal hinges he needed to finish.

Daisy was now home, and her attacker remained behind bars. How long he stayed there was anyone's guess, but the circuit judge wouldn't be through for another two weeks.

When Richard Bentley, the ranch owner where Daisy's attacker worked, found out what happened, he fired the man on the spot. Luc liked a man with integrity, and Bentley possessed that in spades.

And then there was Bea.

It seemed as though they had known each other for ages instead of a few weeks. Everything about her appealed to him. Her poise, her beauty, her grace. Most of all, her humble yet fiery spirit. She possessed a kind and generous nature the townspeople sensed right away. Her unwavering support for Daisy and the desire to help change her lot in life solidified his respect and admiration.

He shook his head and concentrated on securing the two hinge pieces together, then set it aside and began the last one.

Bea intrigued him from their first meeting, and each time since, he discovered something new to like. She was intelligent, witty, and confident. There was hardly a person in town who didn't sing her praises, with the notable exception of Eunice Martin, who didn't like anyone. The stove was now the preferred gathering place for locals, even on mild days when a fire wasn't necessary. When two chairs and an upturned barrel appeared on the sidewalk out front of the store along with a worn checkerboard, that quickly became Amos and Silas's preferred spot.

But it was the woman behind the prim and proper businesswoman who captivated him the most. Their first kiss the night she moved in revealed the passion hidden beneath the genteel persona, and his fascination grew. Her kisses were intoxicating, and he found it a challenge to stay away. They spent hours sitting on the couch, just talking or discussing her plans for the store and Daisy.

The young girl readily admitted she didn't want to get her hopes up, but even he saw the spark of excitement in her eyes and prayed for her sake that Bea's plan worked.

He had helped Bea move Daisy back home Friday night, and after tearful goodbyes and thank-yous, he walked Bea home.

As was their custom, he added wood to the fire and joined her on the couch.

She sighed and rested her head on his shoulder. "Thank you for helping move Daisy tonight, Lucian."

He lightly rubbed her upper arm. "My pleasure."

It was so natural to sit here like this, not speaking, just enjoying each other's company. He'd never experienced anything like it before and couldn't help but wonder if other people experienced such feelings. If not, they were missing out on something special.

Then, she tilted her head and met his steady gaze. "Why is it I feel as though I've known you all my life?"

"Because I feel the same way," he whispered and captured her mouth in a tender kiss.

Her shyness and resistance faded with each touch of his lips until he knew they raced toward a line he should not—could not cross, and he forced himself to leave before things got out of hand.

Unlike Belle, who was self-centered and vain, Bea had no airs. She cared for others more than herself. Her honesty and openness called to his soul. For the first time in his life, he was ready to share himself with someone else, to hold nothing back.

In short, he was besotted with her.

The revelation stopped him mid-swing of the hammer. *Is this love? Is it possible to fall so quickly?*

Maybe so, because he couldn't imagine his life without her now.

Luc stood immobile a moment, then smiled and added a final tap of the hammer to the hinge and stopped again, Bea's face suddenly filling his mind's eye. Had it really only been two days since they last spoke? His frustration and confusion made him stay away so he could think. All it did was increase his desire to see her.

"I'll ask her to the dance on Saturday," he muttered, "before I leave to fix Tyler Roundtree's windmill."

"You gonna use that hammer, boy, or just hold it?"

Amos' gravelly voice cut through his stupor. "I didn't hear you come in."

"Some injun you are," he grumbled and exhaled loudly. "Never knew making hinges could put such a smile on a body's face."

"Just thinking."

"'bout what?" Amos cackled again. "Bet I can guess."

Instead of an answer, Luc tapped the metal with the hammer, then set it aside. "What are you doing here? Isn't it time for your morning checker game with Silas?"

Amos spat toward the bucket at his feet and missed. Again. "Was headed over to the store when I saw Tyler Roundtree." He grinned. "Emma sent him to town for something for the baby, and he had to hurry back."

Tyler Roundtree and Emma Marshall married last spring, and she recently had a baby. Their ranch, Twin Oaks, was one of the finest around. He and Luc were friends and frequently spent time together.

Amos shifted on his seat. "Said you was going out to work on his windmill."

"Yeah. I think it's got a couple of broken blades, or maybe they're just bent. Shouldn't take long to fix."

Amos hooted. "Don't let him talk you into staying for supper unless Lupe's doing the cooking."

Luc joined in the laughter. Emma's lack of cooking skills was well known about town. Until she married Ty, Emma spent all her time taking care of the ranch, and her ailing father, with little time for kitchen duty. Ty claimed she was getting better, but she wasn't there yet.

"Keep an eye on the place for me while I'm gone?" Luc asked.

"Course. How long you gonna be?"

He finished the last hinge. "Probably just a day. I'll leave in the morning and be back on Wednesday."

"You gonna ask Miss Bea to the dance on Saturday?"

"Yep."

"Better hurry."

"Why's that?"

"Couple of cowboys from Bentley's place been hanging around and ole Richard Bentley hisself done took a shine to her when he was in the store 'tuther day." Amos spat toward the bucket and missed. Again. "You might have to get in line."

CHAPTER THIRTEEN

BEA STARED AT THE SMILING WOMAN REFLECTED IN the new hand mirror she just unpacked. *Is this happy woman really me?* She turned her head slightly and studied the scar that previously governed her life. For the first time in a very long time, she didn't cringe in shame.

She squared her face in the mirror. *The scar is barely discernable from this angle. Why did I never see that before?*

Even as the question arose, the answer came. Her parents insisted the scar was so hideous, it was all people saw when they looked at her. They didn't see the person inside; the child who cried herself to sleep with only a doll for comfort. The young girl hiding in the shadows as life passed her by—or the intelligent, caring, and resourceful woman with a keen head for business she became.

All they saw was the scar, and because of what she heard all her life, that was what she saw, as well.

Until Lucian and the people of Bakersville entered her life.

The smile grew, and her heart skipped a beat. Lucian was the first person besides her grandmother to look beyond the scar.

And now, the people of Bakersville did too. When young Josh asked about it at The Yellow Rose that night, she braced herself and simply said it was an accident that happened a long time ago. And that was the end of it. No one mentioned it again.

Maybe word spread, or maybe people didn't see it as the albatross her family did.

Or perhaps they understood the scar didn't signify who she was; that it was merely a part of her like the color of her hair or eyes.

Whatever the reason, she was utterly and truly happy. She had a profitable business, friends, and people who cared about her.

And Lucian, her heart whispered, *you have Lucian.*

Her smile widened as she positioned the mirror for exhibition. Yesterday, Luc stopped by to let her know he will be gone until Wednesday working at Twin Oaks Ranch.

Before he left, he asked her to accompany him to the dance on Saturday. She learned to dance thanks to a kind-hearted nanny and the household staff. However, she only attended one actual dance her entire life when her grandmother hosted a small dinner party in honor of her twenty-first birthday. Though Granny's health was declining at the time, she insisted the celebration go on as planned. Not surprisingly, her parents chose not to come, insisting Newark's distance was too far to travel. Bea was secretly glad they stayed away.

The majority of those in attendance did so out of respect for Granny or because their families expected it. Beatrice Lockhart was a woman few people refused anything.

The single males were respectful but not attentive. The females wore their pity like a new bonnet, and more than one "poor Beulah" drifted over the chatter to her ears. Still, she smiled and pretended everything was okay for her grandmother's sake.

A sudden spring storm rolled in with a vengeance, and the evening ended earlier than planned. Bea remembered thinking at the time that everyone must have prayed extra hard for something to conclude their forced presence.

She shook her head, banishing the painful memory that threatened to dampen her happiness. *The past is gone. There is only today and the future.*

"And I'm going to a dance with Lucian on Saturday," she murmured to herself. "The new dress Daisy made will be perfect."

After a final adjustment to the mirror's position, she scanned the store. The changes she made to the items available for purchase and their displays invited you to browse the aisles. The majority of the stock was, out of necessity, standard farm and ranch items. But she added a small section of extras like teapots and china cups, fine linens, and brightly colored material, including two bolts of silk. The Montgomery Ward Catalogs scattered about the store were a favorite with the ladies, many of whom called them *the wishful thinking books.* While it would never equal Lockhart's, the store was hers, and she was proud of it.

The whistle announcing the train's arrival caused her to glance at the clock behind the counter. Not yet 11 A.M. It was early for a change.

She expected some new items for the store to be on board, so she hurried to make room in the back for them. Silas would ensure they were delivered later today.

The bell above the front door announced a customer, and she called out, "I'll be right there," and moved another box.

Wiping her hands on a rag, she walked to the front. Two cowboys from the Circle B Ranch stood in front of the counter.

"Good morning, Jeb," she said brightly to the one in front. "This is the second time you've been in this week. To what do I owe this pleasure?"

Cheeks pink, he pulled off his hat and stuck out a crumpled piece of paper. "Mr. Bentley sent us in for these supplies, ma'am."

She took the list and nodded. "I'll have this pulled together in no time."

Both cowboys visited the store several times in the last couple of weeks. Their age was a mystery, but she suspected they were younger than her, possibly early-twenties.

Neither displayed any concern with her age or the scar, and both were shameless flirts. Caught off guard the first time it happened, she became flustered and didn't know how to respond. Thankfully, she learned quickly, and got through the experience with only a little embarrassment. The next time, she was better prepared, and their light-hearted banter was an ego-boosting experience.

"That'll be fine, ma'am." Jeb grinned and rolled his hat brim in his hands. "Me and Roscoe here will just hang around in case you need us to help out."

"There's fresh coffee on the stove and cups on the stand there," said Bea. "Help yourself."

She pulled a basket from under the counter and began filling it with items from the list. When she lifted it to carry to the next area, Jeb hurried over.

"Here, ma'am, let me carry that for you."

"I was gonna hold it for her, Jeb," whined Roscoe.

"I got here first."

Bea couldn't hold in a laugh. "I appreciate the offer, boys, but I got this."

"Boys?" asked Jeb, head tilted to one side. "What do the men look like in New York?"

Despite the heat running up her neck, Bea laughed. "Okay. Men, then."

"That's better." Jeb came around the counter and took the basket. "But helping pretty ladies is in the cowboy code."

She shook her head and moved to the next aisle with Jeb behind her, Roscoe on his heels.

"Dang it, Jeb," Roscoe grumbled loud enough for her to hear, "It was my idea."

"Say, ma'am," asked Jeb quickly, "I guess you heard there's a big dance this Saturday. We'll be busy with roundups and branding soon and—"

"It's our last chance to kick up our heels," interrupted Roscoe. "Everyone will be there."

"I heard," said Bea.

"Well, I was hoping maybe you'd allow me to escort you," said Jeb.

"So was I, ma'am," said Roscoe, "So I guess you're gonna have to choose one of us."

She turned around and faced them, unable to control the pleasure caused by having two young men arguing over who would take her to the dance. "I'm sorry, boys, er, men, but I've already agreed to go with someone else."

"Dang it," they muttered in unison.

"Well, can we at least have a dance?" asked Roscoe.

"Of course." She turned and weighed out a bag of coffee beans and added it to the basket. "Though I must warn you, I'm a bit out of practice."

"Don't worry none, ma'am. Roscoe and me are the best dancers in town."

"Yeah," added his companion with no hint of boast, "we'll show you how."

"I can waltz, too," Jeb said with pride. "We had this fella work with us a couple of years ago. He sure did talk funny. I forget where he said he was from, but he taught Roscoe and me the waltz."

"Can you waltz, ma'am?" asked Roscoe.

"It's been a while, but yes, I can waltz."

Before she could react, Roscoe pulled her in his arms and whirled her around the narrow aisle in front of the counter. Initial shock turned to joy as he expertly spun her in the small space, leaving her to wonder how someone as tall and lanky as him could move with such grace.

"See, ma'am," he said with a big grin, "nothing to it."

Happiness surged from the depths of her soul, and she closed her eyes and danced. Laughter, joyful and robust, bubbled up, and she tilted her head back and let go.

"Excuse me," came a cultivated voice dipped in censure, from the direction of the front door. "I hate to interrupt the party."

Lost in the moment, she hadn't heard the clang of the bell above the door. Startled, Bea jerked away from Roscoe and turned toward the voice.

Breath froze in her lungs. Knees weak, she grabbed for the counter to remain upright.

Oh, no. It can't be.

CHAPTER FOURTEEN

"Upon my word!"

Eunice Martin's mortified declaration drew Bea's stare away from the two people who entered in front of her.

"Cavorting with these…these…ruffians!" added Eunice, "And in public no less."

Bea's mind froze, and she couldn't form a decent rebuttal.

Annabelle Blankenship.

And Henry Moreau. Here. In Bakersville.

The first thing Bea noted was that Belle had gotten more beautiful over time. Refined and elegant, she possessed a perfect oval face, creamy complexion highlighted by delicately carved cheekbones and arched brows. Eyes blue as a summer sky framed by golden lashes narrowed as she watched Bea step away from Roscoe.

"I must say," she cooed, "I am shocked you found someone who doesn't mind cavorting with you."

Jeb stepped forward and removed his hat. "Well, now, I ain't rightly sure what cavortin' means, ma'am, but I know they wasn't doin' anything wrong."

"Although," said Annabelle ignoring Jeb's comment, "beggars can't be choosers, can they?"

"Annabelle."

That one word from Moreau silenced further comment. He turned a frosty look to Bea. "Miss Lockhart. I did not expect to find you here." His voice possessed all the warmth of a snowbank.

The man had to be near eighty but held his age well. A slender, austere-looking gentleman, he was clean-shaven, and his silver-colored hair remained full and wavy. A shrewd businessman who built a fortune from the ground up, he was handsome in an elegant, aristocratic way.

Until you looked in his eyes. Distant and callous, their icy blue depths lacked any friendliness or welcome.

"Mr. Moreau," said Bea at last. "What a surprise. What brings you to Bakersville?"

"I told these folks you could tell them where Luc is." Eunice's chin jutted upward, and her smile turned malicious. "Since y'all spend so much time together, I knew you'd know his whereabouts."

Annabelle looked from Eunice to Bea. "Really? My Lucian spends time with…her?"

My Lucian?

Eunice's spiteful glance flitted from Bea to the newcomers as she lapped up the tidbits she would no doubt use later. "They have supper together almost every night," she offered eagerly, as though delivering that statement was significant. "Either at her house or The Yellow Rose."

"Where can I find my grandson?" snapped Moreau, ending Eunice's discourse.

"Your grandson?" asked Bea, the ache in the pit of her stomach growing by the second.

"I have neither the time nor the patience for games, madame," he snapped, "Where is Lucian?"

Dread crawled up her spine like a bug. Surely Lucian couldn't be one of *them*? *The* Moreau's, as in Moreau Shipping. As in one of the wealthiest families in New York. A friend of her father's.

And one of the people caught up in Edmond's failed scheme.

It took monumental effort to control her features and her voice. "Luc is out of town helping one of the local ranchers."

The older man slapped the gloves he held against his right thigh. "When will he return?"

"Sometime in the morning," answered Bea. "He might make it back later tonight, but doubtful."

Moreau's expression darkened. "I suppose there's no point in asking if there is a decent hotel in town?"

Bea took immediate offense to his tone but remained cordial. "Out the door to the right. It's not the Windsor, but it is clean."

"I didn't know Luc had such a fine grandfather," interrupted Eunice, her eyes fever bright as they darted from him to Annabelle. "Who are you?"

Annabelle flinched and turned a sullen face toward her. "I fail to see how that is any of your concern."

"I'll get us rooms at the hotel," snapped Moreau, then turned sharply and walked out, leaving Annabelle standing in the aisle with Eunice taking everything in.

Jeb smiled at her. "Must be my lucky day. Two beautiful women in the same place at the same time."

Belle glared at him, her creamy complexion turning bright pink. "You cannot seriously be comparing me to her." She nodded in Bea's direction.

Jeb's brow furrowed, and he tilted his head to one side. "I ain't comparing nobody, ma'am, just makin' an observation." Then he grinned again. "If you're still in town Saturday, I hope you'll save a dance for me."

"And me, too," said Roscoe as he moved to Bea's side. "Me and Jeb are the best dancers in town."

She pointedly ignored both men and gazed at Bea. "So, this is where you ran off to." She cast a disdainful look around the store. "Your father would be so disappointed to have his name associated with this place." She raked one gloved finger over the counter to her right, and her perfect heart-shaped mouth formed an unattractive twist. "But it seems you have found where you belong."

Bea learned long ago to bury the hurt so deep only she knew it existed and employed that technique now without a second thought. "Yes," she replied, a tight smile on her lips. "I have."

Belle's expression turned dark. "I can't wait to see Lucian again." She fingered the ribbon dangling from her bonnet. "We need to plan the wedding, you know." With that parting shot, Belle turned and bumped into Eunice, who stood at her elbow.

The older woman gave a *humph* of surprise as she stumbled backward. Had it not been for Jeb grabbing her arm, she would have landed on her backside.

Belle never broke stride as she floated out the door without a backward glance.

"Well!" snapped Eunice, "I have never met a woman so rude in my life!" She straightened her bonnet and hurried outside, no doubt anxious to set the rumor mill in motion.

Jeb watched as Belle passed in front of the window. "That woman makes a hornet's nest look cuddly."

"Miss Bea," asked Roscoe, "are you all right?"

His concerned voice helped steady her. "I'm fine, Roscoe." She turned and plucked the basket from the counter. "I only have a couple of things to add."

No one spoke as she completed and tallied the order, then

bundled the items. She placed the wrapped packages on the counter and looked at Jeb. "Anything else?"

"No, ma'am," came the reply, "except that dance you promised me on Saturday."

She smiled despite the turmoil in her stomach. "Play your cards right, and I might even save you two."

"What about me, Miss Bea?" asked Roscoe.

She added Bentley's order to the ledger, giving no hint of the pain the sudden appearance of Annabelle and Henry Moreau caused. "Of course. But I fear I will have to stand in line. Anyone who can waltz as good as you is sure to have a long list of waiting partners."

"Well, now, I don't know about that," said Roscoe, his face beet-red. "But I'll always have a dance for you."

Somehow, that one statement soothed the ache in her heart and brought a sincere smile to her face. "Thank you, Roscoe. I appreciate that."

The rest of the day passed in a slow progression of curious townspeople. Most voiced concern for her well-being, but many wanted to know about the strangers in town. By the time she closed at six, Bea was exhausted and dreaded the thought of going home to her empty house. On a whim, she locked up and walked over to The Yellow Rose. Vi met her at the door and pulled her to a table in the corner. "I'm sorry I haven't been by sooner, child. Are you all right?"

"Yes, Vi, I'm fine."

Viola snapped her fingers at the young woman across the room who helped during busy times. "Mary! Get Miss Bea her coffee and tonight's special." She pulled out a chair and sat down. "Is it true? Is that harridan engaged to Luc?"

CHAPTER FIFTEEN

"I SURE APPRECIATE YOU COMING ALL THIS WAY TO FIX the windmill for me," said Tyler Roundtree as he watched Luc work.

"The blades aren't bent too bad," said Luc. "It's an easy fix."

Ty snorted. "For you, maybe." He watched in silence a moment. "I thought the new metal windmills would be better around here than the wooden ones." He sniffed. "But then I never planned on the wind and storms we've had lately, either."

"The wood might be easier to fix, but the metal will do better for the long haul."

The two friends worked in silence to repair the blades and reattach them to the wheel fan. The sun hovered over the western horizon by the time repairs were finished.

"Supper's almost ready." Emma Roundtree stood on the back steps with her infant son cradled in her arms. "I'm going to put the baby to bed, and then I'll join you." She turned to Luc. "You have the bedroom downstairs. That way, Little Tyler won't disturb you."

"You don't have to do that, Miss Emma," said Luc. "I'll head back to town tonight."

"No. You won't." She smiled at her husband. "Ty has been looking forward to your visit. And you have lots to catch up on." She turned back to Luc. "Like a certain young lady in town who has caught your eye?"

Before he could reply, she turned and disappeared inside the house.

"Just so you know," Ty said with a smile, "Lupe cooked supper tonight. The baby keeps her so busy Emma's given up on learning to cook...thank goodness." He took a breath. "Now, tell me about you and Miss Lockhart."

Luc brought his friend up to date as they packed away the tools and headed to the front porch to sit.

"And you never met her in New York?" asked Ty.

"No. I knew of her, of course, mainly from Belle and her friends, which frankly, was all very uncomplimentary." He shook his head. "From what they said, one would expect a hideously deformed she-witch with claws and horns." *Instead, she's a beautiful and caring woman of great character and purpose.*

"What about your grandfather? When does he arrive?"

"Next week maybe." Luc leaned against a post. "I'm not looking forward to his visit."

"Because you think he wants you to return to New York?"

"Yeah."

"What will you do?"

Luc pushed away from the post and sat down in the rocking chair across from Ty. "My life is here. I've no interest in returning or taking over Moreau Shipping."

"From what you've told me, I can't see him taking no for an answer."

Luc nodded. "He even hinted the engagement with Belle should proceed as planned."

Ty broke the extended silence that followed. "Does Miss Lockhart know about the engagement?"

"Yes, we discussed it one night, but I didn't give any particulars."

"What about the fact that you grew up in New York and knew of her?"

Luc sighed. "No." He rubbed his hands on his thighs. "Everything about my life there ceased to matter to me two years ago, and it doesn't matter now."

"She may see it differently."

Surprised, Luc stared at his friend. "What do you mean?"

Ty shrugged. "Women are hard to figure sometimes. She might not like the fact that you knew who she was and didn't say so."

"But I didn't know her. We never met, and I only heard the name, so I don't see how that makes any difference."

Ty rolled a cigarette, then struck a match to it. He drew in the smoke and blew it out through pursed lips. "You said she comes from a wealthy family. Did she know your grandfather?"

Luc cocked his head to one side and squinted. "Possibly, but I really have no idea."

Ty flicked an ash off his cigarette, then took another puff. "One thing I've learned in my life is that women don't like not knowing things. Makes 'em think you're keeping stuff from them, so you best tell her soon. Otherwise, it could get sticky."

The rest of the evening passed in pleasant conversation that lingered long after the dishes were cleared away.

Luc enjoyed watching Ty and Emma together and silently envied the relationship they forged for themselves. A marriage of convenience evolved into a love as strong and robust as steel. He wanted a love like that for himself and wondered if such a dream was even possible. Then Bea's smiling face appeared in his mind's eye. *Maybe it is.*

After breakfast the next morning, his wagon waited in front of the house.

"I had José bring it around for you," said Emma as she balanced the baby on her hip. "I know you are anxious to get back to town."

He tipped his hat. "Thank you for your hospitality, Miss Emma. It's always a pleasure to see you." He nodded toward the child whose wide eyes took in everything around him. "Thank goodness Little Ty takes after his mama and not his daddy."

"I expect you to bring Miss Lockhart out for supper soon," said Emma. "I haven't gotten to town to meet her yet, and I'm looking forward to it."

He nodded. "I'll let you know." He shook hands with Ty, who stood beside the wagon. "I know the new house is almost done, but if you need help in any way, just let me know."

"I will," said Ty. "Thanks again for fixing the windmill."

"Anytime, my friend. Anytime." Luc climbed in the seat and picked up the reins. "Let's go, Molly." A gentle flick of the leather strips and the dapple-gray mare leaned into the harness and plodded forward.

A route that typically took an hour on horseback took over two in a buckboard. The cold, wet weather of recent weeks was a distant memory as a bright blue cloudless sky stretched overhead. Preoccupied with his thoughts, Luc saw nothing of the landscape around him, not the tiny specks of green on the trees or little blades of grass peeking out from under the winter brown that signaled spring was just around the corner. Not even the joyful song of the various birds zipping through the trees aroused his interest.

His mind focused on Bea, the dance, and thoughts of a possible future.

Together.

A roadrunner skittered in front of Molly, and the horse sidestepped and tossed her head.

The action pulled Luc to the present. "Easy girl," he said softly and adjusted his pressure on the reins. "Just a bird." He was surprised to see he approached the outskirts of Bakersville. He smiled. *Time flies when your mind is preoccupied with a beautiful woman.*

He pulled up to the livery and found the place empty. *Amos must be at the store with Silas for their morning coffee or checkers.*

Despite his desire to see Bea, he unharnessed Molly, brushed her down then gave her a ration of oats and fresh water. He put away his tools and walked to the small house out back where he lived. A far cry from the lavish environment he grew up in, nonetheless, it was home, and he liked it.

He freshened up and hurried back through the livery and turned right toward the store, meeting Silas as he exited the bank.

"Morning, Silas," he called. "I thought you and Amos would be in the middle of a wicked game of checkers by now."

"Humph," the older man snorted and brushed past him without another word.

Luc turned and watched him amble off. Silas never passed up an opportunity to talk. *What on earth has gotten into him?* He shook his head and crossed the street toward the hotel.

Lizzy and Miss Vi stood out front of The Yellow Rose talking but stopped and glared as he stepped up on the boardwalk.

"Morning, Lizzy, Miss Vi."

Lizzy's green eyes spit fire, and her mouth was a straight line across her face. "All I can say is, you damn well better have a good explanation," she snapped.

"I would never, ever have expected something like this from you," added Miss Vi with a *tsk tsk* and shake of her head.

Caught off guard by their unexpected hostility, it took him a moment to gather his wits enough to speak. "Explanation for what?"

"For lying to Bea, that's what!" snapped Lizzy.

He shook his head and stared. "What did I lie about?"

The thought crossed his mind that Lizzy might swat him with the broom in her hands when she changed her grip, knuckles turning white, her breathing rapid and shallow. "How could you?"

"I'm so disappointed in you, Luc," said Miss Vi softly, her face a picture of maternal displeasure.

Frustrated, he took a step toward them, then stopped and glanced toward Bea's store, noting the *closed* sign on the door. Ty's warning whispered through his brain, but he dismissed it. His grandfather wasn't due till next week, and he would tell Bea everything tonight. "What's going on? Why is Bea closed?" Concern morphed to fear. "Did something happen? Is she all right?"

The women continued to glare without answering.

"What the hell is going on? Why are you mad at me?"

Before he could answer, the door to the hotel swung open, and, just like that, his life went to hell.

CHAPTER SIXTEEN

"Lucian, darling!" Annabelle rushed forward with arms outstretched.

He took a step back, one hand out to force distance between them. "What are you doing here?" He made no effort to hide the displeasure in his voice.

One hand fluttered around her mouth, and Belle's voice shook with the false emotion he remembered so well.

"I've missed you, Lucian. I had to see you."

"Excuse me," snapped Lizzy as she moved past Belle. "I need to get back to work."

"Me, too," said Vi as she glared at Belle. "I suppose you'll be wanting tea soon?"

"If it's not too much trouble," said Belle sweetly, but the smile never made it to her eyes.

Vi hmphed and went inside the restaurant.

"Your audience is gone now, so you can stop acting," he growled.

"Acting? How can you say that? You know how much I care for you."

For some reason, her floral perfume irritated his nose, and he took another step backward. "Do you honestly expect me to believe that?"

Some of the starch disappeared, and her shoulders sagged. "You loved me, Lucian. I know you did."

Jaw tight, he flinched when she touched his forearm.

"You and I belong together."

"It was a business arrangement, Belle. Nothing more." He fixed her with a steely look. "And you made it clear you had no intention of fulfilling your part of the agreement."

She straightened and glanced around. "We're on display here. Can we please go somewhere more private to talk?"

He followed her gaze and saw Eunice Martin and half a dozen other people scattered along the boardwalk watching with rapt attention. *Bloody hell.*

"My shop is over there," he pointed toward the smithy and stalked off, not looking to see if she followed.

Inside the familiar surroundings, he jerked an apron off the hook and stoked the fire, idly wondering why Belle would suddenly appear after two years. He didn't think for one minute she'd had a change of heart, for he doubted she even possessed one. She was motivated by money and nothing more and assumed that was the reason behind her visit.

A rustle of fabric said she stood behind him.

"What is this place?"

The distaste in her voice grated on his nerves. "A blacksmith shop."

"There's no place to sit."

He turned around and faced her. "It's a place to work, not socialize. Why are you here?"

She spoke over her shoulder to the young girl standing in the doorway. "Jenny, go to that horrid restaurant and tell them I want a decent pot of tea. I'll be there shortly."

"Yes, ma'am." The girl dipped a short curtsey and fled.

Belle flashed her patented smile that never failed to have men fawning all over her. Thankfully, he was immune.

"Lucian. Darling." She took a step toward him. "I've missed you."

"How did you know where to find me?"

She blinked a couple of times. "Henry told my father he was coming to see you." She paused. "He asked me to come with him."

She's lying. "Where's my grandfather?"

She shrugged. "I have no idea. The hotel, I presume."

"And what did he hope to accomplish by bringing you along?" *As if I didn't know.*

"He wants us to be together."

He turned and worked the bellows to bring the fire to life. "Does he, now?"

She placed one gloved hand on his back and stroked him lightly. "Lucian, you know he's right," she whispered. "We were made for each other."

He stopped and faced her. "No. We weren't."

"Don't say that." She clutched his arm. "We were happy once. We can be again."

"No. We can't, Belle." He took a breath. "Because I don't love you. And you don't love me."

"But I do, Lucian. I do."

He pulled her hand from his arm. "No. You love my money."

Something in her expression flickered.

"That's it, isn't it? The money."

Her gaze flittered around the space. "No, of course not. I—"

"Annabelle," said Henry Moreau stiffly, "Your tea is waiting."

Bea sat at her kitchen table with Lizzy and Vi and studied the wispy vapor rising from the coffee cup in her hand, barely hearing the chatter from her friends. Tired of the endless questions from people who came in not to buy but be nosey, she closed the store after lunch. A note on the door said she was ill and would re-open Thursday morning.

One thought kept circling through her mind. *Lucian was engaged to Annabelle Blankenship.*

"That is the most unpleasant woman it has ever been my misfortune to encounter," grumbled Lizzy. "Do you know she insisted on breakfast in bed this morning! At ten o'clock, no less." Lizzy took a sip of her coffee. "Had the audacity to send her maid, Jenny, down to tell me—*tell* me to bring it to her." She gave a disgusted humph. "Needless to say, I didn't."

"And that man, Moreau," said Vi, "isn't much better. I swear if his nose was any higher in the air, he'd drown if it rained."

"Do you think it's true," asked Lizzy, "what that horrid woman said?"

Bea sighed. "I don't know. He told me he'd been engaged once but broke it off."

"He's been here for over two years," said Vi. "If it were true, something would have happened before now."

"Are you sure you're okay?" asked Lizzy. "You're awfully quiet."

"I'm fine," said Bea. "Just trying to make sense of it all. It's not like we have any kind of—agreement or anything. We're friends." *But I want so much more.*

"Well, if you ask me," said Vi with conviction, "no one in their right mind would choose her over you."

"I'm sure there's a good explanation for all of this," said Lizzy. "As soon as Luc returns, he'll get to the bottom of it."

"That danged Eunice Martin has been spreading malarkey all over town since yesterday," said Vi. "It was so bad this morning I told her to hush up or leave."

Bea snickered. "I'll bet she didn't take it very well."

"No, she didn't. But she hushed, which was what I wanted."

"Well, I've hidden away long enough," said Bea. "And I've kept you both from your work. I best go open back up."

"This is the slow time of day for both of us," said Vi, "and we have dependable folks to look after things." She placed her work-roughened hand over Bea's. "And we want to be here for you."

Tears burned the backs of her eyes but, thankfully, didn't leak out. "I'm so fortunate to have found you both." She chewed her lower lip. "I…I've never had many friends before."

"Well, you got us," said Lizzy as she added her hand to Vi's. "And pretty much everyone else in town, too. You're one of us now."

A light knock on the front door ended the moment.

"I'll see who it is," said Vi, "just keep your seat."

A moment later, she returned. "I need to go. Cook's having a fit about something." She looked at Bea. "You need anything at all, dear, you let me know."

"I will."

Lizzy sighed and stood. "Well, I guess I better go see how things are going. Her highness probably wants something else by now."

After the women departed, Bea cleaned up the kitchen, then stood in the middle of the room. "Now what?" she mumbled. The apron came off with a disgusted yank. "Enough moping. I need to get back to work."

A timid knock on the back door drew her attention. "Daisy," she exclaimed, "what a pleasant surprise." She stepped back from the opening. "Please. Come in."

Daisy clutched a folded garment in her hands. The bruises

on her face had faded to a yellowish-purple tint, and her smile was genuine. "Sorry to bother you, Miss Lockhart."

"You are never a bother, child. Is that my dress?" asked Bea.

"Yes, ma'am. We finished it this morning."

A few minutes later, she stood in front of the big mirror in the bathing room, twisting this way and that. "Oh my, Daisy. I just love it! I'm going to wear it to the dance on Saturday."

The young girl stood off to the side, hands clasped to her chest. "I'm so glad you like it."

"I have another project for you," said Bea as she changed back into her work clothes. "Walk over with me. I need to pay you, and we can talk about it."

The women strolled to the store where Bea counted out the money she owed Daisy. "I found something, and I'd like to see if you can make it." She pulled a pattern from under the counter and showed it to Daisy. "Do you think you can do this?"

"Oh, yes, miss. I made something similar for Rosy. Only I didn't have a pattern." Her voice trailed off. "Well, it was for a working girl, so it was different."

Bea plucked a bolt of emerald green silk covered in a muted gold lacey design from the counter and showed it to Daisy. "I brought this with me from New York. I wasn't sure what I'd do with it, but I think it will look great made into that dress. What do you think?"

Daisy fingered the exquisite material and sighed. "Oh, miss, this is the most beautiful fabric I have ever seen." She looked up at Bea. "And will look gorgeous on you."

"I don't know about that, but I do think the dress will be exceptional when it's finished." She looked at the pattern again. "I may keep it, or I may put it on display for sale here." She shrugged. "I know it's a bit fancy for a small town like Bakersville, but sometimes a woman just needs to look fancy, don't you think?"

Daisy nodded. "Oh, I do, ma'am."

Bea looked around the fabric area. "I have some lace and chiffon, too, in a lighter shade of green that will work well with it." Once she had everything Daisy might need, she bundled it up and handed it to her. "Now, if you need anything else, let me know."

Bea's spirits rose decidedly higher after Daisy left. She changed the sign from *closed* to *open* and grabbed a broom from the back. She swept away dirt tracked in from outside, then dusted shelves and rearranged displays. Something about the mundane actions soothed her frayed nerves and calmed her mind. She still wondered about the unexpected appearance of Moreau and Annabelle, then finally decided it was simply none of her concern.

Luc told her he was engaged but broke it off, so the assertions to the contrary now bothered her more than she cared to admit. But the fact remained it was something over which she had no control.

Young Levi came by after school, and, as had become his habit, he swept the boardwalk out front again, stacked firewood on the rear porch, and did whatever odd jobs Bea wanted. He refused to take any pay, insisting he owed her for taking care of Daisy. She finally persuaded him to take some candy for his efforts before he raced home.

She was thumbing through a catalog when the bell over the door announced a customer. She looked up to find Henry Moreau striding toward her, an ivory-handled silver walking stick in his hand.

His cheek muscles moved as he clenched and unclenched

his jaw several times before he spoke. "I wondered where you ran off to."

"I didn't run," she replied stiffly. "I bought a business."

Moreau looked around the room, his face devoid of expression. "Your father wasn't happy about you leaving, especially under the circumstances."

She gave a non-committal shrug. "His problem. Not mine."

"It was your fiancé—"

Tired of being blamed for things for which she was not responsible, Bea fought back. "My father is an astute businessman, Mr. Moreau, as are you. Any successes or failures encountered in the course of doing business are upon your shoulders alone." Bea was proud of herself for standing up to him, though in truth, her heart raced like a steam locomotive. "It has nothing to do with me."

Something strange flared in his eyes. Amusement? Interest? Whatever it was, it vanished so quickly she may have imagined it.

He tapped the stick lightly on the floor. "How long have you known Lucian?"

Surprised by the change in topic, it took a moment to answer. "A few weeks."

"And you didn't know him before? In New York?"

Heat burned her cheeks as she faced him squarely, hands rolled into fists at her side. "As you are well aware, sir, I seldom ventured out in public, so, no, I did not know him before I arrived a month ago."

"And yet, I understand the two of you spend a great deal of time together."

Indignant, she glared at him. "We are friends."

"Why set up here? In this town?"

Annoyed that he would question her personal business decisions, she took a moment to regain her composure. "Why not here? It's a firmly established business with a constant flow of repeat customers. The nearest competition is over a day's ride from here. The train brings supplies and orders quickly, and, lastly, it's not in New York."

That strange look appeared and vanished again. Moreau stared a moment longer, took another look around the store, and walked out without another word.

CHAPTER SEVENTEEN

WEDNESDAY AFTERNOON WAS A SLOW PARADE OF customers, most of whom wanted to offer support. Some went so far as to say they tried to eavesdrop on Luc and Annabelle's conversation when she followed him to the smithy. Bea did her best to deflect their comments. The last thing she wanted was to talk about it.

The memory of seeing Annabelle's face earlier as she reached out toward Luc was a knife in Bea's heart. From her spot by the window, she couldn't hear their voices, but Luc's stiff posture said he didn't share Belle's happiness about the encounter. Belle hesitated when he stomped off toward the smithy, then followed him, her lady's maid close behind.

"She didn't stay long," said Vi, her voice lowered to a stage whisper, though only she and Mavis were in the store. "That man, Luc's grandfather, walked in, and she left in a huff."

"Well, if you ask me," said Mavis, "that hussy is nothing but trouble."

Bea wiped at the non-existent dust on the counter. "I saw her go into The Yellow Rose after that."

Spine rigid, Vi's voice rose in resentment. "She sat down like a queen and made Mary take back the tea she insisted on because it wasn't hot enough or good enough or some such." She shook her head. "She barely even tasted it. Can you believe that?"

Ever the peacemaker, Bea said, "Well, she's accustomed to a very different lifestyle."

"Then she needs to go where that lifestyle is appreciated," snapped Vi, "cause it sure ain't here."

"What are you going to do?" asked Mavis softly. "About Luc, I mean?"

Taken aback, Bea stuttered, "I…I don't know."

"He sure was in a state before that woman walked out," said Vi. "He'd just seen the closed sign on your door and panicked."

"Panicked?" asked Bea. "What do you mean?"

"He kept asking if you were all right. Before I could answer, her highness come waltzing out the door."

"I don't think there is anything at all between them," offered Mavis. "Why, the look on his face when he stomped off to the smithy would curdle cream."

"I agree," said Vi. "He was not happy."

"What about Luc's grandfather?" asked Mavis, "Do you know him, too? What did he say to you?"

She nodded. "He and my father were business associates. He wanted to know why I bought a store here and asked about my relationship with Luc."

"What did you tell him?" asked Vi quickly.

"That we were friends."

"Oh, honey, you know as well as I do," said Vi smiling, "you and Luc passed friendship some time ago."

"Yes," agreed Mavis, "it's plain as day."

Bea opened her mouth to argue when the door opened, and Belle walked in.

Vi glared at her, then turned and smiled at Bea. "Well, I see you have a customer, and I need to check on supper."

"Yes," said Mavis, gathering up the coffee and sugar she'd

purchased earlier. "Doc should be home soon." She glared at Belle, who remained just inside the door, then turned to Bea. "Remember what we said, honey."

The two women turned and walked side-by-side down the aisle, forcing Belle to move out of the way.

Once the door closed behind them, Belle sauntered toward Bea. "Well, I must say they lack any degree of civility at all." She cast a disdainful look around the store. "But then, this place is so… uncivilized one couldn't expect more."

Angry at Belle's insult, Bea stood straight and fixed her with an icy stare. "My friends return what they receive."

Belle flushed, and her lips tightened a moment. "Well, it wouldn't hurt them to be more cordial to strangers."

"What do you want, Belle?"

The color in her cheeks darkened to bright pink. "You know I hate that name."

Bea tilted her head to the side but remained silent.

"I don't understand why you think you can succeed in anything, Beulah Mae. You're a woman. And your face…"

It took a lot of effort to control her anger. "Who do you think ran Lockhart's for the last five years?" Bea blew out a breath. "And no one here has a problem with my scar."

Belle's eyes widened, and she blinked several times. "They don't?"

"No. They don't."

Belle shook her head and took a deep breath. "What exactly is your relationship with Lucian?"

Bea stared a couple of heartbeats before she replied. "That is none of your concern."

"We are engaged."

"If that were the case, we wouldn't be having this conversation."

Her features tightened, and her eyes narrowed. "He's mine."

Silent, Bea maintained her steady gaze.

Belle's shoulders relaxed, and her expression radiated superiority. Ice blue eyes raked her up and down, then focused on Bea's scar. "No man wants to bed a woman he can't stand to look at."

Stunned into silence by the bitterness in Belle's voice, Bea blinked rapidly.

"And nobody takes what's mine." Belle turned and strode out the door.

Bea gaped at the retreating figure of the woman she once called a friend.

Luc barely hid his shock at seeing his grandfather. The man had aged a lot in the last two years. The hair he remembered as being more salt and pepper was now an all over silvery-grey and full of soft, wavy curls. Gone was the robust figure of the man he remembered. In its place stood a slender man who looked like what he was—an old man whose time ran short.

An unexpected pang hit him square in his chest. Something was dreadfully wrong. He looked for something to work on and grabbed the first thing he touched, a bridle that needed mending. He sat on a barrel and inspected it. "I'm surprised to see you."

"You didn't respond to my letter."

"I didn't know a response was necessary."

Moreau shifted on the barrel. "I assumed you had chosen to avoid me," said his grandfather. "I have been in town since yesterday and had to seek you out on my own."

Luc ignored the jibe. "I was out of town until an hour ago. I wasn't expecting you this soon."

Henry looked around, then sat down on Amos's barrel. "Why here?"

The criticism was difficult to miss.

"I'm happy here."

Moreau watched him with tired eyes. "I was surprised to find Miss Lockhart here yesterday."

Luc couldn't imagine why Bea's presence would mean anything to him but didn't voice it. "She arrived a month ago."

Henry tapped the walking stick against the ground. "Did she tell you how that fiancé of hers tried to swindle me?"

Luc stopped working on the harness and gaped at his grandfather. "What are you talking about?"

He huffed out a disgusted breath. "That so-called fiancé of hers. Sir Edmund Abernathy." He met Luc's gaze, then looked out the door. "He was a smooth-talker that one," he said after a bit. "I very nearly believed him." He brought the cane in front of him and placed both hands on the carved handle. "Thankfully, it only cost me a few thousand before I got wise to his scheme."

Luc allowed his confusion to show on his face. "How is that Bea's fault?"

Ignoring the question, Moreau continued. "I should have known something was off when her father announced their engagement."

Luc waited in silence. There was more to this story, and he wanted to hear it all.

Moreau sighed and removed his top hat. Finding no place around to rest it, he put it back on his head. "I suspect Jeremiah paid the man to court her. What other reason could there be?"

Maybe because she's beautiful, witty, and smart, too.

"Anyway, the consensus was a payoff, but either way, they held an engagement party for them. I think most people there, especially Belle and her friends, came to stare." Moreau shook his head. "I actually felt a bit sorry for her. That man and her parents flitted about, talking to everyone, and left her alone most of the evening. She looked miserable and totally out of place in that silly hat and veil. A few people spoke to her, but it was a very tense evening, which, thankfully, didn't last long."

Luc's heart ached for Bea. Alone in a room full of people.

"The next day, the man dared to approach several of us about investing in this scheme of his. I'll admit, I bought into it at first, but when he came back for more, I sent him on his way."

Luc could only imagine the embarrassment Bea must have endured. Did her father actually pay Edmund off, or did he seek her out? She told him her situation was much like his own. What did that mean? Unable to stop himself, he asked, "What happened?"

"Oh, the truth came out, of course. He was a scoundrel of the first water. Claimed he intended to use the money we invested to purchase various properties, which he would then sell for a generous profit, but no such thing took place. He took the money and planned to sail back to England." He puffed his chest out with pride. "I put a stop to that."

Luc clenched and released his jaw. "You chose to invest," he said tersely. "Bea had nothing to do with it."

Moreau looked at him as though just realizing he was there. "That's pretty much what she said."

"You accused Bea of being responsible for *your* investment decision? To her face?"

He shrugged. "Not precisely." A fleeting smile crossed his face. "Did you know she ran Lockhart's for her father? Her. A woman ran the place."

"Yes, she told me. She's a very astute businesswoman."

"You like her."

"I do."

"You do realize a relationship between the two of you is out of the question."

Luc straightened, anger making his voice stiff and unforgiving. "My life is my life, Grandfather. You have no say in it."

Henry stood and tapped his cane on the dirt floor. "I expect you to join Annabelle and me for dinner promptly at eight." He straightened his hat. "There is only one restaurant in this God-forsaken place, so it will be easy to find."

"I have plans." He didn't but hoped he might.

"I will see you at eight."

He walked out without a backward glance.

CHAPTER EIGHTEEN

Luc glanced at the clock above the mantle. Bea should be closing the store about now. *I'll give her time to get home and settle in a bit.*

He finished dressing early to allow time to see her before joining his grandfather and Belle for dinner. Restless and anxious, he poured himself a brandy—the one luxury from his former life he maintained—and sat in the rocker near the fireplace. He raised the glass and sniffed the complex blend of spices, pepper, and cinnamon, allowing the aroma to fill his mind before taking a sip. The delicate flavor coated his tongue, its beauty and warmth making him temporarily forget how complicated his life became in one short afternoon.

What must Bea be thinking right now?

His anxiety level grew with each new *what-if* that formed in his mind. Unable to stall any longer, he finished his drink and walked outside.

Dusk had fallen, and the air grew chilled as winter refused to release its grip. His long strides ate up the distance, and he quickly found himself standing in front of Bea's house. Lamplight glowed through the front windows, and he made out her slender form as she walked from the living room to the kitchen.

He took a deep breath and walked to the front door, hesitated, then knocked.

She didn't appear surprised when she opened the door. "Hello," she said softly.

"May I come in?"

She moved aside, and he walked in, suddenly unsure of what to say.

The door closed with a soft click, and she turned to face him. "Would you like some coffee?"

He shook his head. "I can't stay long." Heat burned his cheeks, but he met her apprehensive gaze. "Grandfather insisted I meet them for dinner at eight, but I wanted to talk with you first." He looked toward the couch where they shared their first kiss. "Could we sit? Please?"

They sat on the couch, the visible space magnifying the chasm created by Belle's appearance.

"I didn't lie to you, *Chère*," he said softly.

"You weren't completely honest, either."

He sighed. "What do you wish to know? I will answer any question."

She looked at the fire, brow furrowed in thought. "Why didn't you say something about who you were?"

"Who I was is not who I am now. I relinquished that life when I came here two years ago."

"Why?"

It was difficult to get the words out, but at last, he did. "Because my life was a lie." He folded his arms across his chest. "Everything I did, I did for someone else, mainly my grandfather, until I forgot who I was. On the inside." He drew in a fortifying breath. The truth left a bitter taste in his mouth, and his throat burned as his mind replayed the memories. "I was a Moreau. I was wealthy." He turned his head toward her and waited until she met his gaze. "But I was also part white, part Indian. The majority of folks we did business with accepted me, but only because of the money, not me."

"People are blind, Luc," she said fiercely. "Blind and stupid."

Grateful for her understanding, he offered a sad smile. "As you well know." He turned and looked at the ceiling before he continued. "My grandfather and Belle's father agreed to an arrangement. Two powerful families made stronger by marriage."

Voice trembling, she asked, "Did—do you love her?"

"No."

"Yet you agreed to the marriage."

He shrugged. "I wanted a home. A family." He inhaled, blew it out through pursed lips. "I thought Belle did, too. All she wanted was wealth and status." He faced her, unable to hide the hurt and anger that still caused his stomach to roll. "The night the engagement was to be announced, I overheard a conversation between her and her friend, Charlotte. I'll spare you the details. Suffice to say, she vowed never to give me a child."

She reached out and touched his arm.

"So, you see, *Chère*, we are more alike than different."

"What happened next?"

Anger roughened his voice. "When I discovered –" He blinked and looked away. "I told her and my grandfather there would be no engagement. It ended before it began."

"She says you're still engaged."

"I am not, *Chère*. I never was."

She nibbled her bottom lip, removed her hand from his arm, and leaned back. "I've known Belle since we were children." She took a deep breath, released it slowly. "We were even friends once. Until the accident."

He turned his head toward her. After all the cruel things Belle said, he would never have guessed they knew each other.

Bea kept her eyes on the fire. "She has…difficulty seeing beyond what she wants."

On that point, they agreed, but he didn't say anything.

Somehow in the conversation, the distance between them lessened. Luc moved his arm and rested it on the back of the couch, and Bea leaned her head on his shoulder.

"I met Edmund eight months ago," she began, "I told you before he was an associate of my father's. He stayed with us a few times when he was in town. We met by chance in the library one night." She paused. "Looking back now, I wonder if it was accidental at all."

He waited while she gathered her thoughts.

"He was handsome, refined, and so dignified. He didn't seem the least bit put off by the scar. We arranged to meet a few times while he was there, and then one day, he came looking for me at the store. I was shocked when he asked if he might call on me." She scoffed. "For a woman my age, I was pretty naïve. Mother, of course, was thrilled, though she was quick to say I must always wear the veil around him so as not to disgust him with my appearance."

Luc pulled her close and kissed the top of her head. How could a mother be so cruel?

"We became engaged three months later. I thought myself madly in love, though I realize now I was simply lonely and— easy prey. He must have sensed that, too." She paused again. "Anyway, I don't know why Mother agreed to that silly engagement party. She was so ill at ease when I appeared in public. But she and Edmund insisted on it, planned every last detail, even the guest list. He claimed he wanted to show the world how lucky he was." She paused, and her voice lowered. "But he spent the entire evening with everyone but me." She tilted her head back and looked at the ceiling. "Belle was there though she and Charlotte never approached me. Few people did." She shook her head. "It was like watching a child in the schoolyard pointing and making fun of other kids. God, I was such a fool." She waited a heartbeat, then continued. "I received a substantial inheritance when my grandmother died. With the guidance of her banker and lawyer, I discovered I had a head for business, and with their help, it grew over the years." She breathed in deeply. "It was the money he wanted. Not me."

Luc rubbed her upper arm in silent support. The man needed a good thrashing, and Luc would love to give it to him.

"He was a scoundrel and took money from several people. Your grandfather included. When his true nature became known, I ended the engagement. The scandal sent Mother to her bed for days."

"How did you end up here?"

"Grandmother's lawyer was a close relation of the Barkers and knew they wished to sell, so I bought it and never looked back."

The crackle and hiss of the fireplace was the only sound in the room as each processed their thoughts.

Over the last few weeks, he'd discovered there was just as much joy in quiet togetherness as in lengthy discussions. The chime of the mantle clock got his attention, and he glanced up. Seven-forty-five. He would have to leave soon.

"Is it time to go?" Bea asked.

He rubbed his hand over her shoulder and down her arm. "Yes."

She turned and placed both hands on his chest, bringing her mouth up to his. "I shouldn't be doing this." She whispered as her lips sought his. "But I've missed you."

He shifted and clasped her body against him, and a growl of pleasure rumbled in his throat. He drank in the sweetness of her touch and let her control the kiss.

Until he couldn't any longer. He moved his mouth over hers, devouring its softness.

She shivered in his arms as desire spiked.

Raising his mouth from hers, he gazed into her eyes.

Potent desire mixed with something else, something unique, radiated between them.

"You have stolen my heart, *Chère.*"

She raised her hand and caressed his cheek. "As you have mine."

He kissed her again, tender and gentle as a mountain breeze, before once more pulling back. "I have to go."

"I know."

"It may be a couple of days before I can make it back. I have a pretty good idea of what he wants to discuss, and he won't be easily dissuaded. And then I have work to catch up on at the shop."

She rested her hands on his chest and smiled, her cheeks flushed, her breath choppy. "I'll be here."

He kissed the tip of her nose. "I'll see you on Saturday for sure." For the first time tonight, he smiled. "I can't wait for our first dance."

He hurried to The Yellow Rose, anxious to have this ordeal finished. He knew what his grandfather wanted but didn't understand how Belle fit into the picture, though he could probably guess. Regardless, if his grandfather's plans involved Belle in any way, shape, or form, he could forget it.

CHAPTER NINETEEN

Luc spotted his grandfather sitting where Bea typically sat. Irritated by the site, his simmering displeasure grew in volume.

He sat down as Vi came bustling through with two cups. "Saw you come in and knew you'd want your coffee."

"Thanks, Vi," he said, and she bustled off to take care of other customers.

Henry sipped the heady brew, frowned, and looked around with scorn. "I must say I have never eaten in such an establishment before." He faced Luc. "I assume the fare will match the décor."

Luc bristled at the implied slur. "If you mean a hearty meal served with a side of hospitality, then you assume correctly."

"I meant no offense, Lucian, I—"

"I've no desire to go back to New York."

Moreau's jaw clenched, and his eyes narrowed. "You've had plenty of time to get over whatever was the issue," he said firmly. "It's time you take over Moreau Shipping."

"I have a business here."

"A blacksmith shop is not a business. Not for a Moreau."

Luc sat forward and clasped his hands on the table. "I'm sorry to disappoint you, Grandfather. I am. I owe you a lot." He paused, his voice firm. "But not at the expense of my life or happiness."

"It's time you settled down, started a family. Belle—"

"No."

"Lucian—"

"The matter is not open for discussion, Grandfather. I will not marry Belle. Ever. And if you persist in that line of talk, I will leave now."

Henry sighed. "We can—"

He stopped when Belle did what she excelled at—made a grand entrance.

She paused a moment at the door to the diner, clothed in shimmering blue silk, her posture regal as she glanced aloofly around the room. Ivory skin highlighted sky-blue eyes, and curling tendrils of golden hair softened her face. The custom-made gown rustled as she glided toward their table.

All talk ceased as the patrons gawked.

Belle's smile was radiant. She loved being the center of attention.

Both men rose as she approached the table.

"Lucian, darling," she purred and presented her cheek for a kiss.

He deftly ignored the offer and pulled out a chair for her.

She hesitated, cheeks turning pink, then sat down.

Luc met his grandfather's unhappy scowl, his own leaving no room for doubt; he would not be a part of her public display.

"I hope I haven't kept you waiting over long," said Belle. "The hotel leaves much to be desired in terms of service."

"This is a cattle town, Belle," said Luc tartly, "not New York. They are not accustomed or equipped to deal with women of your station."

"Yes, well, it wouldn't hurt them to be a little more accommodating."

The next few minutes drug on as Belle detailed the things she didn't like about the town, the tea, and the people. Done at last, she turned to Luc, a slow secret smile curving her lips as she placed her hand on his arm. "I will be so happy when we are on our way back to civilization."

He pulled his arm free and picked up his coffee. "I wish you both a safe trip."

Her gaze jerked away from him to his grandfather. "I thought—"

"This is not the time or place for this discussion," snapped Henry. "We will meet at the hotel tomorrow." Moreau raised his hand in the air and snapped his fingers as Vi walked by, arms laden with plates. "We'd like—"

She glared at his hand as if it were a snake. "The only creatures 'round here who respond to snapped fingers are dogs."

Luc coughed to hide his chuckle as Vi walked past and set the plates on another table.

"Well!" exclaimed Belle, "I shall most definitely speak to the owner about that woman's deplorable behavior."

"She is the owner," said Luc. "And the cook, so I'd choose my words carefully."

"How can you condone such insulting behavior?" asked Belle.

"Because people respond in kind." Luc looked at his grandfather, who had the decency to blush.

"Whatever does that mean?"

"It means you reap what you sow," said Luc. "Kindness goes both ways."

Luc glanced up when he heard the door open. Bea walked in, looked around the crowded room, and turned as though to leave. Richard Bentley, who sat at a table near the door, called to her, and with an uneasy glance toward Luc, she joined him at the table.

What the hell?

Vi addressed him twice before he noticed.

"Supper tonight is baked ham, carrots, and green beans. And peach cobbler for dessert."

He glanced at Bea, who smiled at something her companion said. "That's fine."

Seemingly unaware of his distress, Vi smiled and nodded, completely ignoring the others. "How's Ty's new baby doing?"

He tore his glance away from Bea's table. "Cute little thing looks like Emma. She hopes to bring him to town soon so you ladies can spoil him."

"Good. Say, Luc, Bea talked me into ordering this fancy wine. Came in today. Would you like to try it?"

"Of course, thank you."

"My pleasure." She glared at his companions and went to the back.

"Fancy wine?" said Moreau with a snicker. "I can hardly wait."

Belle glanced at Bea, then back to Luc. "Well, now that is a surprise." She once more rested her hand on Luc's arm. "Poor Beulah Mae seems to have found a beau after all."

Luc made no effort to temper the coldness in his voice as he extricated his arm. "Why does it surprise you that a beautiful, intelligent, and caring woman would find someone who appreciates those qualities?"

"Lucian, darling, I—"

"Enough." His voice brittle with controlled anger, Luc looked back and forth between his grandfather and Belle. "Not another word about Bea or going back to New York. Not. One. Word."

Thankfully, they accepted his ultimatum, and the stiff conversation consisted of trivial matters such as the trip out and the status of mutual acquaintances in New York.

Any other time, Luc would have enjoyed the hearty meal, and the wine Vi served in plain glasses, but his throat was so tight, swallowing proved difficult.

An unexpected surge of jealousy accompanied each smile Bea bestowed on Richard. By the time the meal ended, his head throbbed, and his jaw ached from constant clamping.

His gut-wrenching reaction upon learning of Belle's plan not to bear his child was nothing compared to the anguish of watching Bea smiling and enjoying the company of another man.

Bea knew the moment she walked into The Rose that she'd made a colossal mistake. The first thing she saw was Belle smiling, her hand possessively resting on Luc's arm. The ache was almost a physical pain. She turned to leave, but Richard Bentley called to her from a table near the door.

"Miss Lockhart? Please, join me. I hate eating alone."

She hesitated only briefly before stepping his way. "Thank you, Mr. Bentley."

He rose and pulled a chair out for her. "Please. Call me Richard."

"Thank you, Richard. And, please, call me Bea."

"The place is pretty busy tonight," he said as he resumed his seat and nodded toward Eunice and her husband two tables away. "Though I'm willing to bet not everyone is here because of the food."

When she sat down, Luc's table was in her direct line of vision. With years of practice in hiding her feelings, she kept her expression neutral. However, when Belle looked at her, surprise etched on her face, followed by a light laugh, she couldn't stop the slow spread of warmth to her cheeks, and she touched the edge of the puckered scar before dropping her hands to her lap.

"It doesn't matter, you know," Richard said softly, his coffee-colored eyes full of kindness.

She furrowed her brow. "I'm sorry. What doesn't?"

He picked up his napkin and placed it in his lap. "The scar. It doesn't matter. And anyone who made you think otherwise is a fool."

His sincerity was touching and produced a grateful smile. She resisted the urge to place her hand on his arm, much the way Belle did Luc. "Thank you. I appreciate you saying that."

He shrugged. "It's the truth."

While he had been to the store several times, she'd never really looked at him until now. Not ruggedly handsome in the way Luc was, he presented a robust and self-confident air. He was tall, broad-shouldered, and lean, with salt and pepper hair that needed a trim. His bronzed and weathered face was clean-shaven, and the crinkles at the corners of his eyes spoke to hours of squinting in the sun. His thin mouth curled as if always on the verge of laughter—all in all, an attractive man.

"Howdy Bea, Richard," said Vi as she approached the table. "What can I get you folks this evening?"

Richard nodded toward Luc's table. "I didn't know you carried wine now."

She smiled. "Bea suggested I order it for folks who want something special from time to time." Her smile widened. "I even got some fancy glasses to put it in." She glanced over her shoulder and winked. "But I'm saving those for special people."

Richard laughed and looked at Bea. "Would you care for some wine?"

"I'd love it."

When Vi brought it out a few minutes later, she carried it on a linen-covered tray with two crystal stemmed wine glasses. Bea hid a smile as the woman made a point of letting Belle see them.

Richard poured the wine and held up his glass. "To chance encounters with beautiful women."

She blushed like a schoolgirl and raised her glass. "To chance encounters with new friends."

He sipped his wine, eyes intent on her face. "And if the new friend hoped for something more?"

She cut her eyes toward Luc and found his fierce expression locked on them. Unable to keep the stammer from her voice, she replied, "Well, I…I'm—"

"That was out of line. I apologize." He glanced at Luc. "I shall be content to enjoy your company this evening." He took another sip of wine and winked. "But if you change your mind…"

Suddenly, the gloom and doom hovering over her head like a storm cloud for days lifted as Richard flirted with her in public. While Luc was always attentive, he never flirted, not even when it was just the two of them in her house. While it didn't alter her feelings for him, it provided a sharp contrast between two men who appeared intent on capturing her attention. Never in her wildest dreams did she ever expect that to happen.

She lifted her glass and took a sip. "You'll be the first to know."

She looked around the crowded room and saw several people she knew and nodded a greeting. She was among friends. At last.

And tonight, she sat next to a charming man who made no secret of his interest.

From the first day she arrived, most people in town accepted her without reservation. True, some eyed the scar in silence, but most gave it no notice at all. Years of being shamed into hiding, of believing her value as a person, as a woman, was severely diminished by her disfigurement faded away. A weight lifted from her shoulders, and she sat up straighter as warmth flooded her being.

"More wine, Bea?"

Richard's gentle voice interrupted her musings, and she blinked. Time spent with Luc was special to her on so many levels. This moment, however, was somehow different. Perhaps it was because she saw herself differently now. *I'm not ugly. I have value.*

Her voice shook as she replied, "Yes, please."

Throughout the evening, Richard entertained her with numerous tales of life on a ranch. He had also visited New York once and shared a different perspective on the city of her birth, and she found herself enjoying his company.

Occasional glances toward Luc's table dampened her spirits, but she refused to let it spoil the evening.

After dessert and coffee, she looked at her companion, grateful for the balm to her soul he unknowingly provided. "Thank you for inviting me to dine with you, Richard. It's been an enjoyable evening."

"Would you allow me to escort you home?"

She was about to refuse when Belle approached, Luc and his grandfather trailing a step behind.

Richard stood when Belle reached the table.

"Beulah Mae."

Belle's sugary-sweet voice grated on Bea's nerves, but she kept her face neutral.

"Luc and I simply couldn't leave without saying hello."

Hands clenched tightly in her lap, Bea's voice betrayed no rancor. "Richard Bentley, may I present Annabelle Blankenship and Henry Moreau."

Richard gave a short bow of his head. "Good evening, Miss Blankenship. Mr. Moreau."

Belle eyed Richard with open interest. "Are you a cowboy, sir?"

"I own a ranch near here." He looked at Luc, his face unreadable. "Evening, Luc."

"Richard." Luc's voice held no warmth at all. "I'll have that harness repaired in a day or so."

"Thanks. I'll pick it up Saturday if that's okay." He gave Bea an expectant look. "I'll be in town for the dance."

"A dance?" said Belle, her voice edging up with excitement as she turned to Luc. "Lucian, darling, you didn't mention a dance." She moved and linked her arm through his. "Why, it will be just like old times. Remember how well we dance together?"

Luc opened his mouth but didn't get the words out before Richard spoke up.

"I guess we'll see you there then."

Luc's jaw clamped tight as Belle turned him toward the door.

"Good night, Beulah Mae." She gave Richard a dazzling smile. "Mr. Bentley, I do hope you'll save a dance for me."

"My pleasure, ma'am."

Henry nodded to them. "Miss Lockhart. Mr. Bentley."

Bea's heart remained lodged in her throat. It was a safe bet Luc would now take Belle to the dance.

Richard sat down, reached for her hand, then halted and rested his on the table. "I'm sorry if I overstepped just now. I suspect you planned on going to the dance with Luc. But it appears that Miss Blankenship…"

She took a breath, tried to calm her racing heart. "Belle is accustomed to getting what she wants."

"I guessed as much."

Bea drained her wine glass, unable to stop the tremble in her hands.

"I have thoroughly enjoyed myself tonight, Bea," said Richard. "Thank you for joining me."

"I'm glad I came in. I almost didn't."

"About the dance," he said softly. "Should you find yourself in need of an escort, it would be my honor."

She took a breath and nodded.

He rose, held her chair for her, then offered his elbow. "May I walk you home?"

Unable to speak for the pain in her chest, she linked her arm through his and walked out.

CHAPTER TWENTY

BEA STOOD BEHIND THE COUNTER AND WAVED AT young Josh Walker and his mother as they exited the store. They came in with a dozen eggs and a small smoked ham to barter for some sugar, beans, and a bar of the new lavender-scented soap that just arrived. Before coming here, bartering was a totally foreign concept to Bea. Thankfully, Mable explained that some folks did that when they didn't have the money to purchase what they needed. It made her happy to help them out. Plus, it made her feel like she belonged and was a part of the community.

She could then add those bartered items to her inventory or use them herself. So far, no one had offered her anything she couldn't use in some manner.

Movement out front caught her eye, and she saw Henry Moreau crossing the street toward Luc's shop. Immediately, her good mood vanished. Unwelcome images of Belle hanging onto Luc's arm last night at The Rose, smiling up at him, filled her mind.

Knowing Belle, Bea was confident she expected Luc to escort her to the dance on Saturday.

Bea hoped he might come back last night, but he didn't. The clock struck noon, and, still, he didn't show, leaving her wondering where she stood with him. He did tell her he had to deal with his grandfather in addition to Belle, so that explained it. Still, she missed his substantial presence.

Richard was pleasant enough company, but he wasn't Luc. Ever the gentleman when he walked her home, they sat on the porch and talked until the chilled air became too much. When he rose to leave, she sensed he wanted to kiss her goodnight, but she quickly went inside. A casual dinner and conversation aside, in her mind, kissing anyone but Luc bordered on betrayal.

"Miss Lockhart?"

The soft question coming from the entrance to the back startled Bea, and she whirled around to find Daisy in the doorway, a wrapped bundle in her hands.

"Daisy," she exclaimed, "what a pleasant surprise."

Eyes sparkling, the young lady stepped inside. "I'm sorry if I startled you, ma'am, but I couldn't wait to show you this," she said eagerly. "I got the dress cut out, and I've more or less pinned it together and wanted to see what you thought about it."

"My goodness, that was fast," said Bea, "I'm impressed."

"I was so excited to work on it that I couldn't stop." She carefully unwrapped the garment and held it up for inspection. "I wasn't sure about the chiffon on the shoulders."

Simple but elegant, the dress was beautiful. Cool to the touch, light bounced off the shimmering fabric like sunshine on an emerald pool. The gently flared skirt was gathered at the back and formed a small train. Pleated silk chiffon, crimped in the center and accented with a green silk rose, adorned the scooped neckline and draped over the upper arm to the elbow. Another length of chiffon cinched in the waist and formed a delicate bow at the back. A small chiffon ruffle on the hemline completed the look.

"Ma made the rose," said Daisy proudly. "She's very good at

that. I wasn't sure about the chiffon on the hem, so I just pinned a small section so you could see it."

"Daisy…I don't know what to say." She lightly touched the gleaming material. "It's exquisite. I wouldn't change a thing."

Daisy's face beamed. "I'm so glad, miss." She began refolding the garment. "I will start sewing on it later today. It will take me several days to finish 'cause I have some other stuff to sew, too."

"Don't put yourself out," said Bea. "I'm in no hurry."

The bell above the door announced a new customer, and Daisy immediately headed for the back but stopped when Bea placed a hand lightly on her arm.

A beautiful young woman wearing a tan split riding skirt strode forward, a sleeping infant in the basket on her arm. Warm chestnut hair pulled into a braid down her back framed a sun-kissed complexion highlighted by emerald green eyes and a welcoming smile.

"Miss Lockhart?" the woman asked, "I'm Emma Roundtree. I've been looking forward to meeting you." At that moment, she spied the garment Daisy held, and her expression changed to one of complete delight. "Oh, my goodness," she gasped, "that is so beautiful." She reached for the dress, then stopped. "May I?"

"Of course," said Bea as she took the gown and placed it on the counter. "Daisy is a very gifted seamstress, and this is her latest creation for the store."

Emma looked at the gown, then at Daisy. "This is beautiful. I can't sew a lick, heck I can barely cook, so I'm envious of anyone who can."

"Thank you, Mrs. Roundtree," said Daisy softly. "I appreciate it."

"Please, call me Emma." She looked at Bea. "Please tell me this dress will be for sale."

"As a matter of fact," said Bea, "it will be. Are you interested?"

Face beaming, Emma looked at the women in turn. "Ty is taking me to Ft. Worth next month. I wear pants and this skirt most of the time and would love to have something like this to wear when we go out to dinner."

"Excellent," said Bea. She quoted a price and heard the gasp from Daisy but didn't turn around.

"I'll take it," said Emma happily. "Can it be ready in two weeks?"

"I'm sure Daisy can do that."

"Oh, yes, ma'am," agreed Daisy. "I can do that."

"Perfect," said Bea. "Why don't you take Emma to the dressing area and let her try on the pieces, and you can make any adjustments needed." She reached for the baby basket. "I'll keep an eye on this little one for you."

Emma handed over the basket. "His name is Tyler, but we call him Ty, like his father. He's getting something from Luc but should be here shortly." She hurried to follow Daisy, leaving Bea alone with the sleeping child.

Bea's heart did a little flip as she looked at the baby. His nose twitched, and his tiny bow-shaped mouth curled up in a smile. She smiled back. One fisted hand moved slightly, and she rubbed a knuckle over it, marveling at its softness. She yearned for a child of her own one day and suddenly realized she wanted a child with Luc. The thought that her dream may die on the vine brought the sting of tears, but she pushed them back when baby Ty made a sound in his sleep, followed by the cutest pout she'd ever seen. "You will be a heartbreaker one day, little man."

"That's what Emma says," came a hearty baritone from the front door.

Bea jerked her gaze up, chagrined to be caught wool-gathering again and not hearing the bell above the door.

"But she's biased." He removed his hat and placed it on the counter. "Nice to see you again, Miss Lockhart." Ty nodded toward his son. "How did you get stuck with babysitting duty?"

"Your wife is trying on a dress. And it's no bother. Your son is adorable."

He rubbed a calloused finger against the boy's cheek. The love he held for the child was almost palpable. "That he is." He looked up when Emma walked in from the room Bea had designated as the women's area. "Find something you like?"

"Definitely, but you'll have to wait until we go to Ft. Worth to see it."

"Will I like it?"

"Absolutely." She turned to Daisy. "I don't own many dresses, and the ones I have are as old as the hills. Most of them need some kind of repair. I would very much like to have some made. Nothing as fancy as that," she nodded toward the bundled fabric Daisy held, "but something I can wear around the house." She looked at Ty and grinned. "I tend to wear pants on the ranch most of the time because it's easier to work in, but Ty prefers I wear dresses at home."

"I'd be honored, ma'am," said Daisy.

Emma spent the next few minutes selecting material and discussing what she wanted. By the time she left, Daisy was bursting with excitement.

"I can't believe she's actually going to pay you that much for the dress," said Daisy.

"It's worth every penny, Daisy. And most of that will go to you," said Bea. "I'll take out the cost of the materials, a small store fee, and the rest is yours."

Daisy gaped at her, one hand covering her mouth. "Oh, no, miss, that's too much."

"No, it isn't. I want to help you get established, and that's how we'll do it for now. Once you can afford it, you'll simply buy your material and such from me at a discounted rate, and we'll both make money. And when Emma wears her dresses in public, it will be an advertisement for your skills, and I will just about bet you will get more orders because of it."

Head bowed, Daisy whispered, "I don't know what to say."

"You don't have to say anything. We're business partners. And that's what partners do."

"You and Mrs. Roundtree are so nice to me. Better than I deserve." She looked up and shook her head slightly. "You're nothing like that fancy woman who come to town with Mr. Luc's grandfather."

Before Bea could reply, Daisy continued. "She may be right pretty on the outside, ma'am, but on the inside, she's ugly as sin." Daisy dropped her gaze, cheeks bright red. "I know I shouldn't talk bad about folks, but she's one of the nastiest people I ever met."

"Daisy," said Bea, ready to defend her friend, "did she say something offensive to you?"

"Oh, no, ma'am, not to me. But I heard her be rude to Mary at The Rose and Miss Vi. And she's pretty demanding to folks at the hotel."

Unable to think of a suitable response, Bea let the moment pass in silence.

"I should be going. Miss Lizzy brought over some of Mikey's pants to mend, so I need to get back to work. And I want to make sure I have Mrs. Roundtree's dress ready on time."

Bea pulled money from the register. "That's our deal, re-member? Half at this point, the rest when Emma picks up the dress."

"I can't thank you enough, ma'am," she said sincerely. "Ever since word got out that I was hurt and now I'm working for you instead of, well, you know, a few folks have asked me to mend things or make stuff for them. Not a lot, but enough that I don't have to go back to the Broken Spur, at least not now." Her eyes filled with tears and her lips trembled. "I will never be able to repay you for that."

Bea pulled the young woman into a gentle hug. "You don't owe me anything, child." After a moment, she pulled back and made Daisy look at her. "I meant what I said about making some dresses for my store. And now Emma wants you to make some for her. And who knows, maybe when she wears that green silk in Ft. Worth, someone may want you to create something for them." She rubbed a tear from the young woman's eyes with her thumb. "You keep your head up, child. Don't ever let anyone make you feel bad about yourself again. You did what you had to do for your family." She took a breath. "And I want you to promise me something, Daisy. Promise me…if things ever get to the point you think you need to go back to that life, you will tell me immediately."

Lips trembling, Daisy nodded. "I will, ma'am."

Bea watched her walk out, head held high, a skip in her step. Daisy would be all right. She'd see to that.

"Hell, boy," quipped Amos, "what'd you expect? That she'd sit home and twiddle her thumbs while you had dinner with another woman?"

Luc swallowed the sharp reproach that surfaced. Amos was right. Bea had every right to have dinner with whomever she chose. He just wanted it to be him. Only him.

Thanks to Belle's untimely arrival, all his plans were now dust in the wind.

"I know," he muttered as he finished the harness. "I was just surprised, that's all."

"Surprised? Why the hell would you be surprised? She's purty as a speckled pup and one of the nicest people around. Bentley ain't the only one who's noticed either." Amos didn't bother aiming for the bucket this time and spat a stream of tobacco juice on the dirt floor. "And now you done dropped her like a hot coal and agreed to take that snobby woman to the dance."

"I didn't—I couldn't—dammit." He pitched the finished bridle onto the table. "I told Belle I planned to take someone else. I may as well have been talking to my horse." He raked long fingers through his hair. "I haven't had a chance to talk to Bea yet, to explain." He didn't mention walking by her house and spotting Richard sitting on the porch with her. Even now, the image made his heart hurt.

"What's to explain?" Amos asked caustically. "She already knows you're an ass."

"Is this a bad time?"

Henry Moreau's tired voice stopped Luc from addressing Amos's remark.

"It's fine," snapped Luc. "He was just leaving."

Amos grunted as he slowly pushed himself up from the barrel and shuffled toward the street. "Guess I'll go see if Silas has learned how to play checkers yet."

Moreau hesitated, then walked to the barrel Amos vacated and sat down. "I hoped we could talk at the hotel."

Luc wiped his hands on a rag and looked at his grandfather. "I have work to do. And I meant what I said last night." He dropped the cloth and moved to the fire pit. "I have no wish to return to New York." He paused. "And I have no intention of marrying Belle. Ever."

Henry sighed and rested his hands on the handle of his cane. "Walking out the way you did put me in a rather awkward position."

Luc remained silent as heat rushed to his cheeks. Common sense said the fiasco would be an embarrassment to all parties, but there was nothing to be gained by dwelling on it now.

"I've known Harper Blankenship for over thirty years," said Moreau. "Takes a lot to ruin a friendship of that length."

Temper escalating, Luc glared at his grandfather. "You were never friends. You were shipping associates who barely tolerated one another." Needing something to do, he grabbed the harness off the table again. "And then one day, you decided a merger was better than being rivals, and Belle was the bargaining chip."

Henry shrugged. "Harper wanted to expand. You needed an heir. Win, win situation."

He tossed the harness back on the table. "Except Belle never had any intention of providing that heir."

"That may have been the case at the time," said Moreau, "but things are different now."

Luc snorted. "One thing you can be certain of, Grandfather, is that Belle's only concern will always be for herself and her position." Struck by a sudden thought, he stood up straighter. "Is that it? They need money, and she's back on the auction block?"

"You make it sound very gauche, Lucian. Arranged marriages are common in England. My marriage to your grandmother, for example."

Luc barely remembered the demur woman with the lovely accent who died when he was eight. "We're not in England."

"It's time to give up this folly and take your place with Moreau Shipping."

"My place is here," he said firmly.

Moreau waved one hand side to side as though to discount Luc's comments, and his temper spiked again. "I'm sorry to disappoint you, Grandfather. I truly am, but I won't be going back. My life is here now." He paused. "And when I do marry, it will be for love, not because it's part of a business deal."

Henry's mouth tightened until it was a straight line across his face. "Love cannot be trusted," he said firmly, "it clouds your judgment."

Luc stared at the man who raised him and wondered what caused him to have such a warped view of love. "We shall have to agree to disagree on that point, Grandfather."

Moreau's voice increased in volume, and he stamped his cane on the dirt floor. "You have an obligation, Lucian, to the company and to me."

"I am very grateful to you, Grandfather. But that gratitude does not mean I must marry someone I don't love or do something I cannot abide."

Henry winced as though in pain, and Luc suffered a pang of sorrow for causing him discomfort.

"I started with little more than an idea and built one of the largest and most respected shipping companies in the country. I dreamed of one day passing that on to your father and then to you." His voice dropped and turned pensive. "Moreau Shipping is your legacy, Lucian." He paused, and sadness pinched his face. "One that is in danger of dying."

"What do you mean?"

Moreau sat up straighter and crossed his hands on the top of his cane. "After you left, there were a series of…events that cost me."

Luc put away the bridle and leaned against the table. "What kind of events?"

His grandfather shrugged. "A lost shipment here, a missed opportunity there, an unexpected storm. At first, it was nothing I couldn't handle." He sighed. "Suddenly, over the last year, people I'd operated with and traded with for years had no use for my services."

"How bad is it?"

He shrugged. "If I make a few changes, I can make it. But it won't be near what it was before." His faded blue eyes locked on Luc's. "Oscar is willing to invest. But he has a price."

Luc knew what that price was, and he had no intention of paying it.

"I'm too old for this fight, Luc. I need you in charge. To bring Moreau Shipping back to where it was."

Luc sighed and shook his head. "I can't go back to that life, Grandfather. It's not for me." He raked long fingers through his hair. "I have more than enough money saved up. You are welcome to it."

Even as he spoke, Moreau was shaking his head, but Luc continued. "Don't you have trusted people in charge now? Can't they run things for you?"

"A Moreau should be in charge. And you need an heir to pass it down to." Henry's eyes narrowed as he watched Luc. "You need a wife who can help you navigate the social waters, who can open doors for you and not be a deterrent." His voice took on a firm edge when he continued. "Someone like Annabelle."

CHAPTER TWENTY-ONE

BEA PLACED THE DAY'S RECEIPTS ALONG WITH HER ledger in the safe and sighed. Today was busy, which helped keep her mind occupied and off Lucian and Belle. However, without activity to waylay her thoughts, her mind conjured countless scenarios in which Belle waltzed off with Lucian, leaving her heartbroken.

She heard the door open and looked up. "We're closed—"

Belle entered and paused.

Terrific. The perfect ending to a perfect day. Bea took a breath and faced the woman coming forward with slow, purposeful strides. "I was just closing. What can I do for you, Belle?"

Jaw tight, Belle's nostrils flared as she sucked in a breath. "I hate that name."

Bea silently raised one brow.

Belle stared in silence a moment, then placed her reticule on the counter. "I can't believe you actually bought this place." She cast a disdainful look around the store. "Your father would cringe at having his name associated with it."

"It isn't his store," said Bea firmly. "It's mine."

Belle's eyes narrowed, and her claws dug deeper. "It's so plain. So ugly." She turned her malicious smile to the scar on Bea's cheek. "You should feel right at home."

Immune to Belle's ridicule, she refused to allow the woman

to spoil her joy. "It's also tough and resilient with hidden beauty beneath the surface. It brings joy to those who enter and provides a vital service to the community." She took a breath. "And it's mine."

Undeterred, Belle straightened her shoulders and glared. "I saw your father recently. He vowed he had no idea where you were, and frankly, I don't think he cared."

Bea pulled on her quickly dwindling reserve of patience. "Well, the feeling is mutual, then."

Belle glanced around the store again, her face broadcasting the fact her mind drifted elsewhere. "I still can't believe he broke our engagement," she said softly and looked at Bea. "No one walks out on me."

Something in her voice made the hair on Bea's neck tingle. "There was no engagement to break, Belle."

She didn't appear to hear as she wandered to the end of the counter and plucked a licorice stick from the jar. "You have no idea the snobbery I endured these last two years." She eyed the candy, then dropped it back in the container and dusted her hands together. "How people laughed at me behind my back."

Bea wanted to say she understood such behavior all too well but didn't waste her breath. Belle didn't care for anyone's feelings but her own.

"My plan is—"

"What plan?"

She cocked her head to one side. "It really wasn't that difficult," she said softly, then stiffened and waved one gloved hand back and forth as though to erase her comment. She picked up her bag and looped her arm through the handle. "He's coming back to New York with me." She said with finality. "His silly honor won't give him a choice. And then the decision will be mine."

It took a moment to get on track with the conversation's change in direction. Something was off about Belle though Bea couldn't put her finger on it. Her unease grew, but she refused to let it show. "Are you sure, Belle?" she asked softly. "Because I don't think you are."

"I always get what I want," she huffed. "And I'll have my…" she stopped mid-sentence, then continued. "He still wants me, you know."

When Bea simply stared without comment, Belle stiffened her back. "What on earth makes you think you have what it takes to hold a man like Lucian?" She raked her gaze over Bea's face and smirked. "That hideous scar would turn any man away."

Bea didn't mean to react to the taunt, but the words rushed forth anyway. "He doesn't think it's so hideous when he kisses me."

The color drained from her adversary's face, then rushed back in, turning her cheeks bright red. "I don't believe you. Lucian would never kiss *you*."

"Frankly, Belle, I don't care if you believe me or not." Patience exhausted, she rounded the counter and headed for the front door. "Now, if you'll excuse me, I need to close up the store." She opened the door and stood aside for Belle to leave.

"I don't believe for one minute he kissed you," she hissed. "But, if he did, it was nothing more than pity." She stopped just outside the door. "And rest assured, it won't happen again." She cocked her head to the side, and one delicate brow arched upward. "And really, why would any man want the likes of you when he can have me instead?"

Bea's mind raced in all directions as she walked home. She still hadn't heard from Luc though Amos told her earlier he'd been in deep conversation with his grandfather for most of the morning.

Belle's comment about a plan kept replaying in her mind. What did she mean?

Shaking her head, she walked into the kitchen. Exhaustion nibbled away the desire to cook, but hunger insisted she do something. Biscuits from this morning rested under a cloth on the counter along with remnants of Mrs. Walker's ham and a jar of canned peas from Mavis. Peach Cobbler from Vi rounded out the menu.

"Ham and biscuits with peas and cobbler for dessert. That will do just fine," she said to the empty room.

Opting for a fire in the fireplace versus the stove, she got coffee going, then sliced ham into a pan along with a biscuit and placed them near the fire to warm. She put the beans in another pot near the coals.

While the items heated, she poured a cup of coffee and was about to sit down when a light knock sounded on the back door. Her heart jumped when she opened it, and Luc stood there, his face pulled into a tight frown. "You look tired. I have fresh coffee. Have you eaten yet?" The words came out in a tumbled rush.

"Not yet. I'm sorry if I have interrupted your dinner."

"Come in." She closed the door behind him and went to the cabinet to retrieve a cup. "Don't be sorry. I'm always glad to see you." She poured his coffee and pulled the cloth from the biscuits. "It's leftover biscuits and ham. Won't take long to warm these up."

"Don't go to any trouble. Cold is fine with me."

"Sit. I won't be long."

By the time she returned with their dinner, he had finished most of his coffee. She placed the meal on the table and brought out plates and utensils. "Would you get the butter off the counter there, please?"

He placed the dish on the table, and they sat down.

"I'm sorry I haven't been by sooner," said Luc. "Things are…" his voice trailed off, and he sighed.

"Let's save the talk for after dinner, shall we?" she said with a smile. "I haven't eaten since breakfast, and I'm famished." That wasn't exactly true, but she couldn't tell him she was terrified of what he might have to say.

Small talk governed the conversation. Bea told him about Emma and the baby coming to the store and how excited Daisy became when Emma wanted the gown she designed. She told him how traffic picked up daily as locals prepared for spring activities. The antics of Silas and Amos always made for an amusing story.

Luc typically had something to offer, but tonight he remained silent, which only added to Bea's concern.

When the meal ended, Luc rose to help right the kitchen, but Bea sent him to the parlor to deal with the fireplace.

Dishes put away, she pulled her prized bottle of French brandy from the pantry, poured two glasses, and carried them to the parlor. He looked up in surprise when she passed him the beautifully etched brandy snifter.

"My one indulgence," she said with a smile.

He nodded in approval and sipped his drink, eyes focused on the yellow flames licking up the sides of the logs in the fireplace, their hiss and crackle filling the tense silence. Luc's posture remained stiff, his face cast in shadow from the single lamp burning on the table behind them.

Unlike other times, tonight's silence bore down like an oppressive weight, turning the meal into a stone in her stomach. She took a generous swallow of the amber liquid, savoring the sweet, fruity tang as it slid down her throat and warmed her insides. Another sip and some of the tension left her shoulders. Eyes closed, she leaned back. Tender hopes of a full life, a child, with Luc flashed through her mind, and pain clogged her throat.

Resignation gnawed at her soul. She would never know the love of a man. She would never birth a child with the man she loved. This man.

Unable to rid herself of the painful images, she brought the glass up and downed the rest of her drink.

The rapid thump of her pulse echoed in her ears like a death knell.

Whatever was coming, she was powerless to stop.

CHAPTER TWENTY-TWO

DESPITE HER RELAXED OUTWARD APPEARANCE, LUC felt the tension rolling off Bea like a tidal wave.

If he explained everything, maybe she would help him make the right decision. Even as the thought crossed his mind, he suppressed a laugh. Like he had a choice.

When she downed the remainder of her drink, he followed suit and reached for her glass. "Would you like another?"

A light sigh preceded a shake of her head.

He took the glasses to the kitchen and spied the brandy bottle on the counter. He poured himself a stiff drink and downed it.

Liquid courage is better than none at all.

When he returned, she rested against the back of the couch, eyes closed, hands clasped tightly in her lap. "Just tell me, Lucian," she whispered. "Whatever it is. Just tell me."

He sat down and pulled her against him, thankful she did not resist. "He insists I return to New York and pull Moreau Shipping out of the dungeon."

"Why is it in the dungeon? I thought it was very profitable."

"It was, but some things have happened recently that strained his resources."

She stiffened. "How bad is it?"

He shrugged. "He said if he made some difficult changes,

155

things might turn around." He blew out a long breath. "But he is getting older, and no longer has the stamina for such an ordeal."

"What does he expect you to do exactly?"

"The short answer is to run Moreau Shipping."

"And the long answer?"

Luc paused to gather his thoughts. "Move back to New York. Take over everything." He inhaled deeply before answering. "I owe him a lot, *Chère*. He took me in after my parents died. But..." He pulled her tighter against him. "I don't belong there anymore." He kissed the top of her head. "My place is here."

She turned her face up to meet his gaze. "Are you sure, Lucian?"

"Very sure, *Chère*. My place is here. With you. That is if you want me."

Eyes glistening, she smiled, and the weight on his heart lifted. Before he could act on the urge to kiss her, a sharp pounding on the front door stopped him.

"Luc?" shouted Roscoe. "Luc? You in there?"

Luc got up and answered the door. "Roscoe? What is it? What's wrong?"

"It's your grandfather, sir. He had some kind of spell at The Rose."

Bea appeared at his side. "What's wrong?"

"Something with my grandfather." He turned to Roscoe. "What happened?"

"I saw him at The Rose with that lady. Looked to me like they was arguing about something. All of a sudden, he stood up and started to leave. And then it was like he just passed out. He hit his head on the corner of a table when he fell." Roscoe's face twisted in sorrow. "I'm sorry I wasn't close enough to grab him 'fore he fell." He took a step backward. "Jeb and some others took him to his room at the hotel and sent for Doc, and I come to find you. Since you weren't at home, I thought you might be here."

Bea grabbed her shawl from the rack by the door and followed him out.

Luc's heart pounded so hard he expected it to burst through his chest. Guilt over his refusal to return to New York tore at him. His grandfather was the only family he had left. He hadn't seen his mother's people since he was a child. They were a small tribe back then, and he had no idea where they might be.

He reached the hotel and bounded up the stairs, Bea trailing behind. Inside the door, he jerked to a stop. Moreau lay in the middle of the bed, minus his jacket. Bright red blood covered his face, down his neck, and onto his stark white shirt. Crimson liquid still oozed from cuts to his mouth and forehead. His chalky white complexion already showed signs of bruising around the raised knot on his forehead, and his chest rose and fell with shaky breaths.

A sudden thought made his heart constrict in fear. Was his grandfather dying?

Doc Morton sat on the edge of the bed and pressed a stethoscope against the older man's chest. Belle stood near the door, twisting a handkerchief in her hands, and Bea waited by the door.

Luc moved to the opposite side of the bed and stared at the man who raised him. "How is he?"

Doc looped the stethoscope around his neck. "Not sure yet. He may have had a spell with his heart. Hard to tell at this point. But, if you rise too quickly, sometimes you can get dizzy and lose your balance." He plucked a rag from the pan beside the bed and dabbed at the cuts on Henry's face. "The cut on his lip isn't bad, but this one on his forehead will need stitches."

"He's so still," said Luc. "Is he unconscious?"

"…t-t-tired," came the soft reply.

Luc nearly collapsed with relief. "Grandfather? You had me worried."

Moreau's mouth twitched, but he didn't speak.

"Don't try to talk, Mr. Moreau," instructed Doc. "Just nod or shake your head to my questions."

Eyes closed, his head moved ever so slightly up and down.

"Do you have any pain in your chest?"

A slow side-to-side roll.

Doc looked at the gradual rise and fall of his chest. "Do you have any difficulty breathing?"

Another no.

"It's hard to say if you've had some kind of episode with your heart," Doc continued. "But your heart rate is a little irregular right now."

Moreau winced when Doc placed the cloth against the cut on his forehead but didn't speak. "The cut on your mouth is minor. The one on your tongue will make eating difficult for a couple of days, but this one on your forehead will need a couple of stitches. You up for that?"

Henry inhaled slowly. "…yes."

"Will he be all right?" asked Luc.

"At this point, I don't see any particular cause for concern. He's not showing any symptoms of heart problems, but we'll keep an eye on him for now." He turned to Luc. "I think someone needs to stay with him tonight."

"I'll be here."

"Good." He lifted the rag and examined the cut on Moreau's forehead. "The blood has slowed enough for me to stitch this up." He dropped the rag in the bowl and reached for his medical kit.

"I'm going to give you some laudanum," he told his patient, "before I start sewing that cut."

Aside from a grimace, his grandfather showed no reaction as Doc finished stitching the gash.

"The best thing for him right now is bed rest and no excitement." Doc turned to the two women by the door. "Ladies, if you will excuse us, we'll get Mr. Moreau situated in bed." He didn't wait for them to leave before turning to Luc. "Help me get him undressed."

Luc was shocked by the paleness of his grandfather's complexion and lack of response as they removed his clothes and placed a nightshirt over his head. *I hope it's the laudanum and not something wrong.*

Doc looked at Luc. "That cut on his mouth will cause some difficulty eating, at least for the next few days." He glanced down at his patient. "The laudanum will help with the pain and will help him sleep." He placed a bottle on the dresser. "Give him no more than six to ten drops every four hours for the pain. If it isn't too bad, you can try some willow bark tea instead. I'll have Mavis bring some over. Roscoe said he didn't eat his supper, so I asked Vi to make some broth for him," said Doc. "I'm not sure he'll be able to eat it but see if you can get him to try."

"I will," said Luc. "Whatever he needs, I'll be here."

Doc's sympathetic eyes met Luc's. "It's difficult to tell at this point if it does pertain to his heart or if there will be any lasting after-effects."

"What do you mean?"

He shrugged. "Well, if it did have something to do with his heart, it can sometimes affect speech or movement." He shrugged and looked at Moreau. "I don't think it's anything like that, but let me know if you see anything that concerns you."

"I will."

After Doc left, Bea walked toward Luc and rested her hand on his arm. "Is there anything I can do to help?"

He covered her hand with his. Just having her near soothed his frayed nerves. He looked at his grandfather then back to Bea. "Would you mind sitting with him a few minutes?" His glacial stare found Belle beside the door. "I need to find out what happened."

Bea pulled a chair beside the bed and sat down as Luc closed the door behind him. She found it difficult to believe the man lying there was the same formidable man she both admired and feared. They met on several occasions over the years, usually at the store, though a couple of times at Bea's few social functions or when he visited her father at their home. Unlike Belle, he never treated her with disrespect, though he was never overly friendly, either. Bea admired his tenacity in business dealings, but his frosty detachment disconcerted her. It was hard to know where you stood with him.

She did know with absolute certainty that Henry Moreau would detest feeling helpless and dependent upon others for anything.

A soft moan drew her gaze to his strained features. "Mr. Moreau? Are you in pain? Do I need to get the doctor?"

"...Lu...Luc..." The whispered word, uttered through his cut and swollen mouth, was slurred and barely audible.

She patted the frail hand resting outside the sheet. "He'll be right back."

He turned toward her voice, and his eyelids fluttered several times before they remained open. His eyes narrowed, and his lips moved as he tried to speak. "...Mi...Mish—."

"Don't try to talk, sir," she said softly. "Luc will be right back. He's talking to Belle."

Henry flinched, and Bea patted his hand again. "Don't fret. He'll be right back. He wanted to find out what happened."

Pale blue eyes locked with hers. "D-don't wa-wa…" Frustration tightened his features as he struggled to speak.

Bea's first thought was, *He doesn't want me here.* She understood his reaction and didn't take the rejection personally. He wanted Luc. "Mr. Moreau, I know I'm the last person you want to see right now, but Luc will be back soon. Please. Don't tire yourself out."

Moreau closed his eyes. His tongue touched his lips as though to moisten them.

"Would you like some water, sir? Do you think you can drink it?"

He nodded slowly.

The glass Doc put the medicine in was half full. Unsure of giving him more at this point, she poured the contents in the bowl with the bloody rag and added fresh water from the pitcher. She placed a clean rag under his chin, then lifted his head to drink. He did swallow a little though more ran down his chin. She gently wiped it off and placed the glass back on the bedside table.

His head moved slightly side-to-side, and he took a ragged breath. "…H-hel Lu…"

Bea blinked, trying to make sense of the corrupted words. "I'm not sure I understand, sir. Are you saying you want me to help Lucian?"

He blinked several times and nodded.

"Help him? How? No, wait, don't try to talk." Instinct drove Bea to make a decision, and she lightly touched his hand. "Mr. Moreau, I must tell you this. I love Lucian with all my heart, and I will do whatever I can to help him. And you." She inhaled a shaky breath. "I know that you want him to marry Belle, possibly for financial reasons." She inhaled quickly. "If that's the case, I might be able to help if you'll allow me. I only want what is best for Luc." She paused. "If, in the end, that means I must step aside, that is what I will do."

Moreau flinched again and turned his hand over to grab hers. The strength there took her by surprise.

"N-n-no."

"No? You don't want my help?"

His grip on her hand tightened, and his pallid complexion took on a rosy hue. Frustration once again strained his features as he struggled to form words, the medication adding to the problem. "N-no tr-trush…"

Bea's eyes narrowed as she stared at Moreau and tried to decipher his words. "I'm so sorry. I don't understand."

He clenched his eyes and sucked in a breath through his nose.

"Please, Mr. Moreau. Don't stress yourself anymore." She patted the hand that still gripped hers. "I know you want to speak, but whatever it is, it can wait until you are better."

His hand trembled beneath hers. "C-cn w-wait."

She leaned forward. "It can't wait?"

His chin dipped.

She remembered Roscoe saying it looked like he and Belle were arguing, so she followed that train of thought. "Okay. It can't wait. Does it concern Belle?"

Another dip of his head.

"Were the two of you arguing at dinner?"

His eyes slid shut, and his grip wavered. "D-don tr-trush…"

She chewed her lower lip, trying to make sense of his mumbled words. "Are you…are you saying not to…not to trust Belle?"

He blinked, opened his eyes a fraction, and nodded once before his eyes closed again.

CHAPTER TWENTY-THREE

"WHAT THE HELL HAPPENED?" LUC DIDN'T bother to temper his speech, and Belle took a step back.

"Darling, it was just awful," she whimpered, hands clasped under her chin. "One minute we were talking, and the next, the poor dear toppled onto the floor." She reached out a tentative hand and placed it on his forearm. "Will he be all right?"

He pulled away from her grasp. "What were the two of you discussing?"

She twisted her hands together. "I don't recall exactly. Just—things. This awful town, the people."

"You weren't arguing?"

She stiffened, blue eyes darting around before connecting with his. "Of course not. We were talking. That's all."

Luc didn't for one minute believe that was all there was to the event. Roscoe didn't imagine what he saw. "He was upset over your conversation." He allowed a small portion of the anger and fear simmering inside to leach into his voice. "You better hope he doesn't have any lasting ill effects from that fall."

"Lucian, darling." She reached for his arm again. "How on earth could you think such a thing? Why I love him like my own father."

"Of course you do," he scoffed.

She did a decent job of faking hurt, but she'd used that expression in his presence once too often.

"I don't know how long it will be before he can travel," he said firmly, "So I think it's best if you took the next train back to New York." He didn't break eye contact as he continued. "There's nothing for you here."

Belle's face contorted, and her eyes filled with tears.

He wasn't buying that, either. He'd seen her summon tears at the drop of a hat.

"Lucian, darling, I couldn't possibly leave you alone at a time like this." A muffled sob escaped, and she took a step toward him, one hand covering her mouth, the other reaching for his arm. "I can't believe this is happening."

He had no choice but to catch her when she collapsed in front of him.

"Lucian?"

Bea's soft voice startled him and cut through Belle's theatrics.

She glanced at Belle's body pressed against his, then back to him. Her muffled sobs grated on Bea's nerves. "He's sleeping now. I'll see that Belle gets back to her room and check on the soup Doc ordered."

Luc pulled Belle into a standing position, but her legs refused to cooperate. Frustrated, he grabbed her by the shoulders and stood her in front of him. "Stand or fall," he snapped and dropped his hands.

Tears gone, she wavered but remained upright, confirming what he suspected. It was all for show.

He faced Bea. "Thank you, *Chère.*"

"He tries to speak," she said and cast a look at Belle, "but between the laudanum and the injury to his mouth, it's difficult."

"He can't talk?"

A hint of surprise in Belle's voice, followed by what sounded like relief, activated warning bells for Luc and further convinced him she said something that upset his grandfather.

Bea took a step toward Belle. "He can speak, but it's difficult to form the words." She took her elbow. "I'll walk you to your room."

Belle jerked her arm free. "I'm perfectly capable of walking myself." She glared at Luc, then turned and stalked down the hall toward her room.

Suddenly, Luc needed Bea close to him, needed her strength to shore up his crumbly defenses. He pulled her into his arms. "*Merci, mon Chère*," he said and kissed her forehead. "*Merci.*"

She wrapped her arms around his waist, and he allowed himself time to soak up the energy and goodness she radiated.

Too soon, she pulled away and looked at him a moment before reaching up and placing a soft kiss on his lips. "He's going to be all right, *Cher*," she whispered. "*Je suis lá pour toi mon amour.*"

The heartfelt comment soothed the ache in his heart. *I am here for you, my love.*

Her hand skimmed his chest before she stepped back. "I'll check on the soup Doc ordered, but, frankly, I don't think he'll be able to eat anything tonight."

He nodded, unable to speak.

"Would you like some coffee?"

"That would be nice."

He watched her walk down the hall, more convinced than ever that he could not leave her behind.

Going back to New York wasn't an option.

So, what was?

Bea balanced the tray against her hip and tapped on Henry's door, then opened it and walked inside.

Luc jumped from his chair by the bed, took the tray from her, and placed it on the dresser. He picked up the coffee and took a healthy drink.

"How is he?" she asked quietly.

He moved to her side and took another drink. "Still asleep."

She nodded. "I saw Doc at The Rose. He said sleep is the best thing for him right now as his body recuperates."

Luc placed the other chair in the room beside his, and they sat down. "I think Belle said something to upset him."

Luc's quiet statement brought Henry's last comment to mind. Even though he didn't say anything specific, Luc needed to know Moreau's concern. She opened her mouth, but before she could say anything, Henry moaned softly.

Luc sat his cup on the nightstand and leaned forward. "Grandfather? Are you in pain? Do you need anything?"

Henry rolled his head slowly side to side, eyes still closed.

"Bea brought some soup. Do you think you can eat?"

Another no.

"That's okay. Doc said you need the rest to get better," said Luc.

Moreau's eyes fluttered several times, then remained open. His mouth moved, but no words came forth.

"Don't try to speak, Grandfather," said Luc softly. "Whatever it is you want to say can wait until later."

"He's right, Mr. Moreau," said Bea. "Don't tire yourself out." Suddenly, two memories rushed forward, and breath froze in her lungs.

Moreau said he didn't trust Belle. Belle told her she had some kind of plan in place. Were the two connected? If so, how?

She leaned forward and placed her hand over his. "I will tell him what you said earlier." She glanced at Luc, then back to Moreau. "You have my word on that. And I'll do everything I can to help."

Luc looked at her. "What are you talking about?"

Moreau's eyes fixed on Bea as she turned toward Luc. "I was about to tell you a few minutes ago." She folded her hands in her lap. "I don't know what happened, but Belle has said or done something that upset him." She looked at Moreau. "And he doesn't trust her."

"Roscoe said he thought y'all were arguing before you collapsed," said Luc. "Is that it? You were arguing?"

Moreau's jaw muscles moved, and he grimaced, then dipped his chin up and down.

"And she said something upsetting to you?"

Another nod.

"Okay." Luc leaned forward and placed his hand on Henry's shoulder. "Whatever it was, don't worry about it now." He glanced at Bea. "We'll keep an eye on her. You just focus on getting better."

"M-my c-cah-cah…" Frustrated, he closed his mouth and lightly pounded the mattress with his fist.

"Your what, Grandfather?"

"M-my c-cah, c-cah…" He closed his eyes again and sighed.

Was he trying to say, "my company"? A logical concern under the circumstances. After all, he was incapacitated, and his company needed leadership. But what if there was more to it than that? She leaned toward him. "Are you trying to say your company, Mr. Moreau?"

His eyes once again locked on Bea as he nodded.

She looked at Luc. "I don't know if this is pertinent or not, but…"

"But what?"

She shook her head. "It's probably nothing, but, well, Belle said something yesterday that I thought strange at the time. In light of your grandfather's distrust, maybe there's more to it."

Luc's voice rang with controlled impatience. "What is it, *Chère?*"

"She said something about my plan, and that it wasn't difficult, but seemed to catch herself and stopped before she said more."

"Did she say anything else after that?"

"No. I got the impression she didn't mean to say it at all and changed the subject."

Moreau hit the bed with his fist again, drawing their eyes toward him.

"Don't worry about Moreau Shipping," said Luc, "Abernathy has run that place like his own for years. I'll telegraph him in the morning, so he'll know what's going on. And he can telegraph here if anything needs your attention."

His eyes slid closed, and Henry shook his head. "N-not th-aat." He took a breath and tried again. "B-Be."

"Belle?" asked Luc.

Moreau nodded.

"I don't understand. What has Belle to do with Moreau Shipping?"

He struggled to keep his eyes open as he focused on Luc. His mouth worked, but no words came forth.

"Mr. Moreau," said Bea softly, "you are trying too hard."

His pale blue eyes flicked toward her, and the expression on his face broadcast his disapproval.

"Please, do as Luc says and wait." Voice calm and steady, she maintained eye contact. "Trying to force the words out is not only frustrating for you, it's also draining your strength. You need to rest. Nothing is going to happen tonight. Tomorrow we'll try again."

"She's right, Grandfather," said Luc. "Tomorrow is soon enough." Luc covered the fisted hand with his own. "I'll have Belle on the next train back to New York, so don't—"

Moreau's face contorted, and he jerked his gaze to Luc. "N-no."

"No?" asked Luc. "You don't want me to send her back?"

Face pinched; he shook his head.

Luc's brows came together in a frown. "I don't understand."

Bea's first thought was he wanted Belle here for Luc, but given his stated distrust of her, she wondered if there was more to it. "Mr. Moreau?" she asked cautiously, "Do you want her here…for Luc?"

Moreau shook his head.

Bea leaned forward. "Okay." A sudden thought made Bea straighten up. "Are you concerned she will…do something when she gets back? Maybe to do with your company?"

His eyes jerked open, and he nodded.

"This is all very confusing," said Luc. "You believe Belle is up to something, and if she goes back, she will…what? Act on whatever it is?"

Henry nodded again, more vigorously than before.

"And it involves Moreau Shipping?"

Another nod.

"Okay," said Luc. "I won't force her to leave, but I'm not sure I can stop her if she wants to go."

"She won't go," said Bea firmly. "Not without you."

CHAPTER TWENTY-FOUR

LEEP AMOUNTED TO SHORT NAPS IN THE STRAIGHT-backed chair beside Luc's before he insisted on walking her home around 2 A.M. Despite the comfort of her new bed, sleep evaded her. Friday morning dawned clear and warmer, so Bea opted for a light shawl as she left the house and headed for the store. Exhaustion dogged her steps, but she forced herself to move.

Luc's grandfather appeared to suffer no significant ill effects from the fall. The cuts to his mouth and tongue may temporarily affect his eating, but that would improve in a few days.

Despite a lengthy discussion, Luc and Bea did not arrive at a suitable strategy to unravel Belle's plan and finally decided to let it go for now and see what happened next.

Bea shook her head to dispel the fog and closed the gate as she exited her yard, stopping when Daisy's brother, Levi, joined her. "Good morning, Levi. On your way to school?"

"Yes, ma'am," he said with a smile, "soon as I sweep off the front and make sure the water crock is full, and you got plenty of wood by the back door."

Bea admired the young man's desire to repay what he considered a debt he owed, but it bothered her, too. "You don't have to do this, Levi," she said softly, knowing it was useless to bring that particular subject up again.

He stopped, and his small frame stiffened. Eyes older than his years met her steady gaze. "I'm the man of the house. It's my job to take care of my family." He swallowed hard, but his gaze did not waver. "I couldn't help Daisy. You did." He started walking again. "I owe you."

Bea slowed to match his shorter stride and thought fast. "I have an idea to run by you."

He glanced at her from the corner of his eye. "Okay."

"Like any business deal, we need to place a dollar amount on what you feel you owe me. Next, we decide on an hourly wage for your time. Then, we figure out how much money you have earned since you started working, so we will know how much you still owe. Each time you work, we'll deduct what you earned from the balance until it's paid in full." Happy with her spur-of-the-moment plan, Bea smiled down at him. "After that, if you want to keep working to earn extra money, we will already have the plan in place. What do you say?"

They reached the back steps to the store, and Levi stopped, his head slowly bobbing up and down as he considered her suggestion. "Okay, ma'am." He stuck out his small hand. "It's a deal."

She took the outstretched hand in hers. "Let's get the details figured out so you won't be late for school."

By the time he left, Bea's mood was decidedly better. Her smile widened as she remembered the way Levi negotiated the terms of their agreement. He wanted a list of chores included, then questioned her figures, ensuring his pay was "what grown-ups would make" and not a cent more. When she quoted a total amount due, he balked again, insisting it was too low. In the end, they settled on the terms and shook hands again.

Tears stung the back of her eyes as she recalled watching

him skip down the lane toward the schoolhouse. He should be playing with his friends, fishing or hunting, or any number of other things instead of worrying about repaying a debt that didn't even exist. Except to him.

When he rounded the corner at the end of the lane, he looked back and waved, and something extraordinary flooded her heart. Love for the child he was, pride for the man he would one day become. She could easily envision him as a loving husband, a doting father and her heart shifted again. His commitment to family, his sense of responsibility was astonishing for one so young. Without question, she knew that he would never shun his children or make them feel unwanted regardless of the circumstances they faced.

Is this how a mother's love feels? Will I ever experience that with my own child?

Dismayed to have her happy mood dissipate, she turned and went inside. There was new merchandise to arrange, and the coffee she put on while Levi worked should be ready by now.

Niggling questions regarding Belle and her unknown plans cluttered Bea's mind as she absently rearranged candy jars on the counter. Annabelle was definitely up to something, but what? And why?

The arrival of her first customer of the day temporarily shelved her internal debate.

But not before the seeds of a plan sprouted.

As had become his habit, Amos dropped by mid-morning and offered to watch the store if she needed a break. She thanked him and hurried to the telegraph office with a letter to mail and hoped there was an answer to the telegram she sent yesterday.

The idea of sending her missive through Barker disturbed

her because she knew every word would eventually make its way to Eunice's ears, which in turn meant secrecy wasn't likely. Thankfully, the Barkers were out of town, and someone new staffed the desk.

"Can I help you, Miss Lockhart?"

"Good morning, Mr. Jones. I just wondered if perhaps there was an answer to my telegram."

"Sorry, ma'am. Nothing yet. I'll let you know just as soon as I hear something."

"Thank you. I'll either be at the store or the hotel."

He nodded and went back to work.

She left the telegraph office and started toward the store. Noise from the smithy drew her toward it, where she saw Luc firing up the forge.

"Good morning," she called from the front entrance.

He turned and smiled. "Good morning, *Chère*." He worked the bellows as he talked. "I like to keep the fire going so it's hot when I need it."

"How is he this morning?"

He stopped working the fire and wiped his hands on a rag. "Better, I think. He ate some of the broth Vi sent over." He smiled. "He didn't even complain about it being cold. The left side of his face is all black and blue, and his mouth appears more swollen, which affects his speech."

"You look so tired. Did you get any sleep at all?"

He shrugged. "Some. I was just about to go home and freshen up, then go back to sit with him."

She moved closer and placed a hand on his forearm, enjoying the feel of strong muscles that flexed beneath her fingers. "Amos is watching the store for me. I'll see if he can stay a bit longer, and I'll sit with Henry until you get back."

He reached for the hand and brought it to his lips. "Thank you, *Chère*," he murmured, then brushed a gentle kiss across her knuckles.

Her cheeks burned under the heat of his gaze, and a delightful shiver of want coursed through her body. "My pleasure," she whispered.

She moved to leave, but Luc pulled her back.

Breath caught in her throat as he lowered his head and kissed her, an intense yet gentle kiss that foretold of more incredible things to come. All too soon, she ended the kiss and took a step back. "I better go."

Giddy with happiness, she turned and walked back to the store. After Amos assured her it was not a bother to remain a while longer, she left to check on Henry.

Her good mood vanished when Belle exited the hotel as she opened the door, her formal afternoon attire entirely out of place in this frontier town. But Belle wore the royal blue and white striped silk with all the style and confidence of someone accustomed to being the center of attention.

She was beautiful, and she knew it.

Belle cast a contemptuous look at Bea. "If you plan to bother Henry, don't. He's sleeping now and isn't to be disturbed."

Bea didn't answer as she moved to walk around her antagonist, but Belle stepped in front of her. "Luc doesn't want anyone to bother him."

"When I hear that from him, I'll believe it." She bypassed her and entered the hotel, nodding to the young man behind the desk as she headed up the stairs. She stopped outside Moreau's door and listened a moment. Hearing no voices, she tapped softly, then opened the door and walked in.

Henry Moreau writhed on the bed as though trying to

get up. His rosy cheeks and the rapid rise and fall of his chest sent a shockwave through Bea, and she hurried to his side. "Mr. Moreau?" she murmured. "Mr. Moreau? What's wrong? Do I need to get Dr. Morton?"

His hand reached out, and she took it, startled at its coldness. "Are you all right, sir?" She glanced toward the door, then back to him. "Are you all right?" she repeated.

He sucked in air. "Sh-she ga-gav…" His swollen mouth quivered, and drool seeped from the corner.

His words were more slurred than yesterday, and Bea's heart jerked. Luc said he was better, but this didn't look better to her. "Don't try to talk, sir," she said softly, "it just frustrates you."

He blinked rapidly, and his brows scrunched together, then his eyes widened as he tried again to speak. "Sh-sh…" he blew out a short breath and made a weak scribbling motion with his hand.

"You want to write something?"

At his nod, she looked around the room but found nothing useful. "I don't see anything here, but I'll bring something back from the store later this afternoon."

His face twisted in frustration as he jerked his head from side-to-side, his voice barely audible. "C-ca-can wa-wa…"

He reached for her hand again and squeezed; this time, his grip wasn't as firm as before. "Are you trying to say it can't wait?"

A slow nod.

She took a deep breath. "Okay. I'll go downstairs and see if Lizzie has something." She patted his hand. "I'll be right back."

She returned a few minutes later with paper and pencil. "Here you go, sir," she said as she walked toward the bed.

His chest barely moved as he breathed, and indecision stopped her. Was he sleeping? Should she wake him or let him rest? Because he insisted this couldn't wait, she reached down and gently shook his shoulder. "Mr. Moreau? I have a pencil and paper. Mr. Moreau?"

No response.

She shook him again, sudden dread engulfing her. "Henry? Can you hear me?"

His head rolled to the side, and a soft breath escaped. Then stopped.

CHAPTER TWENTY-FIVE

Luc's throat tightened as he studied his grandfather's heavily bruised face and swollen mouth. He had no idea a simple fall could do so much damage. He'd never seen him look so frail, his chest barely moving as he breathed. He sat back in the chair and rubbed his face with both hands. When Tommy Owens, the young man who worked for Lizzy, rushed to get him earlier, he feared the worst. Though he was undoubtedly in a weakened state, his grandfather was a tough old bird, and he clung to that positive conviction.

"I thought he stopped breathing," said Bea, her voice cracking. "I didn't know what to do, so I just shook him, and he started breathing again, but slowly like now." She wrung her hands, worried gaze fixed on Doc. "I sent Tommy to get you and Luc."

Luc watched in agonized silence as Doc tried to rouse his grandfather, who merely groaned and didn't wake up.

"What's wrong, Doc?" Luc's voice shook with concern.

"I'm not sure," said Doc, who then turned to Bea. "Did you give him more laudanum?"

She shook her head. "No. He was awake when I went down to get him a pencil and paper."

"Why did he want that?" asked Luc, confusion melding with concern.

"He struggled to say something. When he couldn't, he indicated he wanted to write it down. There was nothing here, so I checked downstairs. When I got back, he was like this."

"Doc?" asked Luc.

Doc kept his gaze on Moreau. "When was the last time you gave him the laudanum?"

Luc rubbed his hands on his thighs. "His mouth hurt, and Mavis hadn't brought the willow bark tea yet, so I did like you said and gave him six drops in some water earlier this morning." He took a breath and continued. "He ate a few bites of the left-over soup and some water, then drifted off to sleep."

Doc exhaled loudly. "I think it's the laudanum. It may be too much."

"I did this to him?" Luc's anguish poured through his voice.

"No, no, it's all right, son," said Doc. "It's all right. I just meant that he's older and hasn't eaten much. He simply had a stronger reaction to the medicine. He'll be fine. Just may sleep most of the day."

Bea moved behind Luc and placed her hands on his shoulders, kneading gently. "He'll be fine, Luc. I know he will."

He reached up and covered one of her hands with his. "What do I need to do, Doc?"

"Let him sleep but watch him. There's a mixture of alcohol and drugs in laudanum. Someone who has never taken it or maybe not accustomed to drinking can easily take too much. I think that's what's happened. He's sleeping pretty deep, so keep an eye on his breathing. If he starts to breathe too slow or too shallow, jostle him until he takes a deeper breath."

"Okay," said Luc.

Doc nodded and headed for the door. "My best guess is he'll sleep most of today. He'll probably wake up slowly, perhaps even come in and out a bit at a time, so don't be concerned if he doesn't wake fully until supper time. Have some water handy, maybe more soup. Let me know if anything changes."

When Doc closed the door behind him, Luc pulled Bea around until she sat on his lap, his arms around her waist. "Thank you, *Chère*," he said softly, resting his head on her chest. "Thank you for being here."

She cradled his head and rocked slowly back and forth, almost like rocking a child. Anxiety trickled away as he inhaled the essence that was Bea. Life, love, vitality, compassion, all the things that made her special.

Once his emotions were under control, he leaned back and faced her. "I don't know what the future holds, *Chère*, but I want it to include you." He glanced at his grandfather's sleeping form. "As soon as he is well enough, I will have to go with him and see what we must do to get the company on sound footing again."

"I know," she replied, "He will need you."

He took a long breath. "And I need you."

Her smile melted his heart.

"You have me, Lucian. I'll be here when you return."

Henry moaned, and they both rose and stood beside the bed. The older man shifted, then stilled, his breathing once again slow and steady.

"I got the old man drunk." Luc couldn't help but smile. "He's not going to be happy with me when the hangover hits."

Bea linked her arm with his. "Under the circumstances, I'm sure he'll understand." She looked around the room. "Is that the soup from yesterday?"

"Yes."

She unlinked her arm and picked up the bowl, placing it on the tray. "I'll take it away and bring something fresh later on."

Before she picked up the tray, Luc pulled her into his arms and kissed her with a hunger that belied his outward calm. He used his lips to tell her what he couldn't put into words right now. He needed her. Desired her. He loved her.

She responded in kind, leaving no doubt of her feelings for him.

And that's when he knew without question.

She was the woman he would marry. Soon.

Bea clung to Luc's shoulders as his mouth continued to do wicked things to hers. Shocked at her passionate response to his kisses, she was nonetheless powerless to stop. Nor did she want to. She wanted more. So much more.

When at last he pulled away, she felt the loss immediately. Her lips still burned in the fiery aftermath of his possession, and her flushed body ached for his touch.

He leaned his forehead against hers and drew in a ragged breath. His muscular arms trembled as he pulled her against him.

"All my life, I have searched for someone like you, *Chère*." His speech was halting, filled with a need that defied description. "Now that I found you, I never want us to be apart." He inhaled deeply and continued. "I will have to go back to New York, at least for a while, but before I go..." He pulled back and met her gaze. "Before I go, I want...will you...be my wife."

At first, she wasn't sure she heard him correctly. She blinked rapidly, and her heart raced like stampeding cattle as the words *be my wife* bounced off the walls of her mind like an echo in a canyon. *Be my wife.*

Before she could reply, a troubling thought intruded. Did

he expect her to leave everything behind and follow him? Leave behind what she worked so hard to build to the care of someone else? Or worse, close it altogether?

Luc's thumbs caressed her cheek. "Your silence scares me, *Chère*. Please, tell me what you are thinking."

Luc's soft statement cut through the haze, and she focused on his face. "I love you with all my heart, Lucian," she whispered.

"...But..."

She cupped his face in her hands and met his hurt-filled eyes. "Nothing would give me more pleasure than to marry you. I know you have a duty, an obligation to Henry, and I understand the need to travel back with him." She paused, hoping her words would not condemn her to a life alone. "But I can't leave. My store, my home is here now."

His hard gaze softened. "I know that *Chère*," he murmured. "I also know how much your independence means to you." He rubbed his hands up and down her arms in a gentle caress. "And I would never ask nor expect you to leave it behind."

Luc's stunning blue eyes radiated unconditional love as he gazed at her. "I want us to live here, work here," he said tenderly. "Together. Always."

She couldn't stop the welling of happy tears as she drew in a fortifying breath. "In that case, Lucian Moreau, of course I'll be your wife."

"*Mon amour, ma vie*," he whispered. "My love, my life." He sealed his declaration with a tender kiss, then pulled back to gaze at her. "If you do not mind, I would like to keep this between us until I can tell Grandfather."

"Of course."

"I would also hope to be married before I leave, but if you'd rather we wait until I return, I will abide by your wishes."

His seductive smile caused air to lodge in her throat.

"But I will not be happy about it."

She gulped fast, then licked her lips. "I don't want to wait any longer than necessary, either."

CHAPTER TWENTY-SIX

BEA COULDN'T SUPPRESS A SMILE AS SHE MADE HER WAY down the stairs, a tray balanced in her hands.

She was getting married. To Lucian. Never in her wildest dreams did she think this day would come.

The front door opened as Bea neared the bottom step, and Belle swept in, Jenny, as always, trailing behind.

Spotting Bea, she stopped and squared her shoulders, her expression shifting from composed to spiteful. "What are you doing with that?"

Today Bea smiled at everyone. Even Belle. "If you must know, I'm taking it to Vi and have her make more soup for Henry."

"I'm surprised he could eat."

"He didn't eat much, but he did manage to eat a little earlier."

"Can he talk?"

"He's asleep." She saw no need to explain any further. "Lucian is with him."

Belle's smile became feral. "Well, maybe I'll go and keep him company." She lifted her skirts and moved beside Bea. "I wouldn't want him to get lonely."

Belle's face clouded when Bea smiled; certain Luc would send her on her way quickly. "You do that."

Belle changed tactics. "I saw that charming Mr. Bentley

a few moments ago." She fingered the silk reticule around her wrist, ice-blue eyes like daggers. "He hinted he would ask me to the dance tomorrow night, but of course, I told him I was going with Lucian." She cocked her head to one side. "But I did promise to save him several dances." She paused as though in thought. "I have this purple silk gown I'm just dying to wear. Luc loves the color on me."

"I'm sure you will be lovely in it, Belle. Now, if you'll excuse me, I need to get back to work."

As she edged past her, Belle bumped the tray, sending the contents clattering to the floor, the remaining soup spilling from the broken bowl.

Jenny squealed and jerked back as though the liquid were a snake.

Belle's lips puckered, and she made a tsk-tsk sound. "You are a clumsy one, aren't you?" She looked at her maid and snapped, "Bring me my tea," then turned and strolled up the stairs.

"I'm so sorry, miss," said Jenny softly as she hurried to follow instructions. Jenny jumped again when the door to The Rose opened, and Roscoe appeared.

He tipped his hat. "Mornin', Miss Jenny. I was hopin' I'd see you today."

The young woman's face turned scarlet, and she cast a worried glance toward Bea. She and Roscoe exchanged a few brief words before she entered the restaurant.

Bea shook her head and bent to pick up the shattered glass as Roscoe hurried over.

"Let me get that Miss Bea. You might cut yourself."

Accustomed to taking care of things alone, Bea found it difficult to accept help but stood aside as he placed the broken pieces on the tray.

Lizzy appeared with rags draped over her arm and a pan of water. She passed a rag to Bea, and the women went to work on the spilled soup.

"That heifer is a piece of work," snipped Lizzy as she cleaned. "I have never met anyone so totally wrapped up in themselves."

"She wasn't always like that," offered Bea. "We were even friends once when we were young."

"What happened?" asked Lizzy as she wiped up the last of the liquid.

Bea shrugged and placed her rag in the pan of water. "I don't know. She just—changed over the years."

Roscoe took the pan from Lizzy and placed it beside the tray on a small table near the stairs, then extended a hand to each woman as they stood.

"Thank you, Roscoe," said Bea. "It's kind of you to help."

"My pleasure, ma'am. I best get back to the ranch. Boss sent me to town to mail a letter. He'll be wondering if I decided to hand-deliver it." He nodded to Lizzy. "Miss Lizzy." He strolled out the door, whistling a catchy tune.

"He's got his eye on Jenny," said Lizzy as she watched him leave. "She really is a sweet girl. Can't imagine how she got tangled up with that she-wolf."

"I'm sure the poor girl could use some special attention."

Lizzy sighed and reached for the pan of water and dirty rags. "Can't we all?"

Bea thought about Luc's proposal and tender declarations of love. She'd never expected to experience the feeling of being loved, even cherished, by someone like him. A future that once held nothing but loneliness now held such promise, her heart soared with joy. And keeping it private for now meant she could treasure their secret in her heart for a while longer.

Bea nodded to acknowledge her friend's comment. "I best get this to Vi then back to the store. Amos will think I've abandoned him."

"Leave the tray. I'll take it back."

"Thanks."

Amos and Silas sat out in front of the store, the worn checkerboard between them. "Ever'thang all right, Miss Bea?" asked Amos.

"Yes. Everything is fine, Amos. Thank you for watching the store."

He nodded and made a move, jumping the last of Silas's pieces to end the game. "I win again," he chortled and clapped his hands.

"Dagnabit," huffed Silas. "You gotta be cheatin.'"

Bea walked around the squabbling friends to enter the store. "Anything happen while I was gone?"

"Miz Walker come in to order something from that catalog," said Amos. "She left a note on the counter about what she wanted." He waited for Silas to make the first move of the next game. "And Miz Morton left you some cookies." He scratched his grizzled cheek and grinned, "Me and Silas sampled one to make sure they were all right for you to eat."

She grinned at the two men who had become like beloved uncles in the last month. "I appreciate that. Did you happen to leave me any coffee to go with them?"

"Fresh pot on the stove."

He gave her a quick rundown of the other customers before she walked inside. She paused to savor the moment. Her store thrived, and she had friends, real friends, for the first time in her life.

Most important of all, Lucian wanted to marry her. The sooner, the better.

Butterflies swarmed her stomach again as realization struck. *I'm going to be a married woman soon.* She fanned her burning cheeks as she absorbed the implications, both thrilled and anxious at the same time.

She walked to the fabric display at the back and fingered the ivory-colored silk that just arrived. *I wonder how quickly Daisy can make a wedding dress.*

Luc crossed his arms over his chest and shifted in the uncomfortable straight-backed chair. He yawned and stretched his long legs out in front. Exhaustion tugged at him, but he would not sleep for fear his grandfather might need something.

A light tap on the door drew his attention. "Come in."

Tommy Owens stepped inside, scooting an overstuffed easy chair in front. "Miss Lizzy said it was okay to bring this to you, Luc. It'll be more comfortable than that brick you're sitting on."

Luc smiled and rose to move the chair out of the way. "It is. Thanks for bringing it up. And please tell Lizzy I said thank you."

He nodded. "I will. I'll be bringing one more up in a bit so the ladies can have one, too."

"Ladies?"

"Miss Bea and that fancy lady that come to town with your grandfather. I saw her coming out this morning when I was going down the hall. Said she'd been sitting with him a while, and the chair was uncomfortable. I asked Miss Lizzy about bringing a couple up from the storage room. And I dusted them off real good, too."

"I appreciate that, Tommy."

"He doing any better?"

Luc shrugged. "Still sleeping. Since Doc said sleep is best, I'm taking it as a good sign."

The young man nodded, then turned for the door. "I'll have that other chair up in a few minutes."

Luc nodded and sat in the new, more restful armchair as one question circled his head. *Why was Belle here this morning?*

CHAPTER TWENTY-SEVEN

STOMACH GROWLING, DESPERATE FOR COFFEE, Luc stood at the window of his grandfather's room, gaze wandering the street below. The anticipated arrival of spring and preparations for the dance tomorrow night had folks out and about this sunny but chilly afternoon. He recognized almost everyone he spotted. A few happened to glance up and wave when they saw him.

Since his arrival two years ago, the people of Bakersville included him and made him feel like he belonged. A feeling foreign to him since he lost his parents.

He looked back to the sleeping form on the bed. In the last hour or so, his breathing appeared more regular, and he groaned more, so Luc allowed himself to hope his grandfather would awaken soon.

He understood how hard he worked to build his shipping empire that guaranteed Luc's education and the opportunity to travel the world. But affection and connection on an emotional level didn't exist in their relationship, and Luc wanted that connection. Very much. He promised himself if God saw fit to give him a chance, he would find a way to make it happen.

He moved back to the chair and sat down, allowing his mind to drift to this morning's conversation with Bea. She said yes. Just the thought of a life with her was enough to lift his spirits and quell the hunger gnawing at his gut. He allowed his mind to wander down the path of life with Bea. Would they have children? He smiled at the thought, then glanced at his grandfather. Would he want to be a part of their lives? He hoped so but lacked certainty.

They agreed not to say anything to anyone until he could tell his grandfather, and he suffered a bit of anxiety at the thought. He had no idea what reaction the news would initiate. Henry said yesterday he wanted Luc to marry Belle. Today, he indicated to Bea he didn't trust her. Why? What changed?

He shifted in the chair as his thoughts centered on that fly in the ointment. Was Belle up to something, and did it somehow affect Moreau Shipping? Maybe she just wanted them to think something was going on to keep them on guard. That was how Belle operated; stir the pot, add drama, stir some more. He shook his head, dismayed at how she so easily duped him in the past.

A soft groan from his grandfather brought him to the edge of the bed. "Grandfather? Can you hear me?"

Henry groaned again, and his eyelids fluttered but remained closed.

Luc sat on the bed and lifted the hand resting outside the covers. Surprised at how cold it was, he rubbed it gently between his warm hands. "I hope you can hear me, Grandfather," he said softly. "Doc says you're just in a deep sleep from the medication."

The older man's hand twitched slightly, and Luc took a deep breath. "It seems I may have accidentally given you too much, and well, basically, you passed out." He paused to gather his thoughts. "We have a lot to talk about, you and I, so you need to wake up soon."

The hand twitched again, though no other reaction happened.

"Just rest, Grandfather. We'll talk when you wake up."

He sat there holding his grandfather's hand and considered a plan of action. First of all, he needed information, starting with the current status of Moreau Shipping. In their last conversation, he'd remained vague on specifics, but getting the information he needed would have to wait until Henry was awake, alert, and able to answer questions.

Earlier today, Luc telegraphed Caleb Oakerson, his grandfather's attorney, and Josiah Abernathy, the shipping manager, to inform them of the accident and that his stay in Bakersville is extended indefinitely.

He knew both men to be trusted employees who would diligently look after things until his grandfather returned. Based on what Doc said earlier, that may not happen for a week or more.

In the meantime, maybe he should telegraph Oakerson again and have him make the trip to Bakersville. His grandfather would undoubtedly disapprove of that action, but Luc needed answers, and Oakerson seemed like a logical place to start.

A light knock on the door, followed by Belle's entrance, interrupted his musings. Jenny followed behind, a cloth-covered tray in her hands.

Jaw tense, he stilled his face to show no emotion. "What are you doing here?"

She stepped aside and motioned for the maid to enter. "I was having tea, and that horrid woman at the restaurant asked a cowboy to deliver this for you to eat. I was coming up anyway, so I offered to bring it."

He didn't bother saying Jenny was the one delivering the tray because it wouldn't matter. In her eyes, Belle deserved the credit.

She pulled off her gloves and gave Moreau a disdainful glance. "I hope he's better soon." She shook her head. "There's food under that cloth."

Anyone who didn't know Belle as well as Luc would think her concern was genuine. He knew better. *Stir the pot, add drama, stir some more.*

Belle motioned toward Jenny, who remained just inside the door. "Put the tray over there and leave us."

Jenny placed the tray on the dresser and looked at Luc. "How is he, sir?"

Her voice, soft and sincere, contained just a hint of a southern drawl. Luc didn't remember her all that well since she'd gone to work for Belle just before the almost-engagement. But he sensed a genuine kindness in her and wished she worked for someone else. "Better, I think. Hopefully, by later tonight, he will be awake and good as new."

"Oh, that is great news, sir. I'm so –"

"My dress needs to be ready for the dance tomorrow night," interrupted Belle, "and you have other work to do."

Cheeks flaming, Jenny dipped a slight curtsy and turned for the door.

"Thank you for bringing up the tray, Jenny," said Luc. "I appreciate it."

She cast a furtive glance at Belle, then nodded and walked out, closing the door behind her.

"Really, Lucian," sniffed Belle, "you seem to have forgotten she's a servant."

He didn't bother to hide his displeasure. "She's a human being first."

"Of course, but they have their place. And we have ours."

He paused and tempered his voice. Upsetting her would not get him information. "Why are you here, Belle?"

She took a step toward him and rested a hand on his forearm. "Darling, I just wanted to check on you. Make sure you are all right." Her fingers tightened on his arm. "I wanted to see if there is anything I can do for you." Golden lashes dipped toward pink-stained cheeks. "Anything at all."

His first impulse was to pull away, but he reconsidered. She likely had at least some of the information he needed. He had to find out, even if it meant playing up to her vanity.

After a short pause, he covered the hand resting on his arm. "As a matter of fact, Annabelle," he said, purposely using the name she preferred, "there is something I need."

Her face brightened with a huge smile. "Anything, darling, anything at all."

He maneuvered them to the two chairs beside the bed and helped her sit. "I'm so worried about him, I can't think straight."

She placed her hand on his arm. "I know, darling, this must be awful for you."

"He's the only family I have left." He allowed his voice to tremble a bit. "I couldn't bear it if something happened to him."

"Well, he is getting older, Lucian. You have to accept that he won't be around forever."

"I know." He blew out a long breath and glanced her way. "He wants me to come back and take over Moreau Shipping."

Her eyes brightened, and she leaned forward. "As you should, darling." Her fingers tightened around his arm. "It belongs to you now."

A chill drifted over him when he realized she spoke as if he were already dead. "I don't know," he hedged, "Grandfather said there are some issues."

She flinched, then resumed her faux-concerned pose. "What do you mean? What kind of issues?"

He shrugged, covered her hand with his. "He said some things happened lately that concerned him."

"What kind of things? Did he tell you anything specific?"

The nervous shimmy in her voice set off warning bells and gave rise to an unsavory possibility. Luc kept his expression concerned as he met her gaze. "I think someone is trying to hurt him. Maybe the company, too."

This time, she didn't manage to cover her frightened expression fast enough.

"Hu-hurt him? Wh-whatever do you mean?"

"I'm sorry, Annabelle. I shouldn't have mentioned that." He patted her hand again. "I don't really know anything yet. I'm sure I'll know more when he wakes up. In the meantime, I've asked his attorney for assistance."

Belle's eyes widened, and she jerked in a breath before she smiled and rose from her chair. "Well, your meal is getting cold. Though, I don't see how you can eat what passes for food here. I will be so glad when we get back to civilization."

He stood beside her and smiled again. "Thank you for bringing it, Annabelle. It was very thoughtful of you."

Her face relaxed into the belle-of-the-ball look she perfected as she stepped forward and placed her hand on his chest. "You know I would do anything for you, darling."

"I thought you might—" Bea's statement stopped mid-sentence as she entered the room, a cup in her hand.

Cheeks flushed, Belle cast adoring eyes on Luc, then reached up and pressed a light kiss on his cheek. "I'm so glad we got to spend this time together, sweetheart." She stepped away and sauntered to the door, a self-satisfied smile on her face as she glanced at Bea then back to him. "And I'm thrilled you're coming back home. With me."

Bea kept her expression neutral as Belle floated past. Common sense said Belle's speech was hogwash; yet, she and Luc did have a history together.

Long-buried feelings of insecurity rose to the surface, reminding her yet again that Belle was everything she wasn't—beautiful and sophisticated. Luc's equal. Maybe he still cared for her? No. He proposed today. He didn't have feelings for Belle. Did he?

Luc stepped forward and took the cup, pushing the door shut with his foot. Placing it on the dresser, he turned to face her. "I see the fear in your eyes, *Chère*," he said softly, taking her hands in his. "But you have no cause for concern." He brought her hands to his lips and brushed a kiss across the knuckles. "You are my life, and my place is with you." He cupped her hands against his chest. "But I am more convinced than ever she is up to something, and I must know what." He kissed her hands again. "And I am not above appealing to her vanity to find out."

Relief coursed through her as she ducked her head. "I am ashamed of my thoughts, Lucian." She looked up and met his soul-searching gaze. "Seeing her with you just now took me back to a dark place. A place where my scar declared—"

He silenced her with a finger to her lips. "Your family was wrong to make you think ill of yourself over such a thing, and they will reap what they have sown."

His grip tightened, and fire blazed in his eyes. "There is no one more beautiful than you, *Chère*," he whispered. "No one. For your beauty is not superficial, it flows from the inside out and touches everyone around you."

Blissful tears burned the backs of her eyes as he held her hands to his chest.

"It comes from your heart, *Chère*. A heart that does not

judge, that gives without question and loves unconditionally. And that kind of beauty is rare and precious."

Her cheeks warmed under the heat of his gaze, and a strange inner excitement sent blood racing through her veins. Desire, foreign yet familiar, ignited. Breath caught in her throat as dormant senses soared to life. When the back of his hand grazed her breast as he moved, she inhaled sharply at the delicious, unexpected contact.

He lowered his head and kissed her temple, then the tip of her nose, and finally, her lips. Tenderly at first, then more firmly, as she gave herself freely to the passion of his kiss.

All too soon, he pulled back, and she breathed loudly through parted lips.

"J´espere qu'on pourra se marier bien tôt, Chère."

His husky whisper warmed her insides like a fine brandy. "I, too, hope we marry soon, *mon amour*. Very soon."

He folded her in his arms, one hand exploring the small of her back, the other resting on her hip.

She wound her arms around his back and pressed her cheek against the corded muscles of his chest, enjoying the warmth and security of his embrace.

His uneven breath ruffled her hair as he held her close.

"Perhaps we should sit and talk about a plan," he said at last, the hint of a smile in his voice. "Less I lose control again."

Regretfully, she pulled away and looked up at him. "That is probably a good idea. Though I was rather enjoying myself."

Once seated, he reached for her hand and held it gently in his lap. "I don't know what to do. I have so many questions that require answers." He leaned back and looked at the ceiling. "I telegraphed his attorney, Mr. Oakerson, to advise him of this situation. Perhaps I should send another and ask that he come here as soon as possible. Perhaps he will have the answers I need."

She paused and considered her next words carefully. "I need to tell you something," she said softly. "Something that may anger you."

Silent, he gazed at her, brow furrowed in concern.

She sat up straight, Luc's fingers still clasping hers. "I telegraphed my attorney yesterday and asked him to look into Moreau Shipping and determine if there was anything I could do to help. I know I should have talked with you first, but I thought time was of the essence, so I acted." She shifted and faced him. "Please don't be angry. I just want to help."

His concerned expression changed to one of pleasure. "You want to help save my grandfather's company?"

"If I can. I don't know what Mr. James will discover or how long it will take, but I instructed him to be very thorough and discreet."

He brought her hand up and brushed a kiss across her knuckles. "That is very kind of you."

"Do you have any idea at all what the status is?"

"No. He was very vague in our conversations. He did say things would work out if he made some changes but didn't specify what changes."

"My knowledge of shipping is limited to things I order for the store. What exactly does Moreau Shipping ship?"

Luc relaxed against the back of the chair. "We run three packet ships between Liverpool and New York. Mostly goods, but passengers, too. And three more that run up and down the coast. Goods like granite or coal, whatever needs shipping. And passengers, too."

"Have you ever considered changing course?"

"What do you mean?"

She straightened, and her voice betrayed her excitement. She loved brainstorming business ideas. "Well, the west is growing by leaps and bounds, and there is room for growth. The railroad links east to west. A shipping company that went overland versus the sea could connect west coast customers with East coast, or East Texas, goods."

He smiled. "I shall bring the matter up to him, *Chère*. Thank you for trying to help him."

She experienced a moment of panic. *Will you still feel that way when you discover I authorized Mr. James to buy the company?*

CHAPTER TWENTY-EIGHT

"He's going to be fine, Luc," said Doc as he prepared to leave. "Though he's been asleep longer than I anticipated, he's showing signs of coming around now, so if he starts to wake up, jostle him, talk to him."

"About what?" asked Luc.

"Doesn't matter. Just something for his brain to focus on. It may help bring him around sooner."

"Thanks, Doc. I appreciate all you've done for him."

The doctor nodded and opened the door. "Try to get him to eat something as soon as he is awake enough. He'll be thirsty but be careful when you help him drink. Small sips at first."

"Okay. Thanks again."

"I'll check back in the morning. Call me if anything happens that concerns you."

"I will."

"Goodnight."

"Night, Doc."

Luc stared at the dark bruises on Moreau's face, pushing down the fear that welled inside. While the accident wasn't life-threatening, it reminded Luc of life's fragility and how quickly things can change. Regardless of the time remaining, Luc vowed he would build a stronger bond with his grandfather—if he let him.

But what if Moreau opposed his plans to marry Bea? The possibility he may have to choose between them tore at his heart. "No," he whispered to the sleeping man, "I won't let it come to that."

Frustrated, Luc walked to the window and braced his hands on either side. Head bent, he drew in deep breaths of musty air. *Why won't he wake up?*

A moment later, he pushed back and tugged on the chain attached to his father's gold watch hidden in a side pocket of his pants. Finding an odd sort of comfort in its slight weight, he ran his thumb over the intricate scrollwork depicting leaves, flowers, and a tiny bird.

The only inscription was his great grandfather's initials, HRM.

He closed his eyes, easily recalling his father's face and his words as he folded the heirloom into Luc's small hand. *My father gave this to me, son,* he had said. *It belonged to my grandfather. Now it's yours.*

He died a few days later, leaving Luc alone with a man he barely knew.

The passing years faded many memories, but Luc still re-called his father's smile, his laughter, the times spent following him around as he checked his traps, and the way he lovingly monitored the time to ensure they weren't late for dinner.

He pressed the top to open the watch. Six-thirty. Over the last hour, his grandfather stayed awake longer, and he tried to speak occasionally but didn't stay alert long.

A soft moan sent Luc to his side, and he sat on the edge of the bed. "Grandfather? Grandfather? Can you hear me?"

He mumbled but didn't open his eyes.

Luc released the breath he held. Maybe Doc was right, and

the tide had turned. He picked up Moreau's hand and gently rubbed the back. "Can you open your eyes for me?"

Pale eyelids fluttered open, then shut again, followed by a soft groan.

Luc tamped down his exasperation with the process and forced patience he did not feel.

Remembering Doc's instructions to talk to him, Luc pulled in a deep breath and began. "Don't worry, Grandfather," he said softly. "You're going to be fine."

A slight side-to-side roll of Henry's head gave Luc hope he heard him, so he continued in a calm, even voice.

"Easy, Grandfather. Doc said it might take you a while to wake up fully, but you will be fine." He chuckled. "You will no doubt have one helluva a hangover, though."

His grandfather's fingers twitched in Luc's hand, and he gripped it a little tighter. "It's the medication, I'm afraid. It has alcohol in it, among other things, and given your age and size, well, I think I gave you too much."

Once again, Moreau moved his head, and his eyes fluttered but remained shut.

Luc patted his hand. "You can yell at me later. Right now, we need to wait for the effects to wear off. I'll be here when you wake up." He paused and gathered his thoughts. "You're all the family I have left, Grandfather, and we have lots to discuss. I know you most likely won't remember any of this, but I'm going to say it anyway."

Moreau's mouth twitched, and the hand beneath Luc's trembled.

"I love you, Grandfather, though you have not made that an easy thing to do. And I owe you a lot. You gave me an education, provided me with the opportunity to travel, to experience life. But the one thing I needed most you couldn't give. You."

Moreau's head lolled toward Luc, and his mouth opened, then closed.

"But it's not too late. There's still time for us to be a family again." Voice clogged with emotion, he paused and swallowed hard. "I'll do whatever I can to help revive the company for you. I owe you that, at least. I'll even make the trip back with you if necessary, but I won't stay. I won't take over the company. My home is here now." He blew out a long breath and continued. "And I can't marry Belle. I don't love her. I never did."

He rubbed the chilled hand beneath his. "I love Bea and want to marry her as soon as possible. She's the most wonderful, caring, and generous woman I've ever known. She's sharp-witted and smart with a shrewd head for business. She even has an idea for expanding Moreau Shipping that I think you'll be interested in."

He paused and stared at his grandfather's still form. "I love her, Grandfather. I want to marry her. And should God bless us with children, I want them to know you, too." His voice dropped to an anguished whisper. "Please don't force me to choose between the two of you. Because as much as I love you, I couldn't bear to live my life without her."

"G'night, Miss Bea," said Amos as he headed for the front door. "I'll see you tomorrow."

"Amos?"

He turned, and she hesitated. "I can't tell you how much I appreciate you and Silas helping me out around here."

He scratched his chin. "Weren't nothin' anyone else wouldn't do, ma'am."

On impulse, she reached out and embraced him quickly, then stepped back.

Face bright red, he coughed and looked away.

"I'm sorry if I embarrassed you, Amos, but I just want you to know how much I appreciate you." She clasped her hands together in front. "You and Silas are like…like precious uncles I never had, and I don't know what on earth I would do without you." She took a breath. "I just wanted you to know that."

A light sheen glazed the earth-tone eyes staring back at her. "That's the nicest thing anyone ever said to me, ma'am." His gaze wistful, Amos stood a little taller. "I never had any kin I know of." He lightly cleared his throat. "I reckon you know we think the world of you, too." He nodded and turned once more for the front door.

"Uncle Amos?" She liked the way the surprised look on his face turned to pure delight. "Goodnight."

Dark eyes twinkling with affection, Amos beamed. "Goodnight…Niece."

Bea followed him to the door and watched as he strolled toward The Rose with confident strides. The impulse decision to call him "Uncle" was the right one. And the best part was, it fit.

About to lock the door, she saw Belle exit the telegraph office, then pause as though in thought. She looked toward the hotel, then walked to a lantern hanging from the corner post and pulled a sheet of paper from her reticule.

Darkness and distance prevented Bea from deciphering Belle's expression as she read, but her lively steps when she stuffed it in her bag and hurried toward the hotel said she was pleased.

"What are you up to, Belle?" she whispered to the night air. "And who will suffer for it?"

CHAPTER TWENTY-NINE

"Thurshty."

Luc's heart did a little jerk at his grandfather's slurred word. Each time he roused now, he stayed awake longer. Luc reached for the water pitcher and glass on the dresser. "Just small sips," he cautioned. He held the glass in one hand and raised Henry's head with the other as he swallowed a few sips. "I'm going to need to get more water, but I'll do that later."

The older man nodded, didn't open his eyes.

Luc lowered his head back on the pillow. "Let me know when you want more."

"…thank you."

The words came out in a whispered rush, and Luc blinked. He couldn't remember hearing his grandfather say that before. "You're welcome." He sat the glass down and pulled his chair closer to the bed. "Bea will be up shortly with dinner for you. Soup most likely because it's easier to eat. But we have to wait until you are truly awake before you try."

"Mouf…hurts."

"I know. You have a cut on your bottom lip and a little one on your tongue. Both are swollen, which is why you have difficulty speaking." Elbows on his knees, Luc clasped his hands together. "Doc's wife sent some willow bark tea over. It will help with the pain if you need it."

"…not now."

"Let me know when you need it." He drew in a deep breath. "You also have a nasty bruise on your face from the fall. The cut on your forehead wasn't too deep but still needed a couple of stitches. All in all, though, you're in good shape." He shook his head. "Except for me accidentally knocking you out with laudanum." He exhaled loudly. "I'm so sorry, Grandfather."

Moreau slowly shook his head. "Not…fault."

"I blame myself." He sat back and rubbed his hands on his thighs. "I'm so thankful you're going to be all right. We have a lot to discuss."

Moreau's chin dipped a couple of times. "Heard…you…"

Luc's heart gave another jerk. "You heard what I said?"

Henry responded with a slight grimace followed by a slow nod.

Did that mean good or bad? Luc chastised himself for saying anything in the first place. What if he misunderstood? What if the medication muddled his brain and twisted the words? He desperately wanted to talk to his grandfather but needed him fully awake and able to communicate.

The damage is done now. I'll just have to wait and see. "We'll talk about everything once you're awake. For now, just rest until that stuff wears off."

"…kay."

A few seconds later, his grandfather drifted off again.

A light knock on the door brought Luc to his feet with a heavy sigh. It was probably Bea with the soup. But, when he opened the door, he found the young desk clerk instead. "Hey, Tommy. What's up?"

"Sorry to bother you, Luc. Miss Bea sent me for you. There's a man at the livery with a broken plow he needs fixed tonight." Tommy nodded toward the sleeping man. "She will be right up to sit with him."

Despite the late hour, it wasn't an unusual request, especially this time of year. Farmers needed to prep for spring planting and sometimes worked until the last light of day vanished. A broken plow was an emergency.

"Okay." Luc walked back to the bed to assure himself his grandfather slept soundly. Satisfied, he donned his coat and hat as Bea walked in carrying a tray.

"I brought soup for Henry and a cup of coffee for you," said Bea. "Vi said Belle brought you dinner earlier."

He plucked the cup off the tray. "Thank you, *Chère*."

She turned toward the dresser and set the tray down.

"Can I get you anything, Miss Bea?" asked Tommy.

"No, thank you, Tommy." She turned toward the young man. "I'm fine."

Luc took a long swallow of the now tepid coffee. "He wakes occasionally but not fully yet. Feel free to talk to him. Doc said that might help him come around sooner." He finished the coffee and handed her the cup. "I shouldn't be more than an hour or so."

Their fingers brushed as she took it from him. "I'll be here."

Overcome by unexpected emotions, he stared a moment, then gave in to the impulse to brush a kiss across her cheek. "I'll be back soon."

Luc turned and hurried out, ignoring Tommy's wide-eyed stare. *I'll be here.* The promise in those three words lifted the doubt and anxiety weighing heavily on his shoulders. Whatever happened, they would face it together.

The love radiating in Luc's eyes as he handed her the empty cup made Bea's heart skip a beat. When he kissed her cheek, breath lodged in her throat as she absorbed the moment.

Luc loves me. He wants to marry me. Can my life be any better?

A glance at Tommy's face told her news of the kiss would spread fast, and she could only wonder how exaggerated the rumor mill will make it.

On the other hand, everyone in town knew she and Luc spent a lot of time together. So what if Tommy saw him kiss her cheek? It wasn't that big a deal. Except it was to Bea.

She turned to the young man. "Thank you for letting Luc know about Mr. Tompkins, Tommy. I thought Amos would be at The Rose, but he'd already left."

"No problem, ma'am. He's probably at the Spur with Silas 'bout now, and that's no place for a lady. Can I do anything else for you?"

"No, thank you." She reached to close the door.

"Mr. Luc's a fine man."

"Yes. He is."

"So are you." His face turned bright red, and he stammered. "I mean, you're a fine woman. Not a man."

She smiled. "I knew what you meant, Tommy. And thank you."

"I'm glad he likes you." He stopped and looked around. "And not that…other lady."

Before she could respond, he smiled. "And don't worry none, ma'am. I won't say anything about Mr. Luc kissing you."

With that, he shuffled down the hallway, whistling a snappy tune.

She closed the door and walked to Henry's bedside. Luc's comment about talking to him swept to the forefront of her thoughts. What does one say to a sleeping man who is a virtual stranger?

Arms folded across her chest, she moved to the window and looked out. Darkness cloaked the town, but more people were out and about thanks to improved weather and the anticipated dance tomorrow night.

The dance brought a frown to her face. *Luc will probably want to stay with Henry. Should I go alone?* She had no desire to attend with anyone but Luc. But going alone lacked appeal. On the heels of that thought came another more distressing one: *What if Luc wanted to escort Belle to gain information?* "I'll just have to cross that bridge when I come to it," she told the darkness.

The fact she contemplated going to the dance at all spoke volumes about the changes she'd undergone in the last month. Changes due in large part to her acceptance by the citizens of this small town. In New York, she was pitied, shamed, and embarrassed. Here she was merely Beulah Mae Lockhart, business owner and upstanding member of the community.

Thoughts scattered, she went back to the chair and sat down, hands clasped in her lap. She studied the sleeping man and tried to ignore the seed of doubt making her pulse skip. What would he say about her relationship with Luc? She shook her head to banish the worries eroding her resolve. *It's out of my hands. I need to focus on what I can control.*

She straightened and began talking. "I'm so sorry you were hurt, Mr. Moreau. I do hope you feel better when you wake." She chewed her lower lip then continued. "I brought you some soup, though, by now, it's lukewarm at best. I'm sure your mouth is no doubt sore, but when you wake up, you really should try and eat something."

A soft groan had her leaning forward. "Mr. Moreau? Can you hear me?" She paused. "Can you open your eyes?"

A couple of jerky movements, a deep breath, and his eyes opened a slit. Bushy grey brows nearly met in the middle as he strained to focus on her.

"...Luc..."

"He had to fix a plow for Mr. Thompkins. He'll return shortly."

A slow dip of his chin indicated he understood. His tongue traced his lower lip, and he spoke again. "Why?"

Bea squinted and tried to decipher his meaning. "Why am I here?"

"Yes."

"Luc didn't want you left alone in case you needed anything, and I offered to stay."

His pale blue eyes opened wider as he stared. "...thank you."

"My pleasure." Though his expression bordered on doubt, she kept her voice cordial and friendly as she glanced at the bowl of soup growing cooler by the minute. "Luc said it was important to talk to you each time you woke to help you rouse quicker."

He blinked several times and nodded. "...kay."

Seeing his pinched expression, Bea asked, "Are you in pain, Sir?"

His eyes closed then opened again. "Mouf, head...hurt."

"Would you like some willow bark tea? It will help with the pain."

A slow shake of his head preceded a soft, "Not yet."

"How about some water?"

"Yes."

She reached for the pitcher and frowned. It was nearly empty. She poured the meager amount into a glass and helped him take a few sips. "The pitcher is empty. Will you be all right for a few minutes while I go downstairs and get more?"

"Yes."

She stood and took the pitcher from the dresser. "Okay. I'll be right back."

He nodded but didn't reply.

It took longer than she intended to get the water because everyone asked about Henry. While she appreciated their concern, it delayed her return.

When she re-entered the room fifteen minutes later, she found Belle trying to give a spoonful of something to Henry, who was not cooperating.

"You have to take your medication," Belle said sternly.

"No."

She tried again. "The doctor said you need this."

"What are you doing, Belle?" Asked Bea as she entered the room and placed the water pitcher back on the dresser. "What are you giving him?"

Flustered, Belle looked at Bea then back to Henry. "I'm trying to take care of him since you obviously cannot. He needs his medicine."

"What medicine?"

Belle stood back. "The doctor said to give it to him every few hours. I gave him some this morning, but he said he hadn't had any since."

Bea saw the bottle of laudanum on the dresser. "You gave him Laudanum this morning? Without talking to Luc first. How much?"

She looked down at the spoon in her hand. "A spoonful."

"Dammit, Belle," snapped Bea. "That's too much."

"It is not. My mother takes this much all the time. It helps with pain."

Bea looked down at Henry. His pinched expression and labored breathing said he didn't appreciate Belle's intervention. "It will also knock him out if he gets too much." She placed a hand on Moreau's skinny shoulder. "Are you all right? Did you take any of it?"

"Fine. No." His face was flushed, and his voice, while soft, was nonetheless tinged with anger.

"Give that to me." She held her hand out for the spoon.

Belle dropped it into the bowl on the dresser and whirled on Bea. "I was just trying to help," she snapped. "He's in great pain and needs his medication, even if he won't admit it." She sucked in a breath. "And you traipsed off to who knows where leaving him all alone to suffer."

"I went down for water."

"Well, I can't wait for Lucian to find out what you did. He insisted someone be here at all times." She paused, nose in the air. "Not only did you leave him alone, you left him in agony."

Bea started to argue with her exaggerated claims but knew it would serve no useful purpose. "Well, I'm here now, so there is no need for you to remain."

Immediately, Belle turned on the charm as she gazed down at Henry. "Why, I couldn't possibly leave him alone with you now. Who knows what you might do to him?"

Anger rose like volcanic lava in Bea, and she straightened her spine. Belle would say or do anything to further her cause.

Before she could utter a word, Henry spoke up. "Don't need you, Annabelle."

Unaccustomed to being dismissed in such a manner, Belle inhaled sharply. Thin lips formed a tight line across her face. Without a word, she turned and strode from the room in a swish of pale blue silk, slamming the door behind her.

Bea's mind raced with questions. Did he remember Belle gave him Laudanum this morning? Is that why he didn't trust her? Why did she do it? Was she genuinely trying to help, or was there another reason for keeping him asleep? Finally deciding it was not her place to ask those questions, she returned to caregiver mode. "Can I get you anything, Mr. Moreau?"

"I'm fine," he said quietly.

Bea wasn't sure what to say or do now. Henry was more awake and alert than earlier. His chest rose and fell in quick succession, so maybe having Belle come in was a good thing, after all. She looked at the bowl of soup. "Do you want to try a few bites of the soup?"

When he didn't reply, she continued. "I know you probably don't feel much like eating, but you've slept most of the last twenty-four hours, and you really need to try and eat something."

"...mouf, head...hurts."

"I'm sure it does." She took a deep breath. "How about we try some of Mavis's willow bark tea first? It has honey in it. It tastes better warm. But, even cold, it's not bad and will help ease the pain. If that doesn't work, we can still try the laudanum."

"Kay."

She poured some tea in a glass and helped him drink. Setting it aside, she sat back down in the chair. "Mr. Moreau, I know you don't like needing help."

"Henwee." His piercing blue eyes met hers. "Pweese."

She gave him a warm smile. "Henry, then. You don't like needing help, especially from someone you hardly know. And, well, in your shoes, I'd feel the same way. But, sometimes, we need to be willing to ask for and accept help when we need it."

His jaw tightened, and Bea feared she'd gone too far, but then he blinked and gave a slow nod.

"Let's get you upright so you can eat." She didn't miss the tremble in his arms as she assisted him into a sitting position against the headboard, supported by pillows. She placed a towel on his chest and reached for the soup. "This has cooled off a lot, and the vegetables are chopped small, so it should be easy to eat." She paused and took a breath. "Okay. I know this will most likely upset you more, but I think I should hold the spoon for you." She held up her free hand, anticipating an argument. "You've eaten nothing since yesterday and have had a lot of medication. Your hands may shake, and we don't want soup all over the bed." Before he could argue, she filled the spoon and placed it near his lips.

For a moment, she thought he might refuse, but he squinted his eyes, and gingerly opened his mouth.

"I'm going to start with just some of the liquid and see how that goes."

He nodded and swallowed the nourishing brew.

"Does that hurt your throat?" she asked before refilling the spoon.

"No."

"Good. Does your stomach feel okay? Any nausea?"

He blinked a couple of times, then opened his eyes wider. "No."

"Good. We'll take this slow. One never knows how the body will react in these situations. Just let me know if you feel ill at all."

When half the soup was gone, he shook his head.

"Are you feeling ill?"

His eyes slid shut, and he shook his head. "I'm full." Though his words were still slightly slurred because of his cut lip, his voice was more robust than before. "Thank you."

"You're welcome." She placed the bowl back on the dresser and turned to him. "It might help you stay awake more if you sat a while. Are you okay with that?"

He considered her a moment, then nodded, his eyes more alert, his complexion no longer an ashen pallor.

"Doc left some salve for the cut on your lip. Do you mind if I put some on it now? It should help it feel better." Without waiting for his response, she took the cream and carefully dabbed it on his lip.

He grimaced. "Stings."

"I'm sorry. But Doc said it would help the swelling."

When she finished, he relaxed against the pillows.

"Let me know if you start to feel sick at all."

Silent, his curious eyes were focused and intent as they studied her.

She squirmed in her chair, overcome with the need to fill the sudden silence. "The weather was much nicer today. I think spring may come early this year."

He blinked but did not reply.

"There's a dance tomorrow night. Some kind of annual thing they do just before spring planting and roundups start." She knew she rambled but couldn't stop herself. For whatever reason, she suddenly felt uncomfortable under his steady gaze. "The ladies in town have been busy decorating all week. I understand they will have musicians and lots of food. I think the whole county will be there." She stopped and racked her brain for something else to say.

Henry moved one hand slowly back and forth on the bed. "I'm sorry," he said at last.

The statement surprised her, and it took a moment to respond. "Whatever for?"

"...you're smart and very kind." His voice, though stronger now, remained low, and his words still slurred. "Sorry I didn't know that."

Embarrassed by his sincere comment, she turned her scarred cheek away from him. "Well, we hardly know each other, so –"

"Your father is a fool. Lockhart's won't be the same without you."

She turned to meet his steady gaze, but her voice refused to cooperate. Try as she might, she couldn't think of anything to say except, "Thank you for saying that."

He closed his eyes, and he sighed. "Lie down now, please."

"Of course." She jumped up and helped him get situated once again on the bed.

He blew out a long breath and closed his eyes. "Tomorrow, want to hear about expanding my company."

Stunned, she sat up straighter. *How does he know about that?*

CHAPTER THIRTY

THE GRANDFATHER CLOCK IN THE LOBBY CHIMED NINE o'clock as Bea reached the bottom step. The last twenty-four hours had been long and eventful.

When Luc returned a short time ago, Henry was dozing, so he tiptoed up to Bea and pulled her in his arms for a long and sultry kiss. When he stepped back, she found Henry's gaze locked on them. Even now, her cheeks burned at being caught, yet Henry didn't seem surprised or even shocked.

Unable to look at him, she quickly excused herself and hurried out the door, barely hearing Luc's promise to come by later.

Mind racing, sleep would be an elusive thing—so much to consider.

Foremost on the list was Luc wanted to marry her. Soon. Whether or not Henry will approve and the repercussions of his stance were a big second. And then there was Belle; her insistence Luc would return to New York with her, and what, if any, involvement she may have with the current state of Moreau Shipping. Rounding out her mental list of worries was Henry's comment about discussing the expansion of his company. How did he know about that?

"Why must life be so complicated?" she muttered, then pulled her shawl tighter and exited the hotel, turning left toward the store. She'd left in a hurry when Thompkins came by looking for Luc and needed to finish closing up for the night.

In the dim light shining through the store's window, she saw a woman pacing near the door of the mercantile and recognized Jenny's slight frame when she turned around.

Curious, she lengthened her steps and met her as she neared the alley between Lockhart's and The Rose. "Good evening, Jenny. Why are you out at this hour?"

Jenny jerked to a stop, holding something to her chest. "I've been waiting for you. How is Mr. Moreau?"

"He is much better."

"That's such good news." Jenny shuffled her feet side-to-side.

"Jenny? Are you all right? Is something wrong?"

She clutched the paper tight to her chest, her face a mask of fear and confusion. "It's not right. I can't let it happen."

"Let what happen?"

Jenny looked over Bea's shoulder when someone exited The Rose, then shoved an envelope into her hands. "I have to go."

Before Bea could react, Jenny hurried past her and entered the hotel.

Bea looked at the envelope as Richard Bentley approached her.

"Good evening, Bea."

"Good evening." She quickly stuffed the envelope into her skirt pocket. "You're in town awfully late tonight."

"I was hoping I might talk you into having dinner with me, but heard you were with Luc's grandfather."

Bea heard the disappointment in his voice but chose not to respond. "Yes, Luc had a plow to repair, so I sat with Henry until he returned. And he's much better tonight. Bruised and sore, but nothing too bad."

"Are you headed home? I'd be happy to walk with you. It is getting late and not much moon tonight."

"Thank you, but I've got some things to take care of at the store."

"I don't mind waiting. Lots of strangers in town to get a head start on the dance tomorrow. I'd feel better if I walked you home."

"I appreciate it, Richard, but Lucian will be here shortly."

"I see."

Again, she heard the disappointment in his voice and felt sorry for him. It wasn't right to give him any false hope either—a no-win situation.

"Well," he said at last, "I'll wait until you are inside and then be on my way."

She unlocked the door and stepped inside. "Thank you, Richard. You are a good friend."

The dim light from the lantern inside and the brim of his hat bathed his face in shadow, but she saw his sad smile as he nodded. "Luc is a lucky man."

He waited until she locked the door behind her, then strolled back toward the hotel.

Thoughts of the envelope faded as she closed up the store, anticipating a visit from Luc when she got home.

Twenty minutes later, she stood on the store's back steps and stared at the darkened expanse of ground leading to her house. It wasn't the first time she'd gone home after dark, but, for some reason, tonight, it exuded a sinister vibe.

"It's only a short distance," she murmured, "maybe thirty yards or so." She glanced up in time to see the quarter moon slide behind a passing cloud, effectively removing the last hint of light. "Great. Just great." She debated going back inside for a lantern but decided against it. Tomorrow, she would make sure there was one at the back door.

"Maybe I should have taken Richard up on his offer," she muttered, then took a deep breath and headed for the beckoning glow of a lamp in her living room. Levi always left one burning for her when he checked the wood box in the evening.

By the time she reached the front steps, her breath burst in and out in rapid succession, leaving her weak and dizzy.

Stifling a chuckle at her unwarranted fear, she opened the door and stepped inside.

"I've been waiting for you."

CHAPTER THIRTY-ONE

"DID YOU EAT ANYTHING TONIGHT?" asked Luc as he gazed at his grandfather. "I forgot to ask Bea before she left, but I see the bowl is gone."

"I did." Henry paused, then looked at Luc with amused eyes. "She didn't exactly give me a choice."

Luc grinned and sat back in his chair. "She's a force to be reckoned with at times."

Henry's eyes narrowed. "You like her."

Luc held his breath a heartbeat. "I love her, Grandfather. I intend to marry her."

He nodded. "I remember something you said."

"You do?"

"Not everything." His swollen mouth formed the semblance of a smile. "You said a lot, and bits and pieces pop in now and again." He paused in thought. "She's not what I expected."

Luc scowled. "What did you expect?"

He lifted one frail shoulder and let it fall back down. "Based on our limited interactions, I expected her to be withdrawn and…distant. But she's very kind." One corner of his mouth tipped up. "I daresay I couldn't pay anyone in this town to speak ill of her."

"She's one of the most giving people I've ever known. She's smart and funny and cares more about others than herself."

Henry turned his gaze to the ceiling as though seeking an answer there. "You didn't give me too much laudanum. Belle did."

Luc jerked upright in his seat. "What?"

"Came in after you left. I vaguely remember saying something about being in pain, and she gave me some of the medicine." Brow furrowed, he shook his head. "Something's not right with her." He squinted and shook his head. "She was mumbling to herself, but I can't recall what she said. I just remember the word plans." He paused again. "But I don't think she intended any harm by giving me the laudanum."

Luc wasn't buying that but didn't say anything. "You two were arguing at the restaurant before you fell."

He nodded. "Insisted I force the engagement." His jaw clenched, and he scowled. "I refused. She got angry."

Confused, Luc shook his head. "I don't understand. I thought that's what you wanted? Why you brought her here."

Henry silently stared at the ceiling so long Luc wondered if he would answer.

His gaze focused on a spot over Luc's right shoulder. "She invited herself." He paused. "The more time I spent with her, the less I liked her." He swallowed and ran his tongue over chapped lips. "Water. Please."

Luc helped him drink, then sat back in his chair and waited.

"Thank you." Henry closed his eyes and breathed deeply. "Belle came back tonight."

"What? When?"

A light chuckle rumbled in the older man's chest. "When Bea went for more water. Said it was time for my medicine. Got upset when I didn't want it." His smile widened, and he grimaced in pain. "Bea told her to leave."

Luc sniffed. "I bet that didn't sit well."

He shrugged, then expelled a long breath and once again closed his eyes. "Did you know Bea ran Lockhart's for the last five years?"

"She told me."

"Jeremiah let something slip a few months ago. I was curious and did some checking." He turned back to Luc. "She's behind their line of luxury items like silver and crystal, even silk from Paris." He paused and continued. "He took credit for all of it. She was about to close a deal to import more items from Europe when that scoundrel came along."

Luc knew Henry's strength faded fast because it took several breaths to get the words out. He needed to say his piece while he could. "I know you're tired, but I need to repeat this to be sure you understand."

"I'm listening."

"I will go back to New York with you if that's what you want. I'll do what I can to help get the company stable again. I've barely touched the money I inherited from Father, and you are welcome to it."

He raised his hand to stop his grandfather's interruption. "But I want to marry Bea first. I want your blessing, Grandfather." He paused and rubbed his hands on the arm of his chair, suddenly feeling like a child asking permission. "Because I want you to be a part of our lives from now on. But—with or without it, I will marry her before I go."

Henry's lips trembled, and his eyes glistened.

Afraid that meant he would refuse his blessing, Luc's heart stopped as he held his breath and waited.

"I'm very proud of you, Lucian," he whispered at last. "I never told you that." He swallowed again and continued. "Would you allow an old fool to be your best man?"

Bea squealed and fell back against the door, one hand clutching her chest as she stared at the man standing in front of the fireplace.

Her father.

Heart pounding so hard she could scarcely breathe, Bea sought her voice. "What are you doing here?"

Jeremiah Lockhart stood with his back to the flames, holding the odd-shaped vase someone had given her during the housewarming party. "It's about time you got here." He placed it back on the mantle and turned to face her. "I've been waiting for over an hour."

Old habits die hard, and she cringed at the censure in his voice, ready to offer apologies and grovel for whatever slight she had committed. But she caught herself in time. No more.

She took a step into the room. The disapproval in his face was nothing new; she'd seen it most of her life. "When did you get here? The train was this morning."

He linked his hands behind his back. "I hired someone to bring me here from Marshall."

She didn't bother to ask any other questions about his travel. She didn't particularly care. But his presence had a purpose, one that did not bode well for her. "I repeat, what are you doing here?"

He didn't speak for a moment as his jaw clenched and unclenched. Even in the muted light, she noted the redness in his face, the coldness in his eyes. *This man, her father, is a stranger.*

"You know very well why I'm here, Beulah Mae," he snapped. "It's time for this foolishness to end and for you to return home."

A thousand thoughts ran through her mind at once, stumbling over each other, trying to be the one on top. Suddenly, she understood. Henry was right. Her father needed her back at Lockhart's. That knowledge gave her the power to remain calm.

"Would you like a brandy?" When he didn't reply, she continued. "Well, I need one. It's been a long day." Without waiting for him to respond, she strode into the kitchen and retrieved the brandy from the counter where she'd left it. She splashed a healthy amount into a glass and then filled another for her father as an afterthought. She walked back to the living room and handed one to Jeremiah before sitting down on the couch and taking a healthy swallow. "I've no intention of going anywhere."

He plopped the glass down on the mantle without taking a sip and took a step toward her. "This has gone on long enough. I am your father, and you will do as I say!"

She nearly strangled on the brandy she'd just swallowed. He spoke as though she were a rebellious teen and not a thirty-year-old woman. "I am long past the age where you can order me around, Father." She took another sip of the expensive liquid courage. "The train heading East doesn't stop here until Sunday afternoon. While the hotel isn't what you're accustomed to, you'll be comfortable enough there." She toasted him with her glass. "Good night."

He straightened and pulled in a deep breath. "Beulah Mae—"

"I prefer to be called Bea."

He jerked back, evidently surprised she would interrupt him. Something else that never happened before.

He changed tactics. "Your mother and I want you to come home. This…this hovel of a town is no place for you."

She settled back against the couch, the brandy warming her insides and loosening her tongue. "This hovel of a town as you call it is more of a home to me than Lockhart Manor ever was."

He opened his mouth, and she held up her hand, palm out. "And the people in it are my family now."

He stiffened, then squared his shoulders. "You would choose these…these people over your own family?"

She stood and walked toward the fireplace, placing her empty brandy glass on the mantel beside his. "Yes. I would."

"How could you do such a thing to your own flesh and blood?"

She stared a moment and then snorted. "How could I? How could you?"

He gave her a quizzical look. "Me?"

"Yes. You. And Mother. You made me feel ugly and unwanted, unworthy of any consideration."

"We only wanted to protect you, Beulah—Bea. We did what we thought was right."

"Is that why I was banned from the floor when customers were about? Why you forced me to remain covered in public? Why you never let me attend parties or balls?"

"You could attend any function you wanted to."

"Of course I could. As long as I stayed out of sight and wore that damnable veil."

"Is that why you left? To punish us for some perceived slight even though your mother and I were only doing what we thought was best?"

She wanted to scream at him *best for whom, Father,* but let it go. "No, Father. I left because I wanted a life of my own. And now I have it."

"Don't be absurd. You're a Lockhart. Your place is with those who care about you."

She met his steely gaze with one of her own. "Which is exactly why I will be staying here."

Bright spots of red dotted both cheeks, and his eyes narrowed. "How can you turn your back on your family when they need you?"

She swallowed the ache in her throat that threatened to bring on tears and ignored the *shame-on-you* tone in his voice. "The same way you turned yours on me," she said softly.

He stared a moment as though just seeing her, then reached for his hat resting on a chair to his right. "Well, there is nothing to be done about the past. We can only move forward." He placed the hat on his head. "We'll have plenty of time to work things out on the way home. I'll get the tickets tomorrow and have my attorney get to work on selling things here, though I dare say we'll lose a bundle on this place." He ran his finger over the brim of his hat, assuring it rested just so on his head. "Make sure you're ready on time. I detest being late."

She laughed, a humorless, I'm-sorry-for-you sound. *He dismissed everything I said.*

"What do you find so amusing?" he sneered.

"You haven't been listening. I'm going nowhere. This is my home now." She took a step toward him, arms folded across her chest. "You can mouth all the nice platitudes you want, but we both know there is only one reason for your presence here, and it's not concern for my well-being."

He flinched, and she continued. "So let me make myself crystal clear. This is my home now. I'm not leaving. Period. The store is mine. It is not for sale to anyone for any price." She took a deep breath and blew it out slowly. "And if it's money you want, Father, I'm sorry. I have none to give."

His eyes widened, and he took a step back. "You lost your grandmother's money? All of it?" He looked around her sparse yet comfortable home; his face pinched with distaste. "That's why you live like this?"

She had no intention of telling him just how wealthy she was. Proper guidance and wise investments paid off. She chose to live simply and give back where she could. "What other reason could there be?"

"You're lying." He waved his hand around the room. "You couldn't have spent all that money on this."

She shrugged. "What can I say? Edmund's schemes rubbed off on me."

He stared a moment longer, then reached for the doorknob. "I want proof there is no money by Monday."

All the hurt she'd suffered over the years was nothing compared to the heart numbing pain that one statement caused. She meant nothing to him. Nothing at all. Shoulders squared, hands clasped so tightly together they ached, she kept her expression unreadable. "Goodbye, Father. I'm sorry you made this trip for nothing."

He jerked open the door. "I want that proof by Monday."

"Proof of what?"

CHAPTER THIRTY-TWO

Luc wasn't sure whose face registered more surprise Bea or her father's.

Jeremiah did a doubletake toward Luc and barked, "None of your concern, Moreau." He then turned to a whitefaced Bea and snapped, "Monday," before he stomped off into the darkness.

Luc started to ask what that was all about but stopped when he saw the color had drained from her face, and she clutched the door for support.

He stepped inside and shut the door, one arm around her waist to keep her steady. "*Chère?* What is it? What's wrong?" He helped her to the couch then sat beside her. "Please. Tell me what is wrong."

She exhaled slowly, and he caught the faint aroma of brandy. He looked around and spied the two glasses on the mantle. He got up and brought the half-full one to her. "Here, sip this. It will help calm you."

She took it, then gave him a trembling smile. "I already had one."

"A little more won't hurt." He pulled her against him and waited for her to continue.

"He was here when I got home." She lifted the glass and downed most of the contents, then hiccupped and relaxed against his side. "I don't know what the exact circumstances are, but I believe he came here expecting money. I told him I had none to give." She downed the rest of the glass. "I lied."

He grinned down at her. "You? Lied?"

"Yes." She paused and took a deep breath. "I told you I inherited some money from my grandmother." She rolled the empty glass in her hands. "It was a sizeable amount. With good advice and guidance, I turned it into a small fortune." She kept her gaze on the crackling fireplace.

"Why do you tell me this, *Chère?*"

She shrugged lightly. "I don't know. I guess I thought you should know. But I prefer a simple life and want to use my money to help others where I can."

He thought of Daisy and Levi and how Bea worked to get them a better life. The people in the community she helped daily by extending credit or adding something extra to their orders without their knowledge.

And then there was Amos and Silas. Her elevating them to favorite uncle status put both men over the moon with happiness, and they wasted no time letting folks know they were now looking out for their niece's well-being. If possible, he loved her even more for that.

He pulled her tighter against him, stretching his long legs out in front. "You have a kind and loving heart, *Chère.*" He kissed the top of her head. "And helping others is a fine thing to do." He paused. "And I think that, together, we can make Bakersville a town to be proud of."

She turned to look up at him, brows furrowed, eyes questioning.

Luc shrugged. "I'm rather wealthy myself."

Her radiant smile faded, and tears clouded her eyes. "I'm

nothing to him, Luc. My own father. I'm nothing but a means to an end." She sniffled and rested her head on his chest.

"It is his loss, *Chère*. His loss."

She took a breath. "I wanted him to…to…"

"To what?"

"I don't know, be proud of me, I guess, of what I accomplished at Lockhart's and here." She paused. "God. I'm thirty years old, and I still wish for a word of praise from my inconsiderate father." She hiccupped again. "How pitiful is that?"

"There is no shame in that, *Chère*. It is natural." He rubbed his hand up and down her back. "I, too, wished for such a thing from my grandfather."

"Did you ever get it?"

He smiled. "I did. Tonight."

"Really?" She turned to face him, her eyes alight with surprise and happiness.

"That's what I came by to tell you. We had a nice long chat before he became too tired to continue." He tipped her chin up, and his gaze fixed on her lips. "It's late, and I know you are tired, so I'll be quick. I will have to go back to New York, but only for a short time."

"How long is a short time?"

He smiled. "No more than a month. But, thanks to you, he has no objection to us getting married before I leave."

Bea couldn't believe her ears and jerked around to look at his face, grimacing when her head spun, no doubt due to the second glass of brandy. "What?"

"He's very impressed with you."

"He is?"

"He thinks you are special."

Overcome by the praise, she grabbed a handful of his shirt and asked, "He said that?"

"He did. He also said you are no doubt the reason behind Lockhart's recent success. And he agreed with me that you are a very astute businesswoman."

Henry Moreau. *The* Henry Moreau thought she was special. And a good businesswoman. It was silly, maybe even childish, to feel such giddiness at his approval. But, except for her grandmother and later her banker and lawyer, no one ever praised her intelligence or business sense, which made Henry's acceptance even more significant. "I didn't do anything special with Lockhart's," she said at last. "I merely worked with what was already in place."

Luc smiled. "You are too modest, *Chère*. Grandfather believes you made it what it is today, and you should be very proud of that."

Once again, pesky tears clouded her vision. "I am, Lucian. I am." She nestled against his chest, enjoying the comfort he provided. Suddenly, she remembered her conversation with Jenny and dug for the envelope in her pocket. "I had a conversation with Jenny earlier, and I am sure Belle is up to no good."

He put a finger to her lips, silencing her. "Probably so, but I do not wish to talk about Belle tonight, *Chère*. I wish to kiss you."

Unable to resist, she leaned into his kiss, one hand resting on his thigh, the other pinned against his side.

The pressure of his hand on her back increased, its warmth penetrating her clothing, turning her insides to mush.

The hunger in his kiss melded with hers and ignited a fire that raced through her veins.

"My beautiful, *Chère*," he whispered. "I love you. You have the heart of an angel." He kissed the tip of her nose. "The soul of a warrior." He brushed his lips across each eyelid. "And the body of a woman. My woman."

His last words, smothered against her lips, accelerated currents of desire racing through her body.

Suddenly, he pulled back, breath coming in rapid drafts. "I should go." He pushed gently against her shoulders, his blue eyes burning with tightly restrained passion. "It's late, and you're tired."

She swallowed hard and acknowledged the truth in what he said and left unsaid. "Could we…just sit here a while longer?" She put a little distance between them and leaned back against the couch, face turned toward the flickering flames. "I really don't want to be alone."

He hesitated briefly, then pulled her against his side in a tender embrace. "Of course."

The hiss and crackle of the fire was the only sound in the room as they sat side-by-side, each lost in thought, savoring the knowledge they were no longer alone.

CHAPTER THIRTY-THREE

Luc woke to the elusive aroma of lavender and roses tickling his nose. Bea snuggled against him on the couch where they had fallen asleep, long, disheveled curls draping over one shoulder. He didn't recall how that happened, but he loved the silky feel of them as he caressed one sable loop between his fingers.

He couldn't deny the desire she ignited in him, but more than that, she filled him with a sense of contentment and belonging he'd never experienced before. Knowing it would not be long until they wed, and a lifetime of making love to her, waking with her in his arms, awaited them, made his heart race in anticipation.

The mantle clock's muted chime said 3 A.M. Few people were out at this hour, but still, he needed to leave. He did not wish to cause her any embarrassment. The problem was, he couldn't bring himself to move.

Bea sighed and snuggled closer, her head under his chin, one hand splayed across his chest, her legs tucked beneath her on the couch.

"*Chère?*" He jostled her lightly. "I should go."

"Ummm."

"People will begin stirring soon, and someone might see me."

She tilted her head and gave him a sexy, sleepy-eyed look. "What time is it?"

"Three."

She tucked her head back under his chin and snuggled closer to him, her arms folded in front of her. "Five more minutes."

"Just five?"

"Umm. I'm cold."

"I'll stoke the fire before I go."

"Okay."

Thirty minutes passed, and Luc knew their special time was over. "Come on, *Chère*," he said, easing her away from his side. "Off to bed with you. I'll fix the fire and let myself out."

The lamp bathed her face in shadows but didn't disguise the heat in her eyes. "I long for the day when you won't have to leave."

He took a deep breath. "As do I, my love. As do I."

"When did your father arrive in town?"

Lizzy's question hung unanswered as Bea's mind drifted back to waking cradled in Luc's arms. Nothing felt more right. And Henry blessed the marriage.

Her mouth curled up in a happy smile. How long did it take to plan a wedding? She attended only three in her life, all friends of her grandmother's. To whom could she turn to for assistance?

"Well, something sure has you preoccupied today."

Her friend's elevated voice got her attention, and heat rushed to Bea's cheeks. "I'm sorry, Lizzy. I'm wool-gathering this morning. What did you say?"

"I asked when your father arrived."

Irritated, Bea kept her voice level. "He hired someone in Marshall to bring him late yesterday."

"Did you know he was coming?"

"No."

Lizzy's brows nearly met her hairline. "So, I'm guessing you aren't happy to see him?"

Anxious about the wedding, Bea cut her off. "I need a favor."

"Of course. Anything."

She took a deep breath. "I have to tell someone, but you can't breathe a word of this yet. Well, maybe Mavis and Vi, but not until I say it's okay."

Lizzy crossed her arms and smiled. "Now, I'm really curious."

She wrung her hands together, then dropped them to the side. "How soon do you think we could put a wedding together?"

Lizzy's surprised gaze turned to worry. "You're not…"

Comprehension sent a blast of heat across Bea's cheeks. "Oh, my goodness, no, nothing like that. It's just, well, Luc asked me to marry him. And I said yes."

Lizzy clapped her hands and came around the corner to wrap Bea in a quick embrace. "I'm so happy for you both. Leave everything to me. I know Reverend Johnson is making rounds to some of the smaller towns this week and next, but we could set something up the first weekend in April." She grinned at her friend. "Your father's arrival is perfect timing. Can he stay here that long?"

"No. I don't want him there," said Bea sharply. "Amos and Silas will give me away."

Lizzy's surprised expression made Bea soften her tone. "It's a long story that I don't wish to go into right now."

"I understand," said Lizzy as she patted her arm. "You know I'm with you all the way. Whatever you need or want me to do."

"I do know that, Lizzy, and it means the world to me."

"Okay, how about April fifth for a wedding date?"

Bea couldn't stop the happy smile on her face. "April fifth is my birthday."

"April fifth it is." Lizzy's happy expression suddenly darkened. "What about that woman? Miss Blankenship? She never misses an opportunity to tell people they're engaged and you're, well, that you're a liar."

"Oh, no!" She jerked off the work apron she wore and tossed it on the counter. "Can you watch the store? We got to talking about getting married last night, and I forgot to give Luc something."

Lizzy winked and snorted. "I bet he didn't complain."

Bea ignored the comment and dashed out the back door. A few minutes later, she returned and stood beside Lizzy, the letter in her hands, and debated what to do.

"Jenny told me to give this to Luc," said Bea, tapping it on the counter.

Eyes on the letter, Lizzy asked, "She didn't say you couldn't read it first, did she?"

"Well, no, but—dang, it! I have to know." Halfway down the first page, Bea gasped. "It's a list of things to do. I can't believe it."

"What? What is it?" Lizzy leaned around and read over Bea's shoulder. "That witch!"

"I have to find Luc," said Bea.

The front door swung open, and Mr. Jones from the telegraph office walked in. "Morning, Miss Lockhart." He extended an envelope toward her. "You got a reply to your telegram."

"Thank you, Mr. Jones."

He dipped his head. "Got one more to deliver at the hotel," then left without another word.

Hands shaking, Bea tore open the message, then sank against the counter as she read.

"Bea? What is it? What's wrong?"

She stuffed both envelopes into her pocket. "I have to find Luc." She looked toward the front. "Is Uncle Amos outside yet?"

"I don't see him, but I saw Silas at The Rose when I walked over here."

"Can you get him to watch the store for me? I have to find Luc."

Without waiting for a reply, she hurried out the door toward the smithy.

CHAPTER THIRTY-FOUR

L UC ADDED MORE COALS TO THE FORGE AND ABSENTLY worked the bellows. He had no pending orders but always kept the fire ready just in case. Once satisfied, he removed his gloves and turned toward his house in the back.

"Hold on, boy," said Amos. "I got a bone to pick with you."

Surprised, Luc turned around. "About what?"

Amos shuffled over to his barrel and sat down. "About that woman in town who keeps saying you're engaged."

Luc blew out a disgusted breath. "I am not and have never been engaged to Belle."

"Well now," tobacco juice dribbled from the corner of his mouth, and he wagged a crooked finger toward Luc. "She keeps sayin' you are."

Before Luc could reply, Amos spoke again. "And if you hurt my niece, friend or no friend, you'll answer to me."

"What the hell are you blabbering about, Old Man?"

Amos sat up straight, pale blue eyes glaring from his weathered face. "Bea. She done said I'm her uncle, and I aim to look out for her." He spat a stream of brown liquid on the floor. "Silas, too."

He stared a full ten seconds before he could form a reply. "Well, if you must know *Uncle Amos*, I intend to marry Bea as soon as possible."

Amos blinked several times. "Since when?"

"Since I asked her, and she said yes." Luc turned back toward his house. "Now, if you'll excuse me, I need to clean up and check on my grandfather." He paused, then smiled at his friend. "And then I aim to talk with my real fiancé about wedding plans."

He grinned to himself when he heard Amos cackle and shuffle off. By the time it occurred to him that Bea may not want it to be common knowledge yet, Amos was gone. *Damn. Nothing to be done about it now.*

Fifteen minutes later, he entered the hotel and stopped when he saw his grandfather sitting in a chair in the lobby. His first thought was the bruising on his face was ugly, but his lip looked much better. Fast on the heels of that came the question, "How did you get down here?"

"I realize you think I am helpless at present, Lucian, but I can dress myself." He nodded toward the young desk clerk. "And Tommy there helped me down the stairs." He settled in more comfortably in the chair. "I needed to get out of that room."

Luc nodded to Tommy then sat in the chair across from his grandfather. "Well, I'm delighted to see you down here. How do you feel? Are you hungry?"

"I'm quite famished, actually."

"When you're ready, we can head over to The Rose."

Doc Morton walked up about then and spoke to both men. "Well, I guess it's safe to say you're feeling much better today."

"I am," said Henry. "Thank you very much for all you did."

"I'm just glad the situation wasn't any more serious." He turned to Luc. "I understand congratulations are in order."

"How did—" Before he asked the question, he knew the answer. Amos. "Thanks, Doc."

Doc turned back to the patient. "I don't foresee any issues, Mr. Moreau, but feel free to send for me if you have any concerns."

As Doc walked off, Luc turned to find his grandfather smiling. "Word travels fast around here."

He ducked his head. "Yeah, well, I didn't ask Bea if she wanted it known yet and made the mistake of telling Amos. The whole town probably knows it by now."

His grandfather chuckled, a warm, happy sound that made Luc smile in return.

"I am happy for you, Lucian." He tapped his cane on the floor. "I believe I have developed a taste for buttermilk biscuits. Let's go eat."

It took a moment for Luc to react to this new, upbeat person. Where was the taciturn, gruff man he remembered?

Seeing Luc's hesitation, Henry spoke again. "I've done a lot of thinking over the last few hours, Luc. I have a lot to make up for. I can't make up for past mistakes, but I can try and make fewer ones in the future." He shrugged. "Or at least not make the same ones again." His expression softened as he gazed at Luc. "I do want to be a part of your life, son. Yours and Bea's."

Luc swallowed past the lump in his throat. "We'd like that."

His grandfather nodded and pushed himself up from the chair. "I'm hungry."

They made their way toward their usual table, frequently stopping to talk to folks who asked after Henry's health or congratulating Luc. By the time they sat down, coffee waited along with fresh biscuits, bacon, and eggs.

"When I saw y'all walk in, I got it ready, so you wouldn't have to wait," said Vi.

Henry smiled and bowed toward her. "Thank you, madame. That is very kind of you."

Vi's cheeks turned pink, and she waved toward the food. "My pleasure, Mr. Moreau. Eat before it gets cold."

Henry nodded again. "Please call me Henry."

Luc stared at his grandfather. Was he flirting with her?

Vi must have thought so because her face turned scarlet as she whirled and headed back to the kitchen.

Henry sat down and looked up at Luc. "Sit. Food's getting cold."

Before he could do more than take a sip of his coffee, Jeremiah Lockhart walked in and made a beeline for their table.

"Henry, what a surprise," he gushed. "I didn't expect to find you in such a place."

"I'm visiting my grandson." His response was cool to the point of rudeness.

Jeremiah turned to Luc, a self-satisfied smile on his face. "Is there something you want to tell me, Lucian?"

Luc set his cup down and looked at Bea's father. "I can't think of a thing."

Lockhart puffed out his chest. "I overheard a conversation just now at the hotel. It would seem you are engaged to my daughter."

Silent, Luc merely stared, refusing to play whatever game he had in mind.

"I think the proper thing to do is to seek my permission first." His unpleasant smile widened, and he looked at the chair across from Luc. "But, under the circumstances, I can tell you I whole-heartedly grant permission."

Luc wanted to knock that patronizing smile off his face. "What circumstances?" Even as he asked, he knew the answer, and his gut churned with anger.

"Well, she can be useful if you look past—"

"Look past what, Father?"

Luc was so focused on Jeremiah he didn't notice Bea's entrance until her icy voice broke through the rush of anger the comment caused. His anger immediately turned to sorrow because he spoke in this public place, with no regard for her at all.

Luc stood and took Bea's hand, kissing her lightly on the cheek. "Ignore him, *Chère.*"

"I've never liked you much, Jeremiah," said Henry, his curt voice coated in distaste, "and I like you even less right now."

Lockhart's face flushed bright red, but he didn't leave. "I meant no disrespect," he said quickly. "I merely thought we should discuss preparations. And you should be in control of her inheritance as soon as possible before she squanders it all." His beady eyes jerked from Luc to Henry and never sought Bea. "Despite her appearance, a Lockhart-Moreau wedding will be the social event of the year, and as such, must be perfect." He glanced at the two men again. "We'll be the two most powerful families in New York." His voice rose on the last sentence, and his face beamed with pride.

Luc felt the shivers of hurt and anger coursing through Bea as he hugged her to his side. Disgust filled his voice when he spoke. "You are the biggest fool God ever made."

Posture rigid, Jeremiah's hands rolled into fists at his side. "How dare you speak to me in such a manner."

The front door swung open and slammed against the wall hard enough to rattle the windows. Belle rushed in, face contorted in anger, hair disheveled, flashing a slip of paper toward Bea. "I'll kill you for this!"

CHAPTER THIRTY-FIVE

Bea instinctively took a step back as Belle stormed into the restaurant, screaming like a banshee. Never had she seen such hate before.

Luc stepped in front of her when she approached Bea. "Stop right there, Belle," he ordered, his voice brooking no opposition.

She leaned around Luc and waved the paper at Bea. "You conniving little sneak! You won't get away with this!"

"Get away with what?" asked Bea, "I have no idea what you are talking about."

Belle tried to get around Luc, but he stopped her with a hand on her arm. "Stay where you are, Belle."

Mortified, Bea scanned the room. So many familiar faces watched the fiasco unfold with expressions varying from shock to amusement.

Roscoe sat with two other cowboys at a table to Belle's right and snickered loud enough to be heard. "How 'bout that?" He leaned back in his chair and crossed his arms. "I think we owe more money for the show, don't y'all?"

Nervous laughter floated around the room, and Bea cringed inside. *How can I look them in the eye again?*

Inhaling deeply, she addressed her antagonist. "Why don't we take this discussion somewhere more private?"

"I think we should continue right here," said Jeremiah. "These people have a right to know who they are doing business with."

Bea's mouth dropped open at her father's statement. He wanted her to be embarrassed, no doubt thinking it would force her to return to New York and fulfill whatever scheme he had in mind. Well, she didn't come this far to give up now.

"Fine. Let's do that," said Bea. "Who goes first?"

Belle ignored everyone but Bea. "It's not enough you stole my fiancé from me," she seethed and shoved the telegram toward her. "You stole Moreau Shipping, too!"

"What are you talking about, Belle?" asked Luc and grabbed for the telegram. His expression remained unreadable as he scanned the note, then handed it to Bea with a raised brow.

Belle slapped a wayward curl from her cheek and glared at him. "She's a conniving little thief."

Bea read the short message: *You're too late. Someone beat you to it.*

"Go ahead, Lucian," snipped Belle, pointing toward the telegram, "ask her to explain that."

Bea ignored Belle and pulled the telegram and letter from her pocket and handed both to Luc. "The telegram came this morning. I went to the livery to find you." She glanced up when Jenny entered the room, her pale complexion ashen as she took in the scene. "The other is a list she and Charlotte compiled that outlines their plan. That's what I wanted to talk to you about last night."

"Wait? How did you get that?" Belle stumbled forward, reaching for the paper. "Give that back!"

Luc glanced around as though an explanation lay hidden somewhere. "*Chère?*"

Bea took a deep breath. "Belle is behind the problems Moreau Shipping experienced recently."

"That's a lie," shouted Belle. "You're a liar."

"It's in the letter," said Bea. "At least most of it."

"How did you get it?" asked Luc as he pulled the sheets from the envelope.

Bea hesitated, and Jenny spoke up. "I gave it to her."

Outraged, Belle turned on Jenny. "How dare you!" Before anyone could stop her, she slapped the young woman so hard she stumbled against Roscoe's table.

Roscoe grabbed Jenny to keep her from falling while another cowboy grabbed Belle. "I ain't never hit a woman in my life, ma'am, but if you say one more word against Miss Bea or even move a muscle, I reckon I'll have to rethink that." He nodded toward Luc.

Bea swallowed hard and chanced a look at Henry and her father. Both men had their eyes fixed on Luc as he read the list.

Finished, he looked at Bea, then his grandfather. "She's been undermining your company for months."

"That's—"

"Not a word, ma'am," said the cowboy.

"According to this, they planned it together. Charlotte put her in touch with men to help carry it out. Belle planned to weaken your company to the point her father could buy it out from under you for a fraction of what it was worth." He paused and fixed his steely blue eyes on Belle. "The success hinged on getting my grandfather to force an engagement. As soon as that happened, she would send word, and he'd buy it before we had a chance to stop him. Once they had control of the company, she'd publicly break the engagement." He paused and slapped the missive against his thigh. "To get even with me."

"That's not true, Lucian," Belle cried, "I love you. I could never do that to you."

Jenny sniffed loudly and spoke up. "It's all true, sir."

All eyes in the room turned to the nervous young woman standing next to Roscoe.

"About a year ago, she started secretly meeting this man. Usually at the park, sometimes at the house. At first, I thought he was a new suitor. But he didn't look like a gentleman caller."

"Shut up, you little—" She glanced at the cowboy and hushed.

"About a month before we came here, I overheard them arguing. Miss Blankenship was mad because he hadn't done something like she ordered."

"What did she want him to do?" asked Luc.

"He was supposed to burn this ship coming from England, but he decided to loot it instead. He got away, but two of his men were captured."

"The *Rose Marie*," said Henry. "It carried passengers and goods, including a shipment of jewels from London. Thieves struck the night it docked. Thankfully, no one was hurt, and the goods recovered."

"What else did you hear, Jenny?" asked Luc.

"Not much, sir. They met several times. She made me stay back so I wouldn't hear, but sometimes I'd sneak closer and listen." She never looked at Belle, only Luc. "She was furious at you for not going through with the engagement and wanted to hurt you."

"And the easiest way to hurt me," said Luc softly, "was to hurt my grandfather."

"I'm surprised you'd think of such an elaborate plan, Belle," said Henry. "And it almost worked."

Belle jerked her arm free but didn't move from her spot. "Tell him how you stole his company, Beulah Mae," she hissed.

Bea turned her gaze to Henry and took a deep breath. "Something Belle said the day you arrived made me suspicious, so I telegraphed my attorney to investigate. I instructed him to do whatever was necessary to protect your company." She paused. "Even if it meant buying up your debts." She nodded to the telegram Luc held but had yet to read. "Evidently, Charlotte cannot keep a secret, and with Mr. James' connections, he quickly ascertained the plan and initiated steps to prevent its success."

"See," sneered Belle. "Your precious Beulah Mae snuck around behind your back and stole the company right out from under your nose."

"How about that?" asked Jeremiah as he rubbed his hands together. "You have money after all, and now we own Moreau Shipping, too. That's fabulous!"

Bea ignored everyone but Henry. "I have no wish to keep your company, sir. My sole concern was preventing Belle from destroying it. Mr. James will be here in a couple of weeks with the necessary paperwork to relinquish it back to you."

"Are you crazy?" snapped Jeremiah. "We'll be the most powerful family in New York, and you won't have to marry that, that half-breed."

Bea took two steps toward her father and stopped. "Get out of my sight."

"Beulah Mae, be reasonable."

Roscoe, the two cowboys, and the remaining customers surrounded Belle and Jeremiah.

"We don't like your kind in our town," said Roscoe, flinty gaze switching between Belle and Jeremiah.

Murmurs of agreement drifted from the crowd.

"And it's best if you left. Now."

Surprised and delighted by her friends' support, Bea faced her father. "I don't care if you have to walk back to New York," she said stiffly. "You and Belle are not welcome here."

Belle's eyes glazed with tears, but Bea felt no sympathy for her.

"This is all your fault!" Belle screeched and took a step toward Bea.

Roscoe grabbed her arm. "Ma'am," he said softly, "it'd be a shame to get that pretty green dress all covered in dirt when I toss you out the front door."

"You wouldn't dare."

"He may not," said Vi as she took a step toward Belle. "But I sure as hell will." She pushed up the sleeves of her blouse. "Get out. Now."

"Come along, Miss Blankenship," said Jeremiah at last. "This is no place for a lady." He emphasized the last word and cast a demeaning glance at Bea, before escorting Belle out the door.

Silence hung in the room like a wet blanket for all of ten seconds, then everyone started speaking at once.

"Good riddance," huffed someone.

"How dare she talk about our Bea that way," came another.

"She's pretty on the outside but ugly as sin inside," said a man to Bea's right.

"Ain't that the truth," said Roscoe, who then turned to Bea and tipped his hat. "Congratulations, Miss Bea. Hope that don't mean I can't dance with you tonight."

It took two attempts to speak. "I'll save a waltz for you, Roscoe."

"Show's over, people," said Vi, waving around the rag she kept hidden on her person. "Let these folks get back to their breakfast." She turned and winked at Bea. "Don't you worry about a thing, honey. We're gonna plan you the biggest, best wedding this town has ever seen."

Bea stood in shocked silence, barely acknowledging the words of encouragement and congratulations spoken by the townspeople as they moved past her to leave or return to their respective tables.

Bea turned to see Luc standing beside her, concern engraved into his handsome face.

He lightly touched her arm. "Are you all right, *Chère?*"

She inhaled and glanced from him to Henry. "I honestly don't know."

He guided her to the table, and Vi immediately appeared with a cup of coffee.

"This here coffee is real special," she said with a grin. "I figured you might need it." She took a breath and asked, "Would you like some breakfast, dear?"

"No. No, thank you. I have to get back to the store."

"Those uncles of yours are taking care of things. Just sit and enjoy coffee with your husband-to-be and his handsome grandfather." She turned and left before anyone could reply.

Bea sipped the whiskey-laced brew, coughing when the unexpected punch hit her throat.

Luc covered her hand with his. "Are you all right?"

She regained her composure and took another cautious sip. "Yes. I'm fine, thank you."

He smiled at her, and her heart skipped a beat. He was the most handsome man she had ever seen. And he loved *her.*

"Thank you, *Chère,* for everything."

She looked at Henry and blew out a deep breath. "Henry, I'd like to—"

"You are about to marry my grandson," he said softly, "which means you will be my granddaughter." He sat up straighter. "I have no objections to you calling me Grandfather. If you don't mind, that is."

She swallowed hard. "I don't mind. Grandfather."

"Splendid. Let's eat."

"But I need to explain."

"You are going to marry my grandson, are you not?"

Unsure what one had to do with the other, she nodded.

"And did you buy up my debts?" he asked with no hint of anger in his voice.

"Yes."

He gave a non-committal shrug. "Then, there is nothing to discuss. You will be a Moreau. The company remains in the family." He picked up a biscuit and slathered butter on it. "And, from what Luc tells me, you have some interesting ideas about expanding that I am most anxious to hear." He raised the bread to his mouth and paused, "After the wedding, of course."

CHAPTER THIRTY-SIX

TWO WEEKS PASSED IN A BLUR OF ACTIVITY. DAISY and her mother worked tirelessly on the gown. Lizzy, Vi, and pretty much everyone else in town worked on decorations and food.

Jenny elected not to return to New York with Belle and now happily divided her time between helping Daisy and working in the store.

Thanks to Bea's help, Jenny and Daisy's family moved into a larger home that provided ample workspace and bedrooms for all.

The night before the wedding, Luc moved his things into Bea's home. Henry took over Luc's small cabin for use when he visited, and Lizzy insisted Bea take a room at the hotel to facilitate the pampering she planned.

Anxiety wore at Bea. *What happens afterward? When Luc and I go home. Together.*

One part of her couldn't wait. Another worried she would not handle it right. She wasn't naïve so much as inexperienced and unsure of herself.

Lizzy said to let nature take its course, and things will be fine. Later, after a glass of brandy to settle their nerves, Lizzy provided a more detailed answer, which both thrilled and frightened Bea.

By four o'clock on the day of the wedding, Bea was ready for it all to be over. Daisy, Lizzy, and Vi took turns helping her dress and fix her hair. It became a little overwhelming at one point, but they were her dearest friends and wanted this day to be memorable, so she kept silent.

"Oh, my," said Vi as she stepped back to take in the full picture. "Bea, that dress is stunning on you."

"Luc won't be able to stop smiling," said Lizzy. She paused and added, "And thinking about getting you out of it."

All three women laughed, and Bea fanned her flaming cheeks. "Y'all are incorrigible."

"Just stating facts," said Lizzy, then turned Bea toward the mirror.

Bea gasped and stared at the image looking back at her. Gone was the uncertainty, the shame that damned scar inflicted on her for years. In its place stood a beautiful, confident, and capable woman about to marry the man of her dreams.

"Oh, Daisy," she gushed, "the gown is perfect."

A simple style constructed of ivory silk with scattered embroidered pink roses featured a square neckline with a rolled chiffon inset and bell-shaped lace sleeves. A fitted bodice emphasized her full bosom, and more embroidered roses graced the shoulder straps. The gently flared skirt flowed back into a short train.

"I can't believe you made this in just two weeks, Daisy," she said to the young woman as she pinned silk roses in Bea's hair. "It's perfect."

"It wasn't just me, ma'am," she said proudly. "Lots of ladies helped. Mrs. Morgan, Miss Vi, and Miss Lizzy, too."

"I think six or eight women did the roses, Bea," said Lizzy. "Everyone wanted to be a part of your special day. And we all worked on decorating the hall."

Lizzy stepped forward and handed her a box. "Luc asked me to give this to you and tell you happy birthday from him." She grinned. "I'm sure you can find a way to thank him later."

Hands shaking, she opened it to find a single strand of pearls. "Oh my," she gushed.

Lizzy took them and placed them around her neck. "Perfect finishing touch."

Bea fought to keep happy tears at bay as she looked at the faces of her dear friends. "I don't know what to say. Thank you seems so inadequate."

"You can thank us by being happy," she said.

"I think I can do that."

A short time later, arms linked with Amos and Silas, who wore their new suits with pride, Bea stood at the hall's back entrance.

Bright green eyes sparkling with delight, Lizzy stepped forward with two bouquets of dried lavender tied with pink ribbons. She smiled and handed one to Bea. "Ready? We don't want to keep that handsome man of yours waiting."

"I'm ready." She turned to the two men escorting her. "Thank you, Uncle Amos and Uncle Silas, for walking me down the aisle."

Amos patted her hand. His cheeks flushed bright red. "Nothing ever gave me so much pleasure, child."

"Same for me," said Silas. "I lost my only girl when she was a babe and her mother not long after. In a way, it's like I'm doing this for her."

Lizzy opened the door and stepped into the large room overflowing with people from miles around dressed in their Sunday best. Because the ceremony itself would be short, they stood on either side of the aisle. A few chairs were scattered around against the walls, and on the right side were tables laden with food. Another table held a beautiful wedding cake and a bowl of punch.

An iron archway covered with bows, streamers, and more dried lavender waited at the end of the aisle, along with Luc and his grandfather. Off to the left, fiddle players began a soft, melodic tune she didn't recognize. Candles burned behind the arch and around the room, the flickering lights adding a muted, romantic glow to the room.

Lizzy walked slowly down the aisle and stepped to the left, then nodded to Bea.

Eyes on Luc, she and her uncles began the slow walk forward. From the corner of her eye, she recognized many people she knew, all wearing huge smiles. Emotion clogged her throat again. She was home, and these people were her friends.

"Who gives this woman in marriage?" intoned Reverend Johnson.

"We do," chimed her uncles, then kissed her on the cheek and placed her hand in Luc's.

"You treat our girl right," said Silas.

"You have my word." Then he turned to Bea, eyes filled with love, and brought her hand to his lips for a gentle kiss. "From this day forward, I am yours, and you are mine."

A collective sigh washed over the room as she fingered the pearls around her neck and replied, "I am yours, and you are mine."

The ceremony passed in a blur of words, and then Reverend Johnson said, "I now pronounce you husband and wife. You may kiss the bride."

Applause and shouts of happy tidings broke out around the room as Luc placed a quick kiss on her lips. "The best is yet to come," he whispered for her ears alone.

And then the crowd surrounded them, everyone talking at once, offering salutations and pats on the back to Luc.

"Congratulations, you two," said Tyler Roundtree as he clasped Luc's hand.

"You are gorgeous, Bea," said Emma Roundtree, "And Daisy did such a fabulous job on the dress." She looked up to her husband and smiled. "Ty loves the green one she made for me."

"She is beautiful, indeed," said Ty as he stepped toward Bea. "Now, may I kiss the bride?"

Before anyone could respond, he placed a chaste kiss on her scarred cheek, that simple act doing more for her self-confidence than all the pretty dresses in the world. "Thank you, Ty," she whispered.

Bea lost track of the compliments, the questions, and even the people as the crowd milled around them. Never in her life did she expect or even hope to feel so totally at home.

When the fiddle players struck up a slow waltz, Luc took her hand and led her to the middle of the room. They barely made three rounds before Amos tapped his shoulder. "May I dance with my niece, please?"

And then it was Silas's turn. Then Richard Bentley, then Roscoe, and someone she couldn't name, though she recognized him as a recent customer.

Lizzy stopped the dancing by saying it was time to cut the cake and eat.

Bea was too nervous to eat more than the bite of cake Luc gave her, followed by a glass of punch, which she quickly discovered was spiked.

Lizzy pulled Bea to the side while Ty and Richard spoke to Luc. "The carriage is out front when you are ready."

Bea's heart did a little flip.

"The house is ready as well, and there is food to last for days."

Bea choked on the punch she swallowed.

Lizzy got Luc's attention, and he quickly made it to her side. "You two should leave before folks realize you're gone, or you'll never get out of here."

He grabbed her hand, and they made their way to the front amid a chorus of well-wishes, whistles, and back slaps.

Outside, Amos sat in the front seat of the carriage. Luc helped her inside then joined her. The ride took all of five minutes, and by the time they reached her front gate, her nerves were a jumbled mess.

Luc lifted her from the carriage and carried her across the yard to the front door. "You don't have to do this," said Bea, "I can walk, you know."

"And chance getting your wedding dress dirty?" His lips curled up in that sexy smile she knew so well. "What kind of husband would do that?"

She gave a light laugh. "Not mine."

They reached the door, and he managed to open it without dropping her, then kicked it shut with his foot. His fever-hot gaze bore into hers in silent expectation. The air around them crackled like lightning in a summer storm as he placed her feet on the floor near the fireplace. He looked around and motioned toward the table in the kitchen. "I see they have set the table for supper. Would you like to eat first? I mean, are you hungry?"

For the first time since she'd met him, his face flushed a warm, rosy color.

I'm not the only one nervous and anxious. She smoothed

down the front of her dress, then met his steady gaze. "Thank you for the pearls."

"My pleasure." He cleared his throat. "You look good in them." Once again, his face flushed, but he didn't say anything else.

"It's barely six o'clock."

Confusion clouded his features, and one dark brow inched upward in a silent question.

She rolled her lips inward, unsure how to proceed. *Okay. Lizzy said just to let nature take its course, but what does that mean?*

How did she tell him it wasn't glazed ham and potatoes she wanted? Weeks of prolonged anticipation and simmering desire left her with an unbearable ache for fulfillment. The realization sent waves of excitement through her, and her pulse skittered, her body suddenly warm and heavy.

Seeming to sense the direction of her thoughts, Luc took a step toward her. "*Chère?*" His large hand caressed her cheek. "Tell me what you want."

Shaken by the impact of his tender touch, she pulled in a shuddering breath. "I want you to kiss me."

He groaned low in his throat and closed the distance between them. His lips brushed against hers, once, twice, then hungrily covered them in a soul-shattering kiss.

She parted her lips and raised up to meet his demanding mouth. Arms around his neck, her body trembled with desire as his warm lips skimmed down her neck. She tilted her head to grant him access to the hollow of her throat, a soft moan escaping at the touch of his tongue, the heat of his lips. The outcry grew in volume when his hand brushed across her breast, the sensitive nipple puckering into a tight bud under her wedding dress. "Lucian," she whispered, wanting more, so much more.

He claimed her lips in a hunger-fueled kiss that left her senses reeling while his hands seared a path down her back, across her hips.

She pulled back and ran her hands over the broad expanse of his chest, her breathing rapid and shallow as she tugged at his jacket. "Lucian…"

He quickly shed the garment and once again lifted her in his arms and carried her into the bedroom. "My beautiful wife," he whispered.

She barely noticed the lamp burning low or the covers turned back on the bed as she stood on shaky legs in front of him.

He kissed her again, then his lips left hers and skimmed her earlobe as he trailed tender kisses down her neck. Long fingers removed the pins holding her hair in place, and he ran his hands through the dark chestnut curls that rained down over her shoulders. "I have wanted to do that for weeks," he murmured.

Knees wobbly, she clung to his arms as his lips slid lower. She tilted her head, then shuddered when his tongue touched the hollow of her throat before trailing down the valley between her breasts.

His fingers toyed with the buttons on her gown, then he pulled back, silently asking permission to continue.

She gasped for air. "I'm not naïve exactly, Lucian, but…I don't…know what I should do."

He took a breath. "You may do whatever you want. Touch wherever you want." He paused, uncertainty replacing the desire of a moment ago. "If you are not comfortable, if you do not wish to continue, please tell me now." His smile held more pain than mirth.

"Don't stop."

Eyes locked with hers, he released the buttons, one by one.

She sucked in a hard breath when he eased the edges over her shoulders, followed by her light corset. The hardened peaks of her nipples were easily discernable through the delicate fabric of her chemise. She noted the rapid rise and fall of his chest, the perspiration coating his upper lip as he gazed at her with desire filled eyes. Emboldened by that desire, she tugged his shirt from his pants, then slid her hands underneath, surprised and fascinated by the heat and smoothness of his skin that contrasted sharply with the coarseness of the hair covering his chest.

His breathing stopped, then started again when her palms slid over his body.

Stepping back, he jerked the shirt over his head and tossed it on the floor behind him.

Her mouth went dry as she gazed at his bare chest, eyes taking in the swirl of dark hair that narrowed into a thin line and disappeared beneath his waistband, and lower still to the tenting in his trousers. "Oh my," she whispered.

He frowned and took a step toward her. "Are you frightened, *Chère?*"

Unable to speak at first, she licked her lips. "More uncertain than frightened."

His work-roughened hands slid over her shoulders and down her arms. "Do you trust me?"

She didn't have to think about her answer. "Yes."

He nodded. "Do you know what to expect?"

"Yes. Sort of." She met his steady gaze. "My grandmother explained part of the ritual to me before she passed away."

"Ritual?" He grinned. "I don't think I have ever heard it referred to in that manner."

"She said it is different for everyone."

"That is true."

"And there may be some pain, but it will be short-lived."

"Also true."

Hands at her side, she took a deep breath, blew it out slowly. "Lizzy said that with the right person, it is something that defies description." Drawing in another jerky breath, she reached up with trembling fingers for the ribbon holding her chemise together in the front.

Slate blue eyes glazed with need, locked with hers. Every inch of her body tingled, and breath whooshed from her lungs.

He closed his hands over hers. "May I?"

Mouth too dry to form words, she lowered her hands.

He pulled the bow loose, then slipped one finger through the lacing to open it further.

She swayed when his warm hand slipped inside and cupped her breast. His mouth lowered to meet hers, his tongue hot and probing as it explored her mouth.

Unsteady on her feet, she clung to him, meshing his urgency with her own unsated needs. His lips, his hands were a dual assault on her body. Fingernails dug into his arms as his mouth seared a path across her exposed flesh. A soft cry escaped when his warm breath tantalized her throbbing nipple before his tongue teased the rosy peak, then he took the bud in his mouth and suckled.

"Luc!"

Supporting her with one arm, he trailed kisses across the top of her chest. "You are so beautiful, *mon Chère*. I want to see all of you."

Before she could object, even if she wanted to, her chemise pooled at her feet. A moment later, her drawers followed, leaving her naked in front of him. Before she could follow through on the sudden urge to cover herself, he lifted her and gently, lovingly, placed her on the bed.

He sat on the edge and removed his boots, then loosened his trousers' flap, but did not remove them.

For the first time in weeks, she thought of the scar and gently touched her cheek.

The bed moved when he lay down beside her and gently pulled her hand away. "*Chère*…It is nothing. It is a part of you, like an arm or leg."

"Oh, Lucian, I love you so." She reached up and pulled him toward her, giving herself over to the urgency of his kiss. Her fingers raked up and down his back as new and exciting sensations pooled low in her belly, eliciting a soft moan of pleasure.

He fondled one firm breast, its dark nipple hard and tight, then slid his hand over her abdomen toward her center. He lowered his head to her breast and took the tender nub in his mouth, kneading it with his tongue as she writhed beneath him, hands fisted in his hair as she held him to her.

"I want to see you, Lucian," she whispered. "All of you."

He moved off the bed, and his pants and drawers joined the rest of their clothing on the floor.

She sucked in a deep breath and let her gaze roam freely over his muscular shoulders, down the broad expanse of his chest, and lower still to the evidence of his desire.

A powerful, virile man, his stance emphasized the strength in his thighs, the slimness of his hips as he waited, silent, watching her intently.

"Lucian…" She held her arms out to him, and he rejoined her on the bed.

His mouth covered hers as one hand explored the curve of her breast before lightly tracing a path over her taut stomach.

She sucked in a breath as a rush of heat flooded her body.

His exploring hand continued its journey downward, leaving a trail of fire in its wake. He paused only a moment before his fingers skated over the dense curls at her center to the hidden nub beneath.

Startled by the intimate touch, her eyes widened, and her stomach muscles clenched. Heat gathered like a building storm, and her whole body hungered for release. Instinctively, she curved toward him, abandoning herself to the passion he elicited.

One finger slid over the responsive flesh, once, twice, three times. She struggled for breath as wonderous new sensations bloomed, the need to move, to get closer to something exciting and unexpected engulfed her.

The promise of fulfillment, of passion yet undiscovered, guided them as they took the time to discover, to arouse, to please each other until her body vibrated with liquid fire, and she cried out. "Lucian!"

"My, *Chère*," he whispered against her lips. "I love you."

His expert touch pushed her past the brink, and she gasped in sweet agony as he lowered his body over hers. Skin to skin, they were as one and found the rhythm that bound them, body and soul, in perfect harmony, until they crested the wave of pleasure together, crying out, breathless, and spent.

Making love to Luc, waking with him beside her, was so much more pleasurable than Bea ever imagined. Never in her wildest dreams did she think she could not only experience such soul-moving passion but stir it in someone else.

The thought of a lifetime of such nights ahead was enough to reignite the alluring flame of newly discovered desire. She heard the mantle clock strike eleven, and they had yet to eat supper. Was he hungry? Perhaps too tired?

She idly ran her fingers through the dark curls on his chest. Soft, yet coarse, they intrigued her.

He slid his hand up and down her back, coming to rest on her hip, then cleared his throat. "Um...are you...in much discomfort?"

"Not particularly." The first time was somewhat uncomfortable, but he quickly found a pleasant way to distract her from it.

"That's good."

She pushed up and rested on one elbow. Eyes the color of a stormy sea locked with hers, and latent desire smoldered in their indigo depths. She drew a circle on his chest with her index finger then nibbled her lower lip. "Lizzy was right." She said at last. "With the right person, the ritual is quite enjoyable."

She hesitated, then leaned down and kissed him, a bashful learning-to-be-seductive kiss that drew an immediate response. When her exploring hand trailed downward and cupped him, all thoughts of eating evaporated in a desire-drenched fog.

EPILOGUE

Three months later

"DID YOU ENJOY YOUR TRIP TO NEW YORK?" asked Vi as she joined Lizzy and Bea at the table.

"Well, yes and no," said Bea. "One of my father's competitors is buying Lockhart's, and my parents plan to leave for London as soon as possible."

"How do you feel about that?" asked Lizzy, placing her hand over Bea's. "It must be difficult for you."

Bea looked at her two best friends and shook her head. "Actually, it wasn't hard at all. They stopped being my parents after the accident. To be honest, I feel sorry for them." She smiled at the women in turn. "My family is here now."

"That's right," said Vi, wiping at her glistening eyes. "We are."

"What about that Blankenship woman?" asked Lizzy. "Please tell me she got what she deserved."

"By the time we got there, she had spun the story to her liking. But Luc let a few people know the truth."

"What happened then?" asked Lizzy.

Bea frowned. "Henry hosted a party for us. Everyone was there." Bea didn't mention how uncomfortable she was at first. Until Luc kissed her in the middle of the ballroom floor and proudly proclaimed his wife was the most beautiful woman in the world.

"When Belle made her usual grand entrance, you could have heard a pin drop." She toyed with her cup. "People shunned her to the point she left in tears."

"Humph," said Vi, "serves her right."

"I felt sorry for her. Crazy, huh?" said Bea.

"No, it's not crazy," said Lizzy firmly. "Because you're a good person, and she is not."

Bea shook her head, refusing to give Belle any more power over her life. "Last I heard, she planned to travel to London with my parents. Oh, what about Eunice? Did she ever get over being mad that she missed all the excitement?"

"Oh lordy, you should have seen her," said Vi. "She was mad as a hornet that no one would talk about it. Being here for the wedding meant nothing since she missed all the excitement." She grinned and winked. "And I heard some folks went out of their way to hint at something, then shut up just to aggravate her."

"Humph," said Lizzy. "She makes my teeth hurt."

Bea laughed and looked at her. "I understand you and Richard Bentley are an item these days."

Lizzy's faced turned bright red, and she glared at Vi. "I wanted to tell her."

Unabashed, Vi shrugged. "Took you too long."

Bea grinned. "I'm happy for you, Lizzy. Richard's a good man."

She nodded. "We're taking things slow." She paused. "The ranch keeps him busy, but he comes to town more now than before."

"What about Moreau Shipping?"

"My attorney got all paperwork completed to turn everything over to Luc, even though he didn't want me to." She took a breath. "But it was only right. He still wants me involved in running things, though. We talked a great deal about expansion plans and decided to focus on overland shipping. Henry—I mean, Grandfather wants to be close to us, so we decided to sell the house there and all but one of the ships. He's going to stay in Luc's cabin until he builds something here. By the fall, we'll be shipping cattle, grain, lumber, even dry goods west from our home base here."

"What about the store?" asked Lizzy. "I know you have Jenny helping out now. How on earth will you do both?"

"Jenny is sharp as a tack," said Bea proudly, "and has some great ideas for expanding our merchandise, including more things from Daisy." She paused, then smiled shyly. "I think I'll be turning more things over to her in the coming months." She looked between the two women and waited for them to understand the unspoken message.

Almost at once, they did.

"You're pregnant!" said Lizzy, clapping her hands together.

"Oh my God. Does Luc know yet?" asked Vi.

"Yes, he knows. So does Henry, and they are both thrilled." She thought of Amos and Silas and their enthusiastic acceptance of the uncle role and couldn't wait to see their reaction.

About that time, they walked by the front window, heading for their afternoon checker game, and waved. Yes, her child would know the true meaning of unconditional love.

Bea listened to the chatter of her two best friends, interspersed with comments from customers who dropped by the table and basked in the warmth of their friendship and love.

For years, she let others convince her the scar somehow defined her worth as a person, as a woman. When she faced Eunice Martin without the veil on the train that day, she unknowingly took the first step in a journey that brought her to this moment.

She came to Bakersville with no expectation beyond escaping the past and being on her own. Instead, she found everlasting love and the missing piece in the puzzle of her life.

Acceptance; not from others, but herself.

THE END

If you read my last couple of books, you know I like to include a recipe or two at the end. Even though the characters didn't make these, I add them because they are quick and easy and so delicious! Enjoy!

BUTTERMILK PECAN PRALINES

Ingredients

1 cup sugar
1/2 cup light brown sugar
1/2 cup buttermilk
1 tablespoon light corn syrup
1/2 tsp baking soda
1/4 teaspoon salt
4 tablespoons unsalted butter, at room temperature
1 tsp vanilla extract
1/2 teaspoon orange extract, optional
2 cups chopped pecans

Instructions

1) In a heavy bottom saucepan, add the sugars, buttermilk, corn syrup, baking soda, and salt. Cook slowly over medium heat until the mixture reaches **235F** on a candy thermometer. Temperature is VERY important for the recipe to work.

2) Stir the mixture constantly with a wooden spoon while it cooks. The mixture will begin to increase in volume as the temperature rises. Keep stirring making sure to stir the edges so the sauce doesn't burn.

3) Remove from heat once it reaches 235F and add the butter, vanilla, orange extract, and pecans. Stir continuously for <u>ten minutes</u> until the mixture becomes thick. Don't fudge on the time.

4) As the sauce cools, it will turn into a thick, silky caramel. Drop by spoonful onto parchment-lined baking sheets or waxed paper.

5) Allow to cool for 30 minutes. (Will keep for three weeks in an airtight container or three months in the freezer in an airtight container. But they never last that long!)

HOMEMADE BUTTERMILK BREAD

Ingredients:

1 ½ cups buttermilk
2 TBSP melted butter
2 TBSP sugar
1 Tsp Salt
3 ½ cups all-purpose flour
1 TBSP yeast

Instructions:

1) Combine buttermilk, butter, and sugar in a bowl. Blend well. Set aside.
2) Combine dry ingredients in a large mixing bowl and whisk well to blend.
3) Add buttermilk to dry ingredients and mix well. You can use an electric mixer with dough hooks if large enough, but I just use my hands.
4) Mix until well combined. You want a little to be sticking to the bottom. If too dry, add a splash of buttermilk until desired consistency is reached.
5) Once desired consistency is reached, knead for 6-7 minutes with dough hooks or 10 minutes by hand. (I just knead by hand). VERY IMPORTANT to knead properly. This is critical to great texture for your bread.
6) Next, place dough in a well-oiled bowl, cover lightly with a cloth, and let rise until doubled in size, about an hour.
7) Punch it down, knead several times, and place it in a well-oiled pan.

8) Let rise in a warm place for another 30-45 minutes.
9) Preheat oven to 350 degrees. Bake dough for 30-35 minutes until the top is golden brown.
10) Cool, slice, and serve!

NOTE: When I start this recipe, I preheat the oven for five minutes, then turn it off. This gets it warm, and that is where I put
the bread to rise. You can simply leave it on a counter or place it
in a cold oven, but it may take a little longer to rise. You want it
kept away from drafts or air as this also affects how it rises.

ACKNOWLEDGMENTS

When I published my first book in the summer of 2016, I had no idea how long my writing career would last. I only knew I wanted to write, and I hoped that people would enjoy what I wrote.

Fast forward almost five years. Five books out, plus a cookbook! Plus, two more books and an updated cookbook are in the mill for the coming months!

But like any endeavor, I did not get here on my own. I cannot express the depth of my gratitude to Patty Wiseman, mentor-extraordinaire, my two favorite nitpickers Beth Howlett and Ruth Buck, and members of my writers' groups. I cannot begin to express the depth of my gratitude to these wonderful people. I would not be able to do what I do without them.

And last, but certainly not least, my biggest fan and most ardent supporter, my wonderful husband, Bud. Your support means everything to me, and I love you more every day.

CHAPTER 1

"O**KAY, MOM. I GOT IT. I GOT IT.**"

Detective Jessie Foster slapped the receiver in its cradle. Two seconds later, she flung a pencil across the room where it ricocheted off a corner of the cushioned cubical wall before it landed on the other desk.

Her mom could turn a good day into a bad one in a heartbeat.

"Whoa, there, Texas. What's got your panties in a wad this time?"

The question from Seth Hamilton, her partner and co-habitant of this padded cell, reminded her she wasn't alone. "Can it, Hammer, I'm not in the mood." She sighed and tugged the red scrunchy from her ponytail, tossed it on the desk, then leaned back and raked trim fingers through dark, shoulder-length curls. A tension headache crept up the back of her neck. *Perfect. Just damn perfect.* "And stop calling me Texas. And Tex."

"I would, but I hear bitch isn't politically correct these days."

Despite her anger, she snorted. "You're such an ass."

"Says you." He sauntered over and rested his hip on the corner of her desk. "She still want you to take that job with the feds?"

Before she could reply, he continued. "And in Dallas no less. You hate traffic."

She caught herself before she blurted out the hard truth. *It's killing me to work side-by-side with you every day and not tell you how I feel.* "A desk job is a place to start." Even as the lie slid off her tongue, her inner voice chided, *'Coward.'*

"You like working in the field, Tex. You'd hate a desk job, and you know it. So, what gives?"

She didn't answer but knew he wouldn't let it go. He was worse than a dog with a bone. "I'm a damn good cop whether I'm behind a desk or out in the field."

She ignored the teasing snicker from Seth. He loved getting her riled almost as much as she loved Mexican food.

"I have my last interview with them next week." She stood and glanced around her work area. Small, crowded, and noisy, it was nonetheless a decent space. The police force in Walker, a town southeast of Dallas, was a small, tight-knit group. Granted, most called her names behind her back, mainly because she refused to take any crap from them, but, if push came to shove, they'd be there for her. Did she really want to start over somewhere else? Or was she just running away?

"You're too good for them," he said. "And we'd miss you here."

She grunted. "Yeah. Right."

He had the audacity to laugh. The throaty, masculine sound made her stomach flutter. *Aw, hell. I've worked side-by-side with him for over a fricking year, and now my stomach flutters when he laughs. Or winks. Or breathes.*

Just shoot me.

If she were perfectly honest with herself—which she always tried to be—he was good looking—handsome even. Five years older than her at thirty-eight, he carried his age well. Cognac colored eyes framed by long, dark lashes she silently envied, and heavy brows were the first thing she noticed about him.

The second was his mouth…those lips. Women paid a fortune to fake what God gave him free gratis. Even a slight overbite and crooked nose didn't detract from his rugged good looks. From the top of his military cut, salt and pepper head to the souls of his cowboy boots, he was six-feet-three inches of blatant masculinity coupled with a compelling sex appeal hard to ignore, but she managed.

Well, most of the time.

Lately, not so much.

One whiff of his cologne, coupled with a provocative man-smell, was enough to send rational thought straight to the gutter.

It took effort on her part to get her wayward mind back on track. "You're just playing nice cause you think you'll get lucky."

"Yeah, right. I relish the idea of sex with a buzz saw."

She flinched and buried the hurt his comment elicited, defensive walls shored and braced. She knew him so well, knew he said it to tease, but still, it gave her pause. Was she so hard? Had the job finally robbed her of all femininity? Desirability? Did Seth see her that way?

Suck it up, buttercup. It is what it is. "Time to rock and roll," she snapped and gave herself a mental shake. Focus on the assignment—pick up Jack Walls in Denver and bring him back to Walker. It took them six months to get the evidence needed to arrest him for the murder of his former girlfriend, Lottie Moore. One step ahead of them, he vanished without a trace. Until now.

"With any luck," continued Jess, "we can get there before midnight tonight and be back late tomorrow night."

The grueling fourteen-hour drive was just another part of the job. Hours alone with her partner presented issues she did not want to dwell on.

Seth looked at her and smirked. "What's your hurry, Tex? Hot date?"

"The sooner this is over with, the better."

He stood, grabbed his jacket off the rack, and draped it over one arm. "Well, personally, I can't wait to spend the next three days trapped in a car with Miss Congeniality and a deranged sociopath."

She lifted the paperwork and purse off the desk, grabbed her backpack, and headed for the hallway, Seth lagging behind. "Wonder why you got stuck with me for a partner."

"Obviously, somewhere along the way, I spit in someone's Cheerios and pissed 'em off."

Jess shook her head. An anomaly, Seth always spoke his mind. She liked that about him, though he sometimes goaded her to no end. For whatever reason, they clicked from the start. Maybe because they were more alike than different. Neither liked all the hoops they jumped through daily to get the bad guys, and both possessed a wicked sense of humor not everyone could handle. Plus, they each tended to call a spade a spade without apology.

Unable to curb the impulse, she cast him a quick sideways glance. Immediately, butterflies the size of a roadrunner took flight in her stomach.

Must be some kind of hormonal-biological-clock thing. I am thirty-three now. It will pass. Probably like a kidney stone, but it will pass.

She gave herself a mental kick and headed down the hallway toward the elevator with Seth following behind. She barely managed to smother the temptation to strut a bit. *What the hell is wrong with me?* She gave the elevator button a harder-than-necessary push. *I don't care what he thinks of my ass in these slacks.*

The doors opened, and she walked in pressing the dial for the garage as she turned.

Seth met her gaze, sensuous mouth curved up in a Cheshire-cat smile. "I appreciate the show."

"Shut up."

He winked.

It was going to be a long three days.

* * *

Seth knew he skated a fine line with Jess. The department's stand on sexual harassment left no room for doubt. One call from her and his ass was in a sling.

But he was just vain enough to believe she enjoyed their suggestive banter. And she gave as good as she got, too. He liked a woman who spoke her mind and didn't get all ticked off when a man did the same.

His transfer to Walker coincided with her last partner's move to Austin. He didn't miss the snickers drifting among his fellow officers after the announcement of their partnership. Later, he discovered most didn't like working with her, calling her names like testy, hardheaded and bitchy. But he never saw that side of her personality. Instead, he saw a first-rate detective, intensely dedicated to the job, with a warped sense of humor to match his own.

She was also a beautiful, fascinating woman who worked hard to hide that fact from the rest of the world. And it was the woman behind the badge who captivated his thoughts these days.

Granted, he sometimes took things a bit too far, like the buzz-saw comment. The brief flash of pain he saw in her eyes tore at his conscience. Filters he found so easy to employ around others failed him completely around Jess. From day one, she took whatever he dished out and gave it back in spades. So much so, that he inched further and further across that invisible line just to see how she would respond.

Lately, though, something was different. *She* was different. An occasional look in her eye that quickly disappeared made him wonder…what if she saw him as more than her irritating partner with a propensity for spouting out useless trivia?

What if she saw *him?*

Finally.

That *what-if* kept him awake most of last night, and he vowed to use this trip to explore the prospect in depth.

After she got over being mad, of course.

Man, she was something when riled. Like now. Her cheeks were a flattering shade of red, and that sexy, sassy mouth formed a tight line across her face. Her anger never lasted, so he'd just wait her out.

And try not to think about other things that could put such an enticing flush on her cheeks.

The door slid open, and she started to exit ahead of him, then stopped and scowled.

He grinned and ambled out. "How about I take first turn at the wheel, Tex. Your driving makes me nervous."

"Since when?"

"Since you go into a cussing rampage in traffic, and we'll hit the start of rush hour through Dallas."

"Whatever. Drive." She pitched him the keys and walked to the passenger side, throwing her bag into the back seat before buckling in.

He placed his go-bag beside hers and climbed behind the wheel of the older model SUV.

Jess dug through the paperwork and pulled out a map. "The GPS is on the fritz again, and cell service may be iffy."

He glared at the map in her hand. "I don't need a map."

"Need I remind you of the last time we had this conversation?"

"That was then. This is now. I don't need the map."

"I promise —you will sincerely regret it if you get us lost and drag this trip out any more than necessary."

"Duly noted."

He put the car in gear and headed out of the garage toward the interstate through Dallas. Traffic would be a bitch, the drive exhausting, but he looked forward to the hours of proximity with his feisty partner who of late pressed every male button he possessed.

It was time he located a few of her female ones.

Coming in 2021

CHAPTER
One

THE FIRST BULLET GRAZED HIS CHEEK, FOLLOWED BY *searing pain and the acrid smell of singed flesh and gunpowder. "Sniper! Three o-clock!" He shouted to the small band of Marines clustered behind the disabled Humvee. "Stay down."*

Jenkins, a kid from Idaho so green his boots weren't even scuffed, looked at him with worried eyes. "What'll we do, Gunny?"

Before he could reply, all hell broke loose. One sniper became six. Pinned down, they waited. And prayed. The whistle of a mortar pierced the roar of a shitload of automatic rifles a split second before Jenkins disappeared in a haze of blood and mangled flesh.

Max Logan jolted awake from the nightmare, a scream lodged in his throat. Heart racing, gasping for air, he threw off the sheet and sat on the side of the bed. The last nightmare happened nearly a year ago. He thought he was over it.

Evidently not.

Control your breathing, lower your heart rate. The shrink's instructions ran through his mind as he struggled to escape the hellhole that nearly destroyed him.

Recurrent pain in his left leg, compliments of shrapnel from the IED, was another reminder of his brush with death. He pushed off the bed and limped to the window.

Must have been my conversation with Big John today. That's what stirred up the memories. He pressed his head against the cold glass. Not for the first time, he asked himself why. "Why am I alive, and they're all dead?"

A sudden light from the kitchen next door ended his introspection and drew his gaze to the woman who paused in the middle of the room, arms straight at her side.

Her name was Skylar Ward, though everyone called her Sky. She worked at the local diner where he took a lot of his meals. Their conversations rarely went beyond did he want the daily special or his usual burger and fries, but something about her piqued his interest. Gut instinct said the awareness was mutual, yet he hesitated to test the waters. He'd come a long way in the last sixteen months but couldn't bring himself to take the next step. Not yet.

A single mom, she had the cutest and smartest little girl who never missed an opportunity to engage Max in conversation at the diner or when they were outside at the same time. Truth be told, the child did most of the talking, usually in the form of a gazillion questions, but he didn't mind. Especially if it meant an opportunity to chat with the mother as well.

He straightened when Sky swiped her cheeks with one hand and dropped into a chair at the small table near the window.

He glanced at the bedside clock, 0430. There were no curtains on the window and the narrow driveway between their houses in this older neighborhood allowed him to see her in sharp detail. She sat drill-sergeant straight, hands clasped together in her lap, auburn hair disheveled, loose-fitting pajamas boasting an animal, maybe a cat, on the front.

It wasn't the first time he'd observed her in the wee hours of the morning. Not that he was a wacked-out Peeping Tom, either. He wasn't. He just had trouble sleeping at times and prone to be up at all hours of the night. Lately, so was she.

Sometimes, she just sat there. Sometimes, she made coffee or did paperwork.

Tonight, though, something was different. She was different.

Rigid as a poplar, she ran slender fingers through shoulder-length hair, then gripped the sides of her head, face contorted as though in agony. She tilted her head back and rolled it side to side. Her chest rose and fell with deep, measured breaths. She crossed her wrists on the table and sat frozen for the space of a heartbeat before her shoulders slumped, and she lowered her head. Her slender body shook with the force of her sobs.

"I know how you feel, ma'am," he whispered to the darkness, "I know just how you feel."

⚜

Skylar Ward hated crying. It never solved anything and left her with red, puffy eyes that no amount of makeup would hide. So what if the rent was due, her car hovered one crank away from the scrap heap, and Christmas loomed a month away? That wasn't reason enough to host a pity party for one. Yet here she sat in the predawn hours blubbering like the world just came to an end. Who knew? Maybe it had, and she didn't know it yet.

Never one to feel sorry for herself, at least not for long, Sky wondered what sparked this infrequent event. The upcoming holidays? Maybe. But in her heart, she knew it went beyond that, beyond monitoring her young daughter's health or pinching pennies.

She loved Maddie more than life itself and did not regret the steps she took to ensure her health and happiness. But more and more lately, she missed not having someone to share her life with, to snuggle on the couch and talk about anything or nothing. She was so tired of watching life from the sidelines, doing everything, facing everything alone, with no one to watch her back or hold her close in the darkness.

"Suck it up, buttercup," she mumbled when the waterworks ceased. "It's not like you have a lot of options." She got up from the table and splashed her face with cold water. A quick glance at the wall clock produced another groan. No point in going back to bed now. She started the coffee maker, then leaned against the counter, arms braced on either side. Surrounded by a sense of imminent doom and a loneliness so profound it bordered on physical pain, she sucked in a ragged breath.

I've been alone practically my whole life, why is it bothering me now?

Her father died when she was young. Her mother was a physical therapist, and they lived in a modest yet comfortable home. A drunk driver turned her once vibrant, happy mother into an invalid a week after Sky turned sixteen. The only relative was a grandmother whom she hadn't seen since her father died, so Sky left her carefree life behind and became her mother's caretaker, working after school and on weekends at a local pharmacy to make ends meet. Despite the burdens she shouldered, she managed to graduate from high school and then enroll in nursing school.

Memories of those dark days threatened to initiate another round of self-pity, and she gave herself a mental shake.

Deal with the problem at hand—how to pay the rent this month—and save the rest for another day. Mr. Jenkins was a kind-hearted older gentleman, but kindness only went so far when money was involved.

A tingling on the back of her neck pulled her to the window where only darkness and the house next door loomed. The occupant,

Max Logan, had moved in about six months ago and was a frequent customer at the diner where she worked. Maddie had more conversations with him than Sky, and when they did talk, it rarely went beyond casual conversation. His demeanor, heightened by tips that exceeded the norm and covert looks cast her way, indicated more than casual interest. Sadly, as a single mother barely making ends meet, she focused on getting through the next crisis, which left no room for a personal life, no matter how badly she wanted one.

Max was the only man she'd met in Bakersville to even halfway draw her attention, and she briefly considered encouraging him. The few men who had expressed interest up to now quickly cooled when they discovered she had a child. Max, however, didn't seem to mind. He would patiently answer Maddie's multitude of questions and occasionally encouraged more. He appeared to enjoy their interactions, which provided Sky an opportunity to get to know him better.

Her friend and neighbor, Gail Brown, said Max was a former soldier. She didn't need that last piece of information since everything about his bearing screamed military.

She guessed him to be a little older than her thirty-three years. Tall, maybe six-three or four, his well-muscled body moved with an easy grace, despite a slight limp. He wore his dark chestnut hair in the traditional buzz cut favored by soldiers, and heavy brows rested above unsmiling, coffee-colored eyes. His features were hard, chiseled like an unfinished sculpture, and he possessed an air of authority that commanded attention.

The beep of the coffee pot brought her back to the counter, where she filled a mug and, with only a brief hesitation, scooted a chair near the window and sat down, calling herself a pathetic fool for pretending she wasn't alone.

CHAPTER
Two

"Hurry with your breakfast, Maddie," urged Sky as she gathered her purse and jacket, "we're going to be late."

"Almost through." Seven-year-old Maddie shoveled another bite of scrambled eggs into her mouth. "You told me not to eat fast, or I'd get sick."

"I also told you not to lollygag around."

The impish smile made Sky's heart lurch. *She'll be a beautiful woman one day.*

"Yes, you said that, too." A last bite of eggs, a gulp of juice, and she slid from the chair. "I gotta brush my teeth and get my backpack. After I put my dishes in the sink."

"Make it quick. We need to get going."

A few minutes later, Maddie followed Sky out the door. "Think Ole Blue will start today?"

Her daughter's question mirrored the one making Sky's anxiety soar. The old Taurus teetered on the edge of done-for, and there was no money to fix it. "Keep your fingers crossed."

The brisk November air cut through her lightweight jacket as they hurried to the car. It wasn't locked since no one in their right mind would want the beat-up old clunker. Once behind the wheel, she said a silent prayer and turned the key.

Nothing. Not even a click.

She gnawed her lower lip. *No, no, no. Please…not this.*

She tried again.

Silence.

"What's wrong, Mama?"

She stifled a groan. "I'm not sure—battery maybe."

"Do we have another one of those?"

"No. We don't." Consumed with dread, she unbuckled the seat belt. "Stay put. Let me take a look." *Like I have a bloody clue what to look for or could fix the damn thing if I did.*

Her stomach threatened to purge its meager contents of toast and coffee. *Please, God, please. Give me a break. Just one small break. That's all I ask.*

She propped open the hood and peered inside. *Yep. There's the motor and the little oil thingy. There's the doo-hickey I put window washer fluid in before it sprung a leak. Yep. It's all there. Now what?*

"Something wrong, ma'am?"

Startled, she squealed and jumped back into the rock-solid wall of a man. Strong hands clamped around her waist kept her upright.

"Sorry, ma'am. Didn't mean to startle you."

His warm breath washed over her cheek. She twisted around and found herself face to chest with Max Logan. She jerked her gaze upward, chilled body sucking the heat radiating from him like a sponge.

"Ma'am? Are you okay?"

The intensely male voice penetrated the stupor robbing her of speech, and she stepped back. "Y-yes. I'm fine. You just surprised me."

He nodded toward the car. "Won't start?"

"No, and I have no idea why."

"Mind if I try?" He folded his huge frame in the front seat without waiting for a reply, only to exit a moment later. "Battery's dead." He walked toward his shiny new F-150 crew cab parked a little farther up the narrow drive.

It took a moment to process what had just happened. *Okay. He tried to crank the car, it wouldn't start, and he just walked off. What the heck?* "Well, um, okay. Thanks for trying."

Before she finished the sentence, the huge engine roared to life, and he backed up. Once even with her car, he got out with the motor still running and pulled long, thick wires from behind his seat.

Jumper cables? Maybe. I think.

Once he had them connected to each vehicle, he looked at her. Didn't say a word. Just stared.

She stared back.

One bushy brow kicked up.

Duh. Crank the car, you idiot.

Slow to respond, Blue did, finally, thankfully, start.

He waited a moment, then unhooked the cables and moved to the driver's side. "Where are you going?"

His question was gruff, and she bristled, about to tell him none of his business, but her mother's ancient speech about manners stifled the impulse. And he did crank her car. And was a good tipper. "I have to take Maddie to school."

"How long will that take?"

She gritted her teeth. "Twenty minutes."

"Don't kill it, or it won't start again."

You could've started with that statement. "Oh. Okay. Thank you, um, Mr. Logan, I—"

"Max. No mister." Hands braced on his hips, the inquest continued. "Are you working today?"

"No. I'm off every other Friday."

"Honk when you get back, and I'll hook up a battery charger. But you'll probably need to replace it soon. It's old, and cold weather is hard on them."

Lips pressed together, she swallowed hard. She could barely pay her bills now. A new battery was out of the question. "How much do they cost?"

"Depends on the battery."

She counted to ten. "Ball park?"

One shoulder rose then fell. "A hundred give or take."

"Dollars?"

His jaw muscles moved, whether to smile or grimace, she couldn't tell.

"No. Pickles."

Maddie's musical laughter floated from the back seat. "You can't buy a battery with pickles, Max."

He glanced at her daughter, and a ghost of a smile appeared then vanished. "No, you can't." He looked back at Sky. "Honk when you get back."

Before she could reply, he got in his truck and left.

Sky watched his exit in her rearview mirror. Despite his brusqueness, she still found herself attracted to him. Just like the first time he came in the diner. There was just something about him…

"Max is really nice, ain't he, Mama?"

"What? Oh. Yes. He is."

"I heard Miss Gail say he got hurt being a soldier. Is that why he limps?"

Thoughts scattered, Sky backed out the drive. "What?"

"Did Max get hurt being a soldier?"

"I don't know." Aware of the child's boundless curiosity, she added, "And don't ask him, either. That would be rude."

Maddie nodded, but Sky could almost hear those inquisitive wheels turning in the little scamp's head and made a mental note to talk about boundaries. Again.

Half an hour later, she pulled into the drive.

Max leaned against his truck, arms folded across an impressive chest. Heat burned her cheeks when he glanced at his watch and then back at her.

She jumped from the car and hurriedly explained. "I'm so sorry if I kept you waiting. Everyone was just so slow today."

He raised the hood without comment. "Go ahead and kill it, then see if it will start again."

"You said it wouldn't if I killed it."

He inhaled and spoke slowly as though she were a child. "When it runs, the battery charges. I want to see if it held anything."

"Oh." Chagrined, she followed his instructions. Blue barely groaned and made no effort to start.

He hooked up this contraption to the battery, presumably the charger he spoke of, without saying a word.

A burst of cold air swirled around her, and she pulled the edges of the thin jacket tighter. Winter was blowing in quicker and colder than usual this year. The weatherman warned of a hard freeze this weekend, with sleet and snow possible. As what usually happened with East Texas weather this time of year, temps would go back up to the forties next week. Still, she needed a warmer coat, but that, too, would have to wait. Something else she couldn't afford.

"I don't think it will hold."

The terse announcement took a moment to process. "And that means?"

"You need a new battery." He wiped his hands on a rag, then threw it back behind the seat of his truck. "But we'll see how it goes. When will you need to go out again?"

"I have to pick Maddie up at three-thirty. I have a couple of errands to run, but they can wait."

"Leave it on the charger. I'll take it off when I get back."

"I don't know how to thank you." Flooded with feelings of inadequacy, she hugged herself a little tighter. "I don't know any of this stuff."

He grunted, then stepped into his truck. "I'll be back in time to unhook it. Don't mess with it."

Before she could reply, provided of course something got past the lump in her throat, he left.

Sky spent the day on housework, crunched a few numbers—such as they were—and tried in vain to figure out how to add a battery to her must-have list. Max came and left a couple of times but didn't speak.

Worse-case scenario, she might ask her boss, Ruby Sloan, to advance her some money, but then she would have to pay it back.

Tips represented the bulk of her income, but with the holidays approaching, folks didn't eat out as much, and tips dropped off.

She had a little money earmarked for the few items on layaway for Maddie's Christmas and vowed not to touch it. If she had to spend that on a new battery…

"Nothing I can do about that right now," she muttered and strived to come up with a way to repay Max's kindness. The list of options was practically nil, and she eventually settled on cookies. Who didn't like cookies? And, thankfully, they wouldn't use up too much of her precious resources.

Around two, she pulled the last tray of peanut butter cookies from the oven and placed them on a cooling rack, when a sharp knock sounded on the kitchen door.

A blast of cold air came through when she opened it to find Max on the steps, hands stuffed in his front pockets. "The battery

Maddie nodded, but Sky could almost hear those inquisitive wheels turning in the little scamp's head and made a mental note to talk about boundaries. Again.

Half an hour later, she pulled into the drive.

Max leaned against his truck, arms folded across an impressive chest. Heat burned her cheeks when he glanced at his watch and then back at her.

She jumped from the car and hurriedly explained. "I'm so sorry if I kept you waiting. Everyone was just so slow today."

He raised the hood without comment. "Go ahead and kill it, then see if it will start again."

"You said it wouldn't if I killed it."

He inhaled and spoke slowly as though she were a child. "When it runs, the battery charges. I want to see if it held anything."

"Oh." Chagrined, she followed his instructions. Blue barely groaned and made no effort to start.

He hooked up this contraption to the battery, presumably the charger he spoke of, without saying a word.

A burst of cold air swirled around her, and she pulled the edges of the thin jacket tighter. Winter was blowing in quicker and colder than usual this year. The weatherman warned of a hard freeze this weekend, with sleet and snow possible. As what usually happened with East Texas weather this time of year, temps would go back up to the forties next week. Still, she needed a warmer coat, but that, too, would have to wait. Something else she couldn't afford.

"I don't think it will hold."

The terse announcement took a moment to process. "And that means?"

"You need a new battery." He wiped his hands on a rag, then threw it back behind the seat of his truck. "But we'll see how it goes. When will you need to go out again?"

"I have to pick Maddie up at three-thirty. I have a couple of errands to run, but they can wait."

"Leave it on the charger. I'll take it off when I get back."

"I don't know how to thank you." Flooded with feelings of inadequacy, she hugged herself a little tighter. "I don't know any of this stuff."

He grunted, then stepped into his truck. "I'll be back in time to unhook it. Don't mess with it."

Before she could reply, provided of course something got past the lump in her throat, he left.

Sky spent the day on housework, crunched a few numbers—such as they were—and tried in vain to figure out how to add a battery to her must-have list. Max came and left a couple of times but didn't speak.

Worse-case scenario, she might ask her boss, Ruby Sloan, to advance her some money, but then she would have to pay it back.

Tips represented the bulk of her income, but with the holidays approaching, folks didn't eat out as much, and tips dropped off.

She had a little money earmarked for the few items on layaway for Maddie's Christmas and vowed not to touch it. If she had to spend that on a new battery...

"Nothing I can do about that right now," she muttered and strived to come up with a way to repay Max's kindness. The list of options was practically nil, and she eventually settled on cookies. Who didn't like cookies? And, thankfully, they wouldn't use up too much of her precious resources.

Around two, she pulled the last tray of peanut butter cookies from the oven and placed them on a cooling rack, when a sharp knock sounded on the kitchen door.

A blast of cold air came through when she opened it to find Max on the steps, hands stuffed in his front pockets. "The battery was shot. I put another one in and fixed the window washer. And you were a quart low on oil. You're good to go now."

Before she worked through his brief statement, he turned toward his house.

"Wait!" She wrapped her arms around herself to ward off some of the chill. She moved to the top step and pulled the door shut behind her.

Max stopped but said nothing.

"What do you mean you put another one in?"

"I thought I was pretty clear."

"I can't—I don't…"

He sighed and stepped toward her. "Look, I work at the auto parts store. I get stuff at a discount. It's no big deal."

"It is to me!" She shivered from the cold and growing anger at his presumptuousness. "I can't pay for it. Take it back."

"And how will you get to work and your daughter to school?"

"I'll—I'll think of something. Take it back."

"No." He headed toward his house.

"What do you mean *no?*"

He ran long, slender fingers through non-existent hair. "Look. You're making a big deal out of this. I don't want anything, *anything* from you. Got that? Call it a neighborly act or whatever. I ain't taking it back." He looked at her a moment, tight features relaxing a miniscule amount. "Your teeth are chattering. Go inside where it's warm."

"Do you like peanut butter cookies?"

The warmth inside the kitchen blindsided Max and it wasn't just heat from the stove or the mouth-watering aroma of fresh-baked cookies. Everything shouted *home* to him, or at least what he thought home would be like, though he had no personal experience with it. Growing up in a broken foster care system, *home* was an unfamiliar concept.

He pulled his thoughts away from that dark corner. Ancient history. He survived. Just like he survived the ambush. Over and done. End of story. Move forward.

A sudden cramp in his leg reminded him he'd skipped the daily stretches, and he swallowed a groan.

"Please, sit down. I'll get you some coffee."

His hostess motioned to the table, and he sat in the chair she had used earlier this morning. He stretched his leg out to loosen the cramp. If she noticed his discomfort, she didn't comment, which suited him fine.

She placed a mug of coffee in front of him, along with a plate of cookies. One whiff of those peanut buttery morsels, and his stomach growled loud enough to be heard, which brought an embarrassed flush to his cheeks.

Once again, if she noticed, she didn't comment.

"I'm afraid I don't have any cream for the coffee since I drink mine black. I do have some milk, though. And sugar."

"Black is fine. Thanks." Suddenly nervous about what to say or do next, he sat there with his hands on either side of the cup.

The chance I wanted is right here, and I'm a tongue-tied imbecile. Just fricking great.

"I hope the coffee is all right. It might be a little strong."

He took the hint. The rich, aromatic brew assailed his nostrils. "If it tastes as good as it smells, I'm sure it will be fine." More than fine. It was perfect. "Great coffee, ma'am."

Her cheeks took on a rosy hue, and her face brightened with a smile that lit up the room. "Thank you."

Not for the first time, he noticed her delicate beauty and extraordinary eyes. A rich, hazel color lit from within with a golden glow, they darted around the kitchen, not focusing on any one thing.

Those auburn curls were trussed up with this weird hair clip do-dad. An insane urge to remove it engulfed him. He reached for a cookie instead.

"About the battery—"

"I love peanut butter cookies." He downed one whole and chased it with coffee.

"How much—"

"They're my favorite." He picked up another. "Especially ones like this with peanut chunks inside."

"I need to—"

"Everyone raves about chocolate chip." He studied the morsel in his hand. "But I bet it's because they never tasted a peanut butter cookie like this."

Her shoulders sagged, and her head drooped a little. "How can I ever repay your kindness?"

Uncomfortable with such sincere gratitude, he finished off the last of the treats on his plate. "Cookies are fine with me."

When their eyes finally met, his breath caught. She was beyond beautiful. She was stunning. He had no idea what prompted the sleepless nights or lonely tears, but in that instant, he desperately wanted to make it all better, and for a split second, he thought it worth the gamble. Hope sparked by the idea shriveled and died when reality set in. *I have nothing to offer her but more problems.*

He placed the empty cup in the sink. "Thanks for the cookies."

"I made some for you to take home." She hurried to the

counter and grabbed a paper plate wrapped with foil. "It's not much, but…"

"Thank you, ma'am. I appreciate it very much."

"Please. Call me Sky." She chewed her bottom lip and lowered thick, dark lashes before she straightened and met his steady gaze.

The bottom fell out of his stomach.

"Thank you…Max."

His name never sounded so good before.

Available Now

ABOUT THE AUTHOR

Dana Wayne is a sixth-generation Texan, admitted die-hard romantic, and a lover of good food, good wine, and good company. She routinely speaks to book clubs, writers' groups, and other organizations and is a frequent guest on numerous writing blogs. A strong advocate for new authors, she started a podcast in 2020 called *A Writer's Life* where she shares her experiences on the road from writer wanna be to award-winning romance author. Her romantic stories are filled with strong women, second chances, and happily ever after.

She published her first book in 2016 and never looked back. Among her accolades are two first-place wins, one-second place, three RONE Award Nominations, Scéal Award Finalist, Top 50 Indie Authors You Need to Read, Reviewers Top Pick, and Five Star reviews from Readers Favorite, InD'tale Magazine and Books, and Benches Magazine.

"I am all about the romance and strive for real in my books. They are entertaining and heartwarming with a splash of humor and suspense. My stories are character-driven with a lot of emotion. They are steamy and typically have one or two love scenes toward the end because I believe romance is about emotion, not sex, and the journey is more important than the destination."

She is a long-time member of Writers League of Texas; Authors Marketing Guild, LLC; East Texas Writers Association; Northeast Texas Writers Organization; and East Texas Writers Guild.

www.danawayne.com

www.instagram.com/danawayne423

www.facebook.com/danawayne423

www.twitter.com/danawayne423

https://anchor.fm/dana-wayne